Nic Tatano

I've always been a writer of some sort, having spent my career working as a reporter, anchor or producer in television news. Fiction is a lot more fun, since you don't have to deal with those pesky things known as facts.

I spent fifteen years as a television news reporter and anchor. My work has taken me from the floors of the Democratic and Republican National Conventions to Ground Zero in New York to Jay Leno's backyard. My stories have been seen on NBC, ABC and CNN. I still work as a freelance network field producer for FOX, NBC, CBS and ABC.

I grew up in the New York City metropolitan area and now live on the Gulf Coast where I will never shovel snow again. I'm happily married to a math teacher and we share our wonderful home with our tortoiseshell tabby cat, Gypsy.

You can follow me on Twitter @NicTatano.

The Empire State Cat's Christmas Gift

Book Two

NIC TATANO

A division of HarperCollins*Publishers*
www.harpercollins.co.uk

Harper*Impulse* an imprint of
HarperCollins*Publishers*
1 London Bridge Street
London SE1 9GF

www.harpercollins.co.uk

A Paperback Original 2016

First published in Great Britain in ebook format by Harper*Impulse* 2016

A catalogue record for this book
is available from the British Library

ISBN: 9780008226688

This novel is entirely a work of fiction.
The names, characters and incidents portrayed in it are
the work of the author's imagination. Any resemblance to
actual persons, living or dead, events or localities is
entirely coincidental.

Set in Minion by Palimpsest Book Production Limited, Falkirk, Stirlingshire

Printed and bound in Great Britain

MIX
Paper from
responsible sources
FSC
www.fsc.org FSC™ C007454

FSC™ is a non-profit international organisation established to promote
the responsible management of the world's forests. Products carrying the
FSC label are independently certified to assure consumers that they come
from forests that are managed to meet the social, economic and
ecological needs of present and future generations,
and other controlled sources.

Find out more about HarperCollins and the environment at
www.harpercollins.co.uk/green

For Gypsy, Pandora, Bella, Buttons, Snoopy, and J.R.,
my furry companions through life...

Chapter One

Socks the cat (full name: Socks Fifth Avenue) had endured an awful night. Fortunately, she had managed to awaken her person after the fire had started in the house. They'd gotten out seconds before lightning hit the large tree which fell and destroyed the bedroom. The storm was bad enough, but spending the night in the hotel with the constant slamming doors and voices from the next room had left her unnerved. The saving grace was that her person had lavished her with so much love and attention, thankful that Socks had saved their lives.

To make things worse, she was now riding in her pet carrier—which all cats loathe—but was hopefully on her way to more peaceful surroundings.

Tish McKenna entered her law office in the Empire State Building with a pet carrier in one hand while wheeling a large suitcase with the other. Her petite doe-eyed assistant, Shelley Downs, got up to greet her tall blonde boss with a hug. "Tish, thank God you're okay. You could have been killed."

Tish held up the pet carrier to eye level. "It's all thanks to this little one. I didn't even know the house was on fire until she woke me and about thirty seconds after we got out a tree fell and crushed the bedroom." She turned and looked at her fur baby, a young black-and-white tuxedo cat with four white paws. "Someone is going to be treated really well for the rest of her eight lives."

"Like you don't already spoil her." Shelley shoved her long chestnut hair behind her ears and poked her finger through the carrier grate. "Hey, Socks. You're quite the little heroine. Much better than a smoke alarm." The cat meowed and licked her finger. "So I guess you couldn't leave her in the hotel."

"No, all the noise from the other rooms freaked her out all night and you know that she'd escape when housekeeping came through."

"So where are you gonna keep her?"

"In my office, for now."

"Seriously, Tish? A cat in a law firm?"

"Look, it will be months before my house is repaired and I can't leave her there with all the construction going on. So I'll be with her during the day and we've got the law student working here in the evenings to keep her company. I already talked to him and he loves cats. She can stay in my office and I'll see clients in the conference room for now. And I'm staying with Madison and Nick on the weekends so she'll come home with me every Friday and back on Monday morning. She can't get out of this office because the cleaning crew only works on Saturdays and she'll be with me then."

"Okay, but what if the landlord finds out you have a cat in the building? I would imagine that would be against the rules in your lease."

"You forget I kept his ex-wife from cleaning him out a few years ago. So the guy owes me big time. I could keep a family of ring-tailed lemurs in here and he wouldn't say a word."

"Right, I forgot you were his lawyer. Hey, I just thought of something…the cat you named Socks Fifth Avenue actually gets to live on Fifth Avenue for a while."

"Yep. Monday to Friday anyway."

"Uh, one more thing. I have one obvious logistical question regarding something unpleasant as it applies to the care and feeding of cats. Specifically the care part."

"Litter box goes in my storage closet."

Shelley's face tightened. "And who—"

"Don't worry, Shelley, you don't have to scoop the litter box. I've got one of those battery powered gadgets that scoops every time she uses it. It's got some sensor so it knows when she leaves. All I have to do is refill the litter and occasionally empty the thing."

"Damn, cats have it better than us."

"In some ways. But a lot of cats aren't so lucky and need a home. You should get one."

"Yeah, I've been thinking about it. It would be nice to have someone to come home to."

"Anyway, the automatic litter box is with her stuff in the suitcase."

"Socks has her own suitcase?"

"Hey, she has her needs. Litter box, litter, food, dishes, toys, bed, it's all in there. Luckily it was all in the part of the house that wasn't damaged, so I went back in after they put the fire out and got her supplies. A cat can't just leave home with the fur on her back, you know. What would the other cats think?"

"So, no car seat? Video games?"

"Stop it. Anyway, I've got to be in court in an hour in front of that new judge."

"That poor witness. Facing you in a bad mood."

"I can take out my frustrations. Anyway, if you can help me get Socks set up I'd appreciate it."

Tish and Shelley headed into her office and closed the door, then let Socks out of the carrier. The cat slowly stepped out onto the plush red carpet and immediately began to explore her new surroundings.

Shelley rolled her dark eyes as she sat on the edge of the desk.

"What?" asked Tish.

"It just hit me. If anyone finds out about this, we're going to be known as the *cat lady law firm*."

"Two single women in their mid-thirties who share an office with a cat. Not exactly a stretch."

"Speak for yourself, Tish."

*

Spencer Capshaw and his partner Ariel Nix headed toward the courtroom on a reconnaissance mission.

The two thirty-five year old lawyers needed to check out the new judge in town, as they had an upcoming case on her docket. If a judge was one who didn't play by the rules, or was a major pain, they needed to know in advance.

Spencer held the door for Ariel as they entered the crowded courtroom and took seats in the last row, already filled with a bunch of lawyers who'd obviously had the same idea. He tried to get comfortable on the ancient, hard wooden bench that was worse than a church pew, stretching out his lean five-foot-ten frame. "So, what did you dig up on this judge from your friends?"

"Not much you're going to like, Spence. The term *ballbuster* did come up a lot."

"So she's really tough on the guys, huh?"

"That comment came from the women."

He ran his hands through his dark, tousled hair. "Wonderful."

"Oh, stop it. You always manage to charm even the crustiest female judge with that boy-next-door persona you've got going. You flash those big olive green eyes, give them the innocent look and it's game over." The tall, slender brunette crossed her legs and rocked a four inch red heel on her toe as she leaned back. Her hazel eyes focused on the front of the courtroom.

"Oh, like you don't flirt with men on the jury."

"I plead the fifth on the grounds you may be right. And that was just one juror." He gave her a disbelieving look. "Okay, maybe two or three."

"I think you've simply lost count."

"All rise!" The bailiff's voice echoed through the ancient courtroom. "Court is now in session. The honorable Rebecca Winston presiding."

Conversation stopped as the judge entered, took her seat on the bench and looked at some paperwork through gold-rimmed bifocals as everyone in the room sat down. Judge Winston looked to be in her mid-forties, a slim, dark brunette with straight hair that curled under her chin.

A tall blonde attorney approached the bench. Spencer sat up straight as he locked in on her. Hair up, horn-rimmed glasses, ultra conservative blue suit with a knee-length skirt, pale silk blouse buttoned up to her neck. "*Who* is *that*?"

Ariel patted his hand. "Down, boy."

Spencer figured what Ariel had heard about the judge was exaggerated, especially since the lawyers for both sides were women and nothing out of the ordinary had happened. Judge Winston appeared to be tough but fair, and ran a tight ship. By the book, followed the law and kept things moving. If she had any political leanings, they weren't evident. His kind of judge. All he ever wanted was a fair trial from someone who didn't have an agenda.

But what captured his attention was the performance of the blonde attorney as she cross-examined the current witness. The middle-aged man on the stand squirmed in his seat and kept mopping his brow, as her laser-sharp questions kept his flop sweat on a steady flow. Spencer leaned over and whispered in Ariel's ear. "Damn, she's amazing. This is like the legal version of waterboarding."

"The witness looks like he's getting a prostate exam with a yardstick."

He crossed his legs as his face tightened. "Thank you for that lovely mental picture."

The attorney continued to hammer the witness, barely giving him time to finish his answer before hitting him with another question. The man stammered as he started to give a long, ridiculous answer to her question.

Then she turned to the jury, her back to the judge, pulled a handkerchief out of her pocket, took off her glasses to clean them and gave the jury a world class eye roll.

They all smiled.

She finished cleaning her glasses as she turned back to the witness.

Spencer couldn't help but admire her.

Ariel cocked her head at the attorney. "You catch that thing with the glasses and the look she gave to the jury? Pretty slick."

"She's got great eyes. I've never seen such a deep blue."

"Oh for God's sake, I was talking about the eye roll to the jury that the judge couldn't see."

"Yeah, that was a neat trick. She still has great eyes. You think she's got colored contact lenses?"

"Duh, she's wearing glasses, Sherlock."

"Oh, right."

"Geez, if you ever have to face her in court you won't have a chance."

The attorney finished up what could only be described as an inquisition of the witness and the judge looked at her watch. "I think this is a good stopping point," said the judge. "We'll recess for lunch and I want everyone back here at one-thirty sharp. And that does not mean one-thirty-one."

The blonde attorney raised one finger. "Approach the bench before we go, your honor?"

"Make it quick, counselor. There's a pastrami sandwich with my name on it in my chambers. Which I assume the bailiff remembered to order. And I hope he got one for himself." The bailiff nodded and smiled as the crowd chuckled. The judge motioned for the attorney to come forward, put her hand over the microphone and leaned toward her. She listened for a minute, then nodded as the attorney went back to her desk. The judge looked up at the crowd. "It has been brought to my attention that there has been a good bit of distracting chatter from the back of the room. Apparently the last row in a courtroom is the same as the one in a classroom, filled with those hooligans who can't keep quiet. Now I understand that since this is my first day there are a lot of attorneys here as you guys want to get a feel for the new sheriff in town. So let me say that if I hear so much as a whisper from a lawyer who is not involved in this case when we return from lunch, I will have no qualms about sending those who can't shut the hell up for a mini-vacation in a rather uncomfortable cell. And speaking of cells, I'd better not hear any of those ring either." She narrowed her eyes at the back row. "Do I make myself clear?"

The blonde attorney looked in Spencer's direction. He turned and looked to both sides, as if searching for the culprit.

Ariel shook her head, wrote on her legal pad and slid it onto his lap.

Bus-ted.

Spencer handed his lunch menu to the waiter and turned to Ariel. "So, what did you think?"

"I thought the judge was very fair. I don't think she was biased either way. If she has an agenda it will take a while for everyone to figure it out. And obviously she has no tolerance for people who disrupt her courtroom. I think she got a bad rap from the people I talked to. I wouldn't have a problem with her."

"Not the judge. What did you think about the attorney?"

"The short brunette? Eh, she was okay."

"I meant the other one." His eyes widened as he flashed a slight smile.

"I know you did. Ah, I knew she was your type."

"I don't have a type."

"Oh, bull. She's just like all the other women you've dated."

"I've never been out with a blonde."

Ariel shook her head. "Nothing to do with hair color, sweetie. When it comes to what gets your motor running, they all have the same common denominator."

"Enlighten me, counselor."

"Let's see…she checks all the boxes for you. Conservative outfit, skirt to the knee, practical heels, strand of pearls the only jewelry, pure old-school class. The kind of woman who wouldn't be caught dead in a bikini or miniskirt even though she might have a killer body. Not stunning but attractive in a classic way. What you always refer to as *quietly beautiful*. Strong and independent, obviously in control. And the big one that really turns you on, she's obviously smart and spunky as hell. Kicks ass and takes no prisoners. You have to agree the woman owned the courtroom. What she did to that witness probably violated the Patriot Act. I can't believe I'm saying this, but she was tougher on a witness than you are, and you're ruthless."

"I can't believe I'm agreeing with you."

"Anyway, did I just describe your perfect woman?"

"Okay, I admit I'm attracted to really smart women who are pretty but aren't flashy. However, that's a really broad brush."

"Ah, but the thing that drives all guys nuts…hair up and glasses. You fantasize that once the hair comes down and the glasses come off, she's a hellcat in bed."

He couldn't hold back a sly smile. "Hence the term, *let your hair down*. And I've found it to be true in most cases."

"What about women who never wear their hair up, like me?"

"I plead the fifth on the grounds that I already love you. You're the sister I never had."

"Good answer, Mister. Oooh, I almost forgot. Added to all that, she's got another quality you can't resist."

"What else?"

"That scratchy, lives-in-a-smoky-bar whiskey voice. Demi Moore meets Lorraine Bracco meets Angie Harmon. Hell, if she ever got disbarred she could get a job with a phone sex company."

"Fine, I'll give you that. Her voice was sexy as hell. Now can we get back to the case we have tomorrow? We've got a long night ahead of us already."

"Sure. But this is a lot more fun." Ariel flashed a grin as their lunch order arrived. She picked up her fork and stabbed at a piece of salad. "Oh, before I forget, I wanted to run something by you. I have a possible case coming up with a man who... well...is pretty much a horrible person."

Spencer shrugged. "We represent a lot of people who are long way from being decent. Hey, unless he's murdered someone, what's the big deal?"

"Yeah, but this one—"

"Will the client's checks bounce?"

"No, he has extremely deep pockets."

"Well, then, I think that ends the discussion. We are in business to make money, after all."

Ariel nodded. "Hmm, that we are..."

*

Tish finished her research around six just as law school intern Brian Stevens entered her office. She reached over to pet Socks, who had claimed the corner of her desk as her own for the last several hours. "Hi, Brian. Meet your new assistant."

"Ah, this must be Socks." The short, sandy-haired, third-year law student moved forward to pet the cat. "So, she actually saved your life, huh?"

"Yep. I could sleep through an atomic bomb. If she hadn't

woken me up I'd be taking a dirt nap because the smoke alarm didn't go off. I owe her big time."

"Well, I love cats and I'll keep her company tonight. She's in good hands."

"Thanks, Brian, I appreciate it." Tish pointed to the round table on the other side of her office. "I've left all the stuff for the upcoming case over there. If you could finish by the end of the week that would be great."

"I'm on it and ahead of schedule."

"You sure this won't interfere with your studying for the bar?"

"I'm fine. Trust me, I know how to manage my time."

"Great, but if you need study time just let me know. Oh, all the cat supplies are in the closet if she needs anything. I've already put out plenty of food and water, so you're good to go in that department. But do give her a handful of treats before you go. That's been her usual bedtime snack."

He started to laugh. "Glad you don't spoil her, Miss McKenna."

"Hey, she deserves every bit of it. She's got nine lives and saved the only one I've got."

Three hours later Brian wrapped up his duties. He lifted Socks off his lap, as she had been there the entire time. "Okay, kitty, gotta go. Don't mess with the paperwork." He carried the cat to her bed under the desk and set her on it. She immediately curled up into a ball. "Night, Socks. See you tomorrow."

Socks raised her head as soon as the man closed the door. With all the attention she'd had today, there hadn't been enough free time to thoroughly explore her new surroundings. The room wasn't nearly as interesting as the one in which she'd been raised. But at least it was quiet. After all the commotion last night, she needed a peaceful sleep.

But something captured her attention behind the bookcase, and being as curious as any other cat, she had to investigate. She easily fit between it and the wall and saw the open vent that was dimly lit, then heard a voice coming through it. Her ears perked up. It was not her person, but a male voice.

She decided to follow it and entered the vent.

A noise caught Spencer's attention. He looked up from his notes and turned to Ariel. "You hear that?"

"Your stomach growling? Yeah. Let's head out for dinner."

"Not that. Something's in the wall. Listen." He cocked his head in the direction of the sound. "Aw, hell. Probably a damn rat. That's all we need."

She turned her head toward the bookcase. "Yeah. It's coming from over there. Well, it is New York City. Though I wouldn't expect rats in this building."

Then they heard the meow and saw a cat emerge from behind the bookcase. "Well, I'll be damned." Spencer got up and crouched down next to the cat. "Where did you come from?" It meowed again and nuzzled his hand. Spencer noticed it had a red collar. "This isn't a stray."

Ariel got up and looked behind the bookcase. "Oh, I see what happened. It obviously came through the vent. They must have forgotten to put the covers back on when they did all the remodeling on this floor last month. And since the bookcases are built-in, the vents are gonna stay open."

"I guess it's somebody's office cat."

"Someone has an office cat in the Empire State Building?"

"Hey, why not?" He picked it up and looked at the collar, turning it all the way around to see if there was an ID tag. "There's nothing to identify the owner. But obviously it's gotta be someone on this floor."

"Sounds right. Can't imagine a cat can climb up or down in a steel vent."

He looked at the cat. "You hungry, kitty?" It meowed.

Ariel headed out the door. "I've got some cans of tuna in the break room. And milk for coffee. I'll go get it."

Spencer sat down and put the cat on his lap, then started to stroke its soft fur. He was rewarded with a purr. "Y'know, an office cat is not a bad idea. So who do you belong to?"

Ariel returned with some food for the cat, putting a saucer of milk and some tuna in a dish on the floor. "See if she'll eat something."

Spencer put the cat near the food. It ate about half of the tuna, drank a little milk, then took off behind the bookcase. "Well, that was a quick visit. So much for trying to find her owner."

"She must know her way around."

"Maybe so. Guess I'll pick up some cat food in case she drops by again."

Ariel shook her head as she shot him a smile. "You crack me up."

"What?"

"I know what you're thinking."

"You do, huh?"

"Now you want an office cat, don't you?"

"Not terribly practical for a law firm, but if that one likes to hang out here I won't complain. We always had cats when I was a kid, and to be honest I've been meaning to get a pet."

"Well, don't spoil her. You can't get a reputation as the lawyer who stole someone's cat. There are laws against that, you know."

"What laws?"

"Catnapping."

Chapter Two

Tish saw that her three closest friends had already arrived at the restaurant. Normally they went out on the weekend, but in light of the situation with her house, Rory, A.J. and Madison insisted they get together for moral support on Tuesday evening. Tish couldn't help but agree; being literally driven from her home in the middle of the night was beyond stressful. Even though no one had been hurt, living in Madison's guest room on weekends for a few months and a Manhattan hotel during the week while her home was being repaired would be disorienting. Her home had been a second office with everything impeccably organized; now it was a water and smoke-damaged disaster. If she hadn't had a hanging bag of a few outfits she'd just bought in her car, she would have had nothing to wear.

Of course, Tish had no choice but to count her blessings. She had adopted a cat who had literally saved her life.

Everyone got up to hug her as she arrived. "Thanks, guys. Really appreciate all your help."

Madison, the tall redheaded network television reporter who had given her Socks, patted her on the shoulder as they all sat. "You're good to go in our guest room. Nick's got everything squared away. He took your clothes that survived to the cleaners and hopefully they can get the smoke out of them. I've got some outfits for you in my car, enough to get you through the rest of the week. Y'know, since the insurance company is going to buy you some clothes, you might consider jazzing up your wardrobe a bit."

"Nice try. Anyway, your fiancé is a saint. I'm jealous. But I hate that I'm cramping your style moving into your love nest on weekends for a few months."

"You'll get used to Madison screaming," said Rory, Madison's best friend who lived across the street and worked at home as a copywriter. The slim brunette flashed a wicked grin.

"Yeah," said A.J., the petite New York Italian gal who ran the family delicatessen. "So much for keeping the windows closed during sex to keep it a secret."

Madison started to blush. "Stop it. Anyway, Tish, my network wants you and Socks sometime this weekend, probably on the Saturday morning show."

"What for?"

"Cat saves owner's life, film at eleven. It's an incredible tale. Or tail, as the case may be. And you know the story of my litter of orphaned kittens refuses to die. The dominoes of their effect on people continue to tumble. They're a bunch of furry good luck charms."

"No argument here."

"Besides, you can throw in a plug for the local shelter and talk about pets that need adopting."

"Sure, I'll do it."

A.J. handed Tish a business card. "My cousin Angelo says he should have you back in your house around Christmas. He pulled some of his guys off another job and got the insurance company out there already. He said everything is covered and you get replacement value. Don't worry, they won't cut corners. Your house will actually be better than new. He'll be getting in touch with you to pick out paint colors, flooring and that sort of stuff."

"Thank God you're related to a contractor. This means a lot, A.J. Thank you so much for getting him over so fast."

Madison leaned back as she studied a menu. "So how's the furry little lifesaver doing in her new weekday home?"

"Socks seemed to really like being in the office instead of at home by herself during the day. And my law intern is keeping her company in the evening. She already sleeps at night. You sure I can bring her home on the weekends?"

"Of course. You can't leave her in the office and she'll love playing with Bumper again. And my cat will be thrilled. You sure you don't want to leave her with me full time?"

"She'd miss me too much."

Rory rolled her eyes. "Wait for it…"

"Fine," said Tish. "And I'd miss her too much."

A young brunette waitress arrived at the table with a water jug and filled their glasses. She pulled an order pad from her apron. "Good evening, ladies. Can I start you off with something from the bar?"

Tish nodded. "Big bottle of bourbon. No glass."

The waitress laughed. "I'm sorry, but we don't allow drinking right from the bottle. Though I could wrap it in a brown paper bag and you could go out back."

"Then a nice chilled bottle of Pinot Grigio with four glasses please."

"Sure." She wrote down the order. "Let me tell you about our specials this evening. Tonight our chef has prepared— "

"Hey! Waitress!" The man at a table in the middle of the room interrupted her, waving frantically while looking angry. He pointed at her. "You! Right now!"

The waitress turned and her face dropped. "Excuse me a minute. We have a problem customer at one of my tables and I need to deal with him."

Spencer and Ariel stopped eating as the portly middle-aged

bald guy at the next table was making a scene chewing out the young waitress. The eating in the entire restaurant had stopped, as everyone was watching the man.

"I ordered the steak well done, and it was medium! Can't you people get anything right?"

The waitress was shaking a bit. "Sir, if you'd told me that when I brought it to you, I could have sent it back to the chef—"

"You should have checked it before you brought it out, you stupid bitch!"

Spencer threw down his napkin. "Okay, that's it." He stood up and approached the guy. "Hey, buddy, that's enough."

The man turned to him. "Why don't you mind your own business. It's my problem."

"You just made it everyone's business with your big mouth and rude behavior." He pointed to the man's empty plate. "And if you had such an issue with your steak, why did you wait till you ate the whole thing before complaining?"

"What difference does it make? It tasted awful. She couldn't even take a simple order!"

"Obviously you just want a free meal."

"I want what I ordered!"

"That doesn't give you an excuse to talk to the young lady like that. You owe her an apology."

"Like hell."

Spencer turned to the waitress who now had her arms wrapped around her waist. She was pale and trembling. "How much is his check?"

"Thirty-eight dollars."

Spencer pulled out his wallet and handed her a one-hundred dollar bill. "Keep the change." He turned back to the man. "Now, since you got your free dinner, why don't you get the hell out and let the rest of us eat in peace? And do everyone a favor. Don't come back. Next time go buy a hot dog at Coney Island." He tossed two dollars at the man. "Here, it's on me."

The man got up and stormed out to a round of applause.

The waitress put her hand over her chest and exhaled as Spencer sat down. "Sir, thank you so much for sticking up for me. And picking up the check. That was incredibly nice of you."

"Not a problem."

"You sure you don't want change?"

"I think you earned a big tip for dealing with that idiot."

"Well, thank you again. If you need anything, let me know."

Ariel reached over and patted his hand as the waitress headed back to work. "My partner, legal shark by day, Boy Scout by night."

"Just doing the right thing. He had no right to talk to her that way."

"I know, I was giving you a compliment. While every woman wants to be treated like an equal, every woman wants a man who will stand up for her. I'm proud to have an old fashioned guy like you as a partner. And a friend."

Tish wore a dreamy look as she stared at the man who had rescued the waitress. "Damn, that was some old fashioned chivalry over there. And he's awfully cute."

Madison nodded as she sipped her water. "Yeah. Too bad he's sitting with some babe."

Rory turned back to the menu. "And now we know the reason some babe is sitting with him. White knights are hard to find."

A.J. shook her head. "Yep. The good ones are always taken."

Madison playfully slapped her arm. "Hey, Nick wasn't taken when I snagged him."

Tish patted her hand. "He snagged you, sweetie. You swallowed the hook and practically jumped into the boat."

"Okay, no argument here. But come to think of it, we don't know if that woman is his girlfriend."

The waitress returned with their wine. "Sorry about that, everyone. Our manager says drinks are on the house tonight."

"Hey, not your fault," said Tish. "You okay?"

"Just shaken up a bit. I think I'm the one who needs the big bottle of bourbon. Thank goodness for Mr. Capshaw taking charge of the situation."

Madison cocked her head at the man. "You know the guy?"

"He's one of our regulars. Very nice guy and really good tipper. And of course he just saved me from a jerk and getting stuck with the check, which I really couldn't afford."

Rory looked at the pretty brunette sitting across from the man. "Do you happen to know if the woman sitting with him is his wife or girlfriend?"

The waitress shrugged. "No clue. But if she isn't, take a number. What woman wouldn't want a guy like that?"

*

After a supportive dinner with her friends, Tish had a spring in her step the next morning as she headed into the office, but it vanished when she saw the worried look on her assistant's face. "What's wrong? Oh my God, is Socks okay?"

"She's fine. And I already fed her."

"Then why do you look like you just ate the cat food?"

Shelley handed her a newspaper. "Because we just lost our biggest and nicest client."

Tish's eyes grew wide as she saw the headline. "Oh my God! His company went belly up?"

"Apparently some of his employees embezzled a ton of money while driving the company into the ground. Dammit, I hate that it happened to such a good guy."

"I know. But that was part of his problem. He was too damn trusting." Tish scanned the article. "I told him he couldn't be such an absentee owner. But he said he had good people running things. What a shame."

"Anything we can do?"

"I'll give him a call right now. Maybe I can get my friend in the DA's office to help him recover the embezzled funds. Not sure what I can do about the company shutting down."

"Damn, this has been the week from hell. First your house and now this."

"Yeah, and with this new development my house is now on the back burner. I gotta make some rain, Shelley. He was responsible for more than fifty percent of our revenue. We're gonna need some new clients."

"Speaking of new clients, you've got one coming in shortly."

"I know, but that's a contingency. We have to win to get paid."

"You usually win, Tish. Hell, you're way over ninety percent."

"Yeah, but right now we need some definite income. And that case is going to take a ton of time. Plus, it's a David and Goliath case and I'm going to need a big friggin' slingshot to win or even get a settlement. Damn, now I almost wish I hadn't taken it."

"You took it because you've got a good heart. You could always refer her—"

"I said almost. The poor woman was turned down by lawyers all over town and she's really in a bind. I can't do that to her. But if the case doesn't pan out, well…"

"Don't worry, we'll be fine. You have too good of a reputation. Meanwhile, there's something on your desk that demands your immediate attention."

"What, we heard back from the judge on the Carson case?"

"No. Your cat is waiting for you."

Tish headed into her office, finding Socks sitting on the corner of her desk. "I see you have permanently claimed that spot." She reached out to pet the cat and was rewarded with a lick on her hand. Then she sat behind the desk and Socks immediately climbed in her lap. She picked up the phone as the cat looked up at her. "Okay, kitty, gotta find some clients to keep you in that high end cat food."

*

"Do you think we have a chance? I mean, really? No one else wanted this case." Tish noted the woman's eyes were sad and desperate.

She had almost considered Shelley's suggestion to refer the client to another law firm with which she had a great relationship, one that could handle a loss of both considerable time and money. But the moment the woman entered her office, shook hands and locked eyes, she knew she couldn't abandon her.

Especially when the new client told her why time was of the essence.

She was dying.

A big settlement would get her the medical care to save her life.

If Tish lost the case, well…

Her friend Madison hadn't abandoned helpless orphaned kittens, and that was how she'd ended up with a wonderful cat like Socks.

In much the same way, she couldn't in good conscience abandon this client who was basically an orphan seeking a lawyer. Who would die without her help.

And right now, Tish needed to give the woman an injection of confidence because she couldn't possibly look this defeated in a courtroom. The woman was forty but the stress she'd gone through made her look ten years older. Face drawn, eyes drooping, dark brown hair a ragged mess. Tish knew she'd be very attractive with a little attention and a smile. She leaned forward and nodded. "Cynthia, I think we have an excellent chance. And I want you to focus on that when we come face to face with the defendant. If you look defeated, you give them an advantage. Hold your head up high and always look like you've got the upper hand. Confidence is key."

"I'll do my best, Miss McKenna."

"Tish, please."

"Okay. Tish. I can't thank you enough for taking me on a

contingency. I'd been through six law firms and everyone wanted a huge retainer. I'm broke or I'd give you something. Maybe later this year—"

Tish smiled and waved it away. "Don't worry about it. I didn't become a lawyer just to make money. Sometimes you have to do the right thing, and in this case that means representing you. What was done to you was unconscionable."

"You're a good person, Miss McKenna. I could tell the minute I met you. And people say you're an incredible lawyer. When I heard your nickname I was expecting…well…"

Tish laughed. "Well, that's my name in the courtroom. I'm pretty much a softie when I'm off the clock. Anyway, I want you to stop worrying. You're in good hands. And I have an excellent assistant to work on this case. Even my law intern is helping out."

The woman finally smiled a bit. "Thank you. I can tell you really care. How long do you think this will take?"

"Well, that depends on the other side and who they hire. If they get the right attorney who doesn't play games, we could be done by the holidays. And hopefully have something in your Christmas stocking."

"That sounds good. I don't want one of those cases that lingers on for years and years."

"Don't worry, this one's pretty cut and dried. We might not even have to go to court if I can get a decent settlement offer. Would that interest you?"

"Depends on the offer, but I'll listen to anything. And of course, defer to your advice."

"Well, remember, I work for you. I can offer advice but any final decision will be yours. If something doesn't feel right, tell me. Anyway, I'll get things filed shortly and then we'll see who we're up against."

"I know who we're up against, and he has deep pockets."

"I meant the lawyer. But I'm gonna pick the defendant's pockets."

Spencer's eyes narrowed as tossed his pen on the stack of papers. "I can't wait to get this guy on the stand and rip his throat out."

Ariel reached across the desk and patted his hand. "Someone's inner shark gets cranky when he doesn't eat."

"Sorry, I will not lose this case. But you're right, I'm starving. You wanna go get some dinner or order in?"

Ariel pulled out her cell phone. "I'll order some Chinese. If we go out to a restaurant we'll get too relaxed and then we won't get home till midnight. It'll set us back two hours."

"Then again if you get Chinese I'll want a nap. Get something from the Italian place." He reached under his desk, grabbed a bag, got up and moved to the bookcase, then pulled a bag of cat treats from the bag and shook it.

"What have you got there, cat food? What are you doing?"

"Playing Pavlov and the cat. Seeing if our furry friend wants to come visit."

Ariel laughed. "You are too funny. Six hundred dollar an hour attorney trying to lure someone else's cat through an air vent. I should take a picture of this and write it up for the law review."

"The cat's owner might sue us if you make it public."

"For?"

"As you said, catnapping." He shook the bag again, then stopped to listen. "I think I hear something."

"Yeah, but it might be a rat."

"If it is a rat, the cat will get it."

Ariel looked up and sure enough, the tuxedo cat emerged from behind the bookcase. "No one would believe this."

Spencer shook some treats into his hand and held it out. The cat quickly gobbled them up, then nuzzled his arm. "Hey there kitty, how was your day? You want a few more?"

"Y'know, that cat is going to get fat enjoying the smorgasbord between you and her owner, who has no idea someone else is feeding her."

"I'm just giving her a few treats, that's all."

"Right, that's how it starts." She noted the pure joy in his face as he fed the cat. "And I cannot believe you're actually sacrificing part of a billable hour to spend time with a cat."

"It's just a little while."

Ariel looked at the clock and leaned back in her chair. "Spence, speaking of time, what the hell are we doing here still working after nine o'clock?"

"We've got a lot to do."

"Not what I meant. We don't need to kill ourselves anymore. And frankly, I'm sick of eating dinner out of a Styrofoam container or a pizza box at my desk. Listen to me for a minute. Look, you left the District Attorney's office and I quit the *pro bono* world of Legal Aid to start this firm so you could make enough to take care of your father. But you got him the expensive medical care, he's cured, you even bought him a house, he's retired and happy…I mean, we make a ton of money working normal hours. Why are you still in that mindset that we have to take every client who walks in the door and need every dollar we can possibly make?"

"Because it could happen again."

"Your dad is fine and you got him the best health insurance money could buy. And the doctor told you his illness was a one-in-ten-million thing."

"One of *us* could get sick."

"And we're both covered by the same insurance. Besides, I'd always take care of you and you'd do the same for me." She sat back and looked at him. "Have you forgotten why you wanted to be a lawyer and why we took the first jobs that we did?"

He slowly nodded but didn't respond as he kept petting the cat.

"Y'know, Spence, that cat makes you look like your old self."

"Huh?"

"Relaxed and happy. You've got that same look you used to have when you helped the good guys win at the DA's office. Can you honestly say the people we're representing in this case are the good guys? Would you even want to be in the same room with them if they weren't clients?"

"Not really. To be honest, I can't stand them personally."

"Hell, I feel like I need a shower every time they come by. Spence, this kind of work is making us a lot of money, but we're not really making the world a better place. And I know that's why you became a lawyer."

He looked back at the cat. "I guess I've kinda gotten away from what I used to believe."

"You still believe it. Money, and the people you help with it, is just clouding your memory." She pointed at the cat. "While your furry friend there is a perfect example of what makes you happy. Yesterday you said you've been meaning to get a pet. That means taking the time to be with it. Time away from this office. You can't just get a cat and leave it alone in your apartment all day. When you adopt a pet you make a commitment to be part of its life. It's not an accessory. It's a living creature that needs love and attention. And if we don't slow down you won't have the time. But if we do then you'll be able to enjoy the unconditional love of a cat."

He turned to look at her. "I'm sorry, Ariel, but once you go through something like my dad's situation—"

"I know and I understand. You're terrified it could happen again. But you can't go through life worried about what might lie ahead. Take some time to smell the roses. Or play with a cat. You make a lot of money, so it's time you started enjoying it. Even your dad says you work too hard. Hell, you haven't taken a vacation in three years."

He exhaled and nodded a bit as he scratched the cat's head. "I guess we could…scale things back."

"Good. Let's start by not taking any more clients and that will take things off our plate by attrition."

"Sure. No new clients."

"And even better…let's send a few clients to some other firms and add a few *pro bono* cases to replace them. You know that helping desperate people is what makes you happiest, so let's get back to that a little."

"You're right, Ariel."

"Meanwhile, the hell with ordering in. Let's go to dinner, relax, have some wine, and then actually go home. Maybe once we clear some of these cases we might be able to eat dinner before the sun goes down instead of like a bunch of vampires." She pointed at the cat. "Meanwhile, you gonna call the little furball Kitty?"

"Well, there's no name on her collar. I'll come up with something. I guess we need to find out if it's a boy cat or a girl cat. Do you know how to tell?"

Ariel folded her arms. "Do I look like a veterinarian to you?"

Spencer moved back to his laptop and did a search. "Hang on a minute. Okay, here we go. How to sex a cat."

"I hope you don't get arrested. If the Feds look at your search history and see that, God knows what they'll think."

Spencer chuckled and continued reading. "It says to look directly under the tail. If it looks like a colon, it's a boy. Upside down exclamation point, it's a girl."

"Well, I'm not doing this punctuation search of a cat's nether regions. Knock yourself out."

He picked up the cat and took a look. "Our guest is a young lady."

"Well, you do need a nice girl on your lap."

"Very funny."

"Speaking of which, you want me to track down the name of that lawyer with the great eyes who turned your head? I mean, if you think you can sacrifice the billable hours in order to actually go on a date with her and have a social life."

He offered a slight smile. "Okay, okay, you've made your point. But yeah, it would definitely be worth it."

Chapter Three

By Friday morning, cabin fever, or rather hotel room fever, had set in. Tish hated living out of a suitcase and couldn't wait to get to Madison's house for the weekend. Her friend had offered her the chance to stay there all the time, but the commute would take too many valuable hours away, especially in light of her lost client. She needed every minute to dredge up new business and work on her big case if she was to get her law practice back on solid ground. The only good thing about living in a hotel was that it was very close to her office. She determined the only way to make the next few months livable was to spend as little time in the hotel as possible.

The early morning jog along the river had brightened her spirits. She had fallen out of an exercise routine and though she had maintained her one hundred and forty pounds on her five-eight frame, she had gotten a bit soft and out of shape sitting at a desk or in a courtroom all day. Time to get toned again and getting away from the hotel was a good incentive. Besides, it was a pretty fall morning, sunny and unseasonably warm. She finished her run, out of breath and soaked with sweat, hair matted to her face. She was parched as she spotted the soda cart in front of the hotel. She made her way over to get a cool drink, finding herself behind a man in a suit who was talking on a cell phone.

The burly, fiftyish guy with salt-and-pepper hair operating the cart handed a cup of coffee to the man as she moved forward. He gave her a warm smile. "Can I help you, young lady?"

"Thank you for calling me young."

"No charge for compliments."

"You got a cold club soda, or sparkling water?"

"Sure." He reached into the cooler, pulled out a can and handed it to her. "Dollar."

She reached into her pocket. Empty. "Damn it. I forgot some money. I'm in the hotel, I'll be right back."

The man in the suit apparently overheard. "Hang on a minute." He put the phone against his chest, reached in his pocket and handed the guy a dollar bill. "I got it."

She turned to face him. "Thank you, that's very kind of you—"

And then it hit her.

Her eyes went wide as she looked into the face of the white knight from the restaurant.

She had called him *awfully cute*, but up close he was *beyond* cute.

And here she was looking like absolute crap in the paint covered sweatpants and old t-shirt she kept in her car.

"No problem," he said, flashing her a smile. "Excuse me." He turned away and went back to his phone call as he looked at his watch. "I'm back. Anyway, I'll see you Saturday night but I gotta go." He started to walk away. "Love you too."

Tish shook her head. "Well, damn. Can this week get any worse?"

The soda cart guy studied her face. "Something wrong, Miss?"

"My luck just needs to change, that's all."

*

Spencer waited until Ariel left the office for a deposition. She'd be gone an hour or so, more than enough time for him to follow through on her idea.

Finding out the identity of the lawyer who had seriously kicked ass in the courtroom the other day. Ariel was right about the woman being his type. Intelligence trumped everything with him, and that woman was off-the-charts brilliant. Her combination of street smarts and knowledge of the law was impressive. Toss in some New York City spunk and her appeal skyrocketed.

And she was quietly beautiful with those spectacular eyes.

He logged into the New York City justice system database and called up the docket for the new judge, then clicked on the case that had been scheduled for her first morning.

A quick read reminded him there was a female attorney for both the plaintiff and the defendant. One of the names was somehow familiar. "Where the hell do I know that from?" He paused a minute, but couldn't place it.

He opened another window on the laptop and logged into the New York Bar Association website, then typed in the name of the defendant's lawyer, Jolene Davis.

He drummed his fingers on the desk as he waited for her bio to load. Then shook his head as the screen featured a photo of a brunette in her fifties. "Nope, not her. Gotta be the other one." He typed in "Tish McKenna" and waited.

There she was.

His pulse quickened a bit as he started to read her bio—

Which stopped him dead in his tracks. His jaw dropped as he saw the name of the law school and the year she'd graduated.

"You gotta be kidding me. She was in my class? How the hell did I miss someone like that?"

Because you were young and stupid. And into flashy bimbos back then like most men of that age.

He simply couldn't remember her at all. Next stop, the website for his law school's alumni association. He pulled up the photo of the graduating class, read the caption to find the name and her place in the photo. When he saw her face he instantly remembered the woman.

"Oh." His eyes narrowed as his jaw and fists clenched. "*Her.*"

There she was, middle of the picture in a cap and gown standing next to the Dean of the law school. She was the valedictorian, her grades so far ahead of the other students it wasn't even close. The one person who had kept him in second place. Known back then as *Mrs. Spock*, nicknamed after the Star Trek character who had no emotions and was driven by pure logic. She had been all business, all the time. Never socialized with any of the other students. Never smiled, cracked a joke or made any comment in class regarding anything other than the law. Didn't go to any of the parties. As far as anyone knew, she never dated. It was like having a nun as a classmate. She sat in the first row, her hand always shooting up like a rocket a nanosecond after the professor asked a question. Answers always perfect. Able to cite obscure legal precedents in a single bound. The woman was a walking law library who got a perfect score on every single exam.

Everyone had hated her. Part jealousy, part lack of personality. Okay, mostly jealousy.

He'd admired her performance in the classroom and actually tried to strike up a conversation with her in the law library during his first year, just to be nice since he knew she hadn't made any friends. He sat down across from her and slid a cup of coffee next to her book. She'd told him, "No offense, and don't take this the wrong way, but I prefer to study alone." She'd picked up her books and moved to another table, leaving him with two cups of java. She was the most driven woman he'd ever seen.

Her.

But the graduation photo didn't remotely look like the woman he'd seen in the courtroom.

The law student with the long, stringy blonde hair who had always looked like an unmade bed in cargo pants and bulky sweatshirts had blossomed like the proverbial ugly duckling into a swan.

"Okay, where is she now?"

Spencer did a search for her firm and his eyes bugged out.

"She's in this building? On this floor? You gotta be kidding me!"

He stared at the photo on her website, the same woman he'd seen in the courtroom.

Actually smiling a bit.

The website was nothing fancy, pure business. No surprise there. She apparently ran a one-person firm. No surprise there either, as he couldn't imagine anyone wanting to work with her and the attitude that came with it.

Back to the justice system website for a search of her cases. "Let's see what kind of clients she likes."

The list was impressive. Tish McKenna obviously wasn't in it for the money—he used to be the same. All her clients seemed to be on the side of good. Lots of pro bono work for charities. A few high profile cases he remembered.

And she won almost every time. Just like law school.

"Bus-ted! Again!"

He swung his chair around and saw Ariel smiling at him. "What happened to your deposition?"

"Canceled. Much to your dismay." She pointed at the laptop. "Ah, stalking the classy attorney, I see."

His face immediately flushed. "I was just curious since, uh, you know, you said we should hire her."

"Oh, gimme a break, Spence, you've got a thing for her. We've been friends too long for me to miss the signals. Those glasses came off and it was game over. If we'd stayed in the courtroom any longer you would have needed a drool cup." She pulled up a chair and sat next to him. "So, what'd you find out about the mystery woman?"

"You're not going to believe this, but we were in the same class at law school."

"You gotta be kidding."

"Nope."

"Let me get this straight…you're hot for this woman and you spent three years in law school with her? Why didn't you go after her then?"

"She wasn't exactly the same person." He clicked on the laptop and brought up the graduation photo, then pointed at the woman.

"*That's* the lawyer we saw in the courtroom? Damn, I want some of what she's drinking. Talk about getting better looking with age."

He patted Ariel's hand. "Just like you."

"Awww, you're such a sweetie. I really do have you trained and ready for a wife." Ariel leaned forward and pointed at the photo. "And apparently she's not the only one who gets more attractive. Is that really you?"

"Yep."

"Doesn't even look like the same person. But could you not afford a razor? That is one sorry looking beard. You look like you're trying out for Occupy Wall Street."

"Yeah, it seemed like a good idea at the time. I got rid of it right after graduation. My adviser said it wasn't good for job interviews."

"Anyway, back to your infatuation with the young lady who has the great eyes. May I remind you about the last time you dated a lawyer."

"I would rather you didn't. I've tried very hard to forget her."

"You're not the only one. Dinner with you two was like a trip to the Supreme Court. All you did was argue, and half the time it was over what to order from the menu."

"That doesn't mean all lawyers are like her. Thank God."

"Well, tread carefully. So, what was Miss Spectacular Eyes like back then?"

"She wasn't friends with anyone. I tried being nice to her once in the law library. Brought her a cup of coffee. She picked up her books and walked away. Totally focused on school. Zero personality. Remember the woman I told you about who beat me for valedictorian?"

"*That's* the woman who kept you in second place?"

"Yep. And it wasn't even close. Then she gets the number one score on the bar exam for the entire state of New York. Smartest person I've ever met."

"Which, when you add it to the features she already has, makes you want her even more."

"Hey, I like brilliant women. That's why you and I get along so well."

"You're just full of compliments today. Of course if she *still* has zero personality the point is moot."

"Very true. But she didn't show that kind of spunk in law school when we had mock court. She was more like an android. Since then she's developed an attitude."

"Honey, we all do as we get older."

"Oh, one more thing." He pointed at the monitor. "Check out the address of her firm."

Ariel's jaw slightly dropped. "She's down the hall?"

"Yep. And I've never run into her. I'd remember a woman like that."

"Well, we've only been in this building for a year. So, you gonna walk down to her office and say hello?"

"Are you out of your mind?"

"Why not? You've got a great excuse. You saw her in court, and we could use another lawyer for the firm to take things off our plate. Go pay her a visit, tell her she impressed the hell out of you and see if she might be interested in joining us. Even better, ask her to lunch but call it a job interview."

"Yeah, like that situation couldn't blow up in my face. Dating someone I work with."

"You have a point. Hey, wait a minute."

"What?"

"Since you two went to the same school, I've got an idea how you can meet her."

*

Tish tore into her plate of ziti and meatballs while Socks and Bumper were busy batting a ball of aluminum foil around the living room. "Madison, I cannot tell you how great it feels *not* to eat in a restaurant or be in a hotel room after work." She looked at her plate. "Oh my God, this is fantastic. Did you make this?"

Rory rolled her eyes. "Get real. You know her specialty of the house is burnt toast."

"Nick cooks for her every night," said A.J. "She's one step away from being a kept woman."

Tish took a bite of a meatball and washed it down with some wine. "Damn, Madison, you're gonna be three hundred pounds by your first anniversary."

"Trust me, they work it off," cracked A.J.

Madison slapped her on the shoulder. "A.J.!"

"Hell, Madison," said Rory. "We all know you can't keep your hands off him."

Madison blushed. "Fine. We have an…active lifestyle."

Tish laughed. "Yeah, you hit your target heart rate without leaving the bedroom. Thank God he's not around to hear this. Where is your darling fiancé anyway?"

"Poker game with the guys from his precinct."

"Ah." Tish dabbed her mouth with a napkin. "Speaking of men, I, uh, ran into our white knight from the restaurant."

Conversation stopped. Madison leaned forward. "Really. Do tell."

"Well, I went for a run before going to work and on my way back to the hotel I stopped at a soda cart to get a drink. He was there talking on his cell phone. Anyway, I go to pay for the soda and realized I'd forgotten to bring some cash. He notices, stops talking, pulls out a dollar and pays for it."

Rory locked eyes with her. "And…then what happened?"

"I thanked him, he went back to his phone call and walked away."

A.J. frantically waved her hands. "Whoa, hang on. You just let him walk away?"

"Well, for one, I was soaked with sweat and looked like crap wearing some old clothes I keep in the trunk of my car and he's in a thousand dollar suit. Then I hear him on the phone say, '*I'll see you Saturday night, love you too.*'" Her face dropped. "So you were probably right about that babe he was with in the restaurant. He's obviously taken and the woman he was with was stunning."

Madison shrugged. "He could have been talking to his mother."

Tish shook her head. "Oh, come on. What single guy goes out with his mother on a Saturday night?"

"Could be a sister," said Rory. "Or a close platonic female friend. Or maybe he was going to a party."

"Stop it," said Tish. "Guys like that always have someone." She leaned forward and rested her chin in her hand. "But I tell ya, that guy had the most spectacular olive green eyes I've ever seen. If you thought he was cute from across the restaurant, you should have seen him up close. This great thick hair and he filled out a suit like a model. A real boy next door look, on the line between cute and handsome. The kind of guy you want to take home to meet your parents. And you know your mother will fall in love with him."

Madison stopped eating, pointed her fork at Tish and talked through a mouthful of pasta. "You. Are. Smitten."

Tish's face tightened as she sat up straight. "Pffft. I don't get smitten."

Rory laughed. "Yeah, she's got that dreamy look she had freshman year over that guy in the dorm. Haven't seen it since, but it's back. Schoolgirl crush. Definitely smitten."

"I am not…smitten! And this is not a simple crush. I don't even know the guy."

A.J. patted her on the shoulder. "It's okay, sweetie. You're not on the witness stand. Just admit you're attracted to the guy and wanna jump his bones."

Tish waved her hand in disgust. "Pffft. Like it will make any difference. The odds of running into him again…and of him being unattached…that's a wild daily double with some pretty long odds."

"Serendipity happens," said Rory. "But sometimes you gotta give it a little help. Look at Madison and Nick. I mean, if their ending up together wasn't a wild turn of events…well, you still have hope."

"What do you mean, give it a little help?"

"Tell you what, next time we all go out to eat we'll hit that restaurant again. The waitress said he was a regular. If he's there we'll ask to get seated next to him. At least if that woman is with him we can eavesdrop and see what the story is and if she's his significant other."

Madison nodded. "And you should go jogging at the same time on the same route. If you ran into him near your hotel and he was in a suit, chances are he works in the neighborhood. He's not going to walk ten blocks to get coffee."

"So, what, I just run up to the guy and hit on him?"

"Geez, for someone ruled by logic you sure miss the obvious," said Rory. "You offer to pay him back for the soda. Then you buy him a cup of coffee. Only make sure you don't look like crap this time."

"Pretty hard to do after I run two miles."

Madison rolled her eyes. "Duh. Again, missing the obvious. You stop at the drink cart *before* you run."

Tish shook her head and sipped her wine. "Wow, the things a girl has to do to get a date…"

*

Madison entered the guest room just as Tish pulled back the covers. "Nick and I are going to turn in. So, you need anything?"

"I'm good." Tish gave her a strong hug. "Can't thank you

35

enough for this. Really nice of you, though I feel like I'm putting you out."

"Hey, what are friends for? By the way, hope you didn't mind us yankin' your chain on the smitten thing. But, to be honest, you've got that look."

Tish shrugged as she sat on the corner of the bed. "I guess it's been so long since I had a decent boyfriend it shows."

"Yeah, your choices haven't always been the best. When's the last time you dated a guy more than once?"

"Probably three years ago. I dunno, Madison, I guess I've reached the point where I can tell right away. I've become an expert on spotting red flags after those poor choices you referred to. Subconsciously I guess I'd given up."

"You've been like me, too obsessed with a career to take time to smell the roses." Madison slid next to her and patted her hand. "Well, when you least expect it, the right guy will show up in your life. I mean, look how I met Nick."

"True. Talk about serendipity. You guys had it in spades."

"Well, maybe it's your turn. You certainly had enough bad luck this week. Things can only get better."

Just as she said that, Socks jumped onto the bed and started kneading the comforter with her front paws. "At least I have *someone* who wants to sleep with me on a Friday night."

"Oh, stop it. So why all the interest in a guy all of a sudden?"

"I dunno. I guess I see you and Nick, how happy you two are, how much he's changed you in a good way…how this house has turned into a home. I'm jealous of what you have and lately I want it for myself."

"Yeah, he has made me a better person. And a very different person. Of course, the kittens got the ball rolling on that."

"Socks seems to be doing the same for me. I look at you and how you used to be so obsessed with your work and now you balance your job and your love life so well. You've got it all. All I've got is a career. It's all I've ever had."

36

"You have good friends, Tish."

"I didn't mean it that way. Now I want it all too. Maybe I need someone to show me there's more to life than a law practice, y'know? And since the fire I've been thinking about where I live. It's not really a home, but just a place where I sleep and work on my cases. It's really been no more than a second office. You two have made a real nest here."

Madison wrapped one arm around her. "Yeah, I must admit life is a lot better now that I take time to enjoy the little things. But don't worry. The fact that you realize there's more to life than a career is a big step. Actually, you already took the first step."

"Huh?"

Madison reached over to pet Socks. "You adopted a cat. You've already started making yourself a home. Remember, a home without a cat is just a house." She stood up. "Anyway, get some rest, we gotta get up early since you and Socks are on the Saturday morning show."

Chapter Four

Tish couldn't help but smile as she held Socks while the Saturday morning show anchor began to interview her. "Today we're joined live from Staten Island by Tish McKenna and her cat Socks to share an amazing story. Tish, welcome to the show. So tell us why you're talking with us this morning."

She held up the cat. "Because of this little fur baby. Earlier this week my house was struck by lightning and caught fire. The smoke alarm never went off. I'm a very heavy sleeper but Socks obviously knew something was wrong. She jumped on me and woke me up. Once I realized the house was on fire I grabbed her and headed out the door. And about thirty seconds later the storm knocked over a huge tree that crushed my bedroom. Without my cat waking me up I'd be dead from the fire, the tree or both."

"That's an incredible story," said the anchor. "Now our viewers have met you and Socks before as the cat is from reporter Madison Shaw's famous litter of orphaned kittens. Can you tell us why you chose this particular cat to adopt?"

"I needed a smoke alarm." She saw the anchor laugh in the monitor. "No, seriously, she's a sweet cat and since I'm kind of a formal person and Socks looks like she's wearing a tuxedo, I thought we were a good match. But actually, she chose me rather than the other way around. A cat chooses its person, you know. Humans really have no say in the matter."

"I didn't know that about cats. And I assume she has been rewarded for her heroism."

"Oh, she'll never be without her favorite cat treats. And she absolutely goes wild over salmon. I have to share it with her whenever I have it for dinner."

"Is Socks your first cat?"

"The first in several years. We had cats when I was a kid but I haven't had a pet since I got out of college. I'd forgotten how much I enjoyed having one around and this cat is a wonderful companion since I live alone."

"We all know how the experience taking care of the kittens changed Madison, so what has sharing your life with a cat done for you?"

"Well, it's very special getting unconditional love from an animal. And cats are very perceptive creatures. This one seems to know when I'm down, and to be honest this has been a very stressful week. It's been great having her to help me get through this ordeal. She seems to know that I'm the one needing extra attention." Tish smiled lovingly as Socks nuzzled her hand and purred.

*

Spencer was half asleep as he carried his coffee and the morning paper to the den. He plopped down in a reclining chair, placed his coffee on the end table and unfolded the paper in his lap, then turned on the television. He was bleary-eyed and barely paying attention as the screen cleared, revealing a woman holding a cat. The bottom of the screen read *Cat Saves Owner's Life From Fire.*

"And remember, a home without a cat is just a house," said the woman. "So go to a shelter and adopt one today."

"Words to live by from a cat owner," said the anchor, as the story ended.

Spencer began to nod, his thoughts going to the little cat that had visited him in his office. He realized he missed seeing the kitty on the weekend. "Yeah, I need to get a cat once things slow down. It's too damn quiet around here."

He turned back to his newspaper, not having noticed anything in particular about the cat on television or the owner.

*

Spencer was greeted by several looks of surprise as he walked into the annual law school cocktail party on Saturday night.

"Whoa, look who's here!" His old study buddy Jim Hartselle quickly moved in his direction, hand extended.

Spencer shook his hand. "Hey, Jim, how've you been?"

The tall, lanky lawyer nodded. "Doing well. Still working for the Governor in Albany and fighting politicians at every turn. Not wild about the upstate winters which never seem to end but it's a cool job. Wow, I never expected to see you here. Is this the first time you've made it to one of these?"

"Yep. Figured I'd check on you and some of the others."

"Well, good to see you after all these years. So what are you doing?"

"I'm partner in a two-person firm in Manhattan. Things are going very well."

"Good to hear. I'm in town from time to time so we'll have to get together for lunch."

"Sounds good." Spencer looked around. "So who's here from our old gang?"

"Most of the midnight oil study group. Denise, Frank, Carrie. They're over at the bar. C'mon. I know they'd love to see you."

Spencer kept looking around the room as the group shared

stories at a table but he didn't see Tish McKenna. "Hey, does our class valedictorian ever show up at these things?"

Everyone laughed as Jim shook his head. "Seriously, Spence? Mrs. Spock? She had no friends in school, why would she ever come to a reunion? Who would she reunite with? A law book?"

He shrugged. "Y'know, people change."

"Who cares? And not sure she could change her personality since you need one to start with," said Denise, a corporate attorney. "I mean, talk about a cold fish. I invited her for lunch once and she blew me off. Said she couldn't spare the time and had to study. Maybe that's why she was valedictorian. Personally I'd rather have friends than that designation."

"Wonder what ever happened to her," said Frank.

"I saw her in court the other day," said Spencer. "The woman was amazing. She absolutely destroyed a witness. By the way, you wouldn't even recognize her. Looks very professional now. I was shocked when I found out she was that frumpy girl in our class."

"Someone in my firm went up against her awhile back," said Denise. "She wiped the floor with him."

Carrie nodded. "I had a trial against her last year. I thought my case was a slam dunk but the woman kicked my ass. I mean, I'll be honest, I didn't know what hit me, and I was well prepared. She's a damn chess player. It was like she was three steps ahead of me the whole time. Cited a whole bunch of obscure cases and I found myself painted into a corner. Oh, she's no longer Mrs. Spock. She's got a new nickname around the courthouse."

"What's that?" asked Spencer.

"Jaws."

"Why Jaws?"

"Because a tough lawyer is a shark and she's the deadliest shark in the ocean. Just like in the movie. The bailiff said when she walks into the courtroom you can almost hear the theme music."

*

Tish actually felt like some sort of stalker, but her friends had insisted she at least try to run into the cute white knight. But she had to know if the guy was attached. Men like that didn't grow on trees.

She decided to look her best without going overboard. While she wouldn't go so far as to put on makeup to go running, she did at least pick up a new pair of sweats, a cute red sweatshirt with the hotel logo and a Mets baseball cap. Bright sunshine and a cool breeze greeted her as she headed out of the hotel lobby on Tuesday morning, early enough that she could hang around for a while if he was there. She spotted the drink cart across the street and headed for it.

No white knight in sight.

Still, she might be able to find out who he was or if he was a regular.

The guy running the cart looked up and smiled as she approached. "Morning, young lady, what can I get for you?"

"Some orange juice, please."

He handed her a container and she paid for it. "Hey, by any chance do you remember me from last week?"

He studied her face and smiled. "Though I am a happily married man I'm not dead. I do tend to remember the pretty women. You're the one who forgot her cash."

"Right. And there was a guy in an expensive suit who paid for it. Dark tousled hair, olive green eyes, slender, mid-thirties. You know who he is?"

"I do. He stops by just about every morning for coffee."

"Ah. Well, I was hoping to pay him back."

"I don't think he's the type to miss a dollar. But I'll be happy to pass it on if you like."

"I was hoping to thank him personally."

"What, you don't trust me with a buck?"

"No, it's not that. I, uh…"

He smiled and nodded. "I see what's going on here."

"Nothing's going on. I just want to say thank you in person—"

"Young lady, I may look like a guy who runs a soda cart, but I'm a hopeless romantic. If you're interested in meeting him, just say so."

"Why do you think I'm interested?"

"The way you described him. Very detailed. And you got this dreamy look."

She shook her head. *Busted.* "Fine, I'm interested. Nice guys don't grow on trees and I actually saw him doing a good deed in a restaurant. So what's he like?"

"Extra cream, two sugars."

"Very funny. I meant what is he like *as a person*? What can you tell me besides how he takes his coffee?"

"Sorry, I couldn't resist. Like I said, he's a regular. Name's Spencer but likes to be called Spence. He works on this block, and he's a helluva tipper."

"You get tips running a soda cart?"

"Only from him. He told me his dad did this for years and he knows how hard I work. Every time he buys a dollar-fifty cup of coffee he gives me five bucks and tells me to keep the change. He actually talks to me, unlike most of my customers who act like I'm the hired help. He could probably buy and sell me ten times over but he treats me like an equal."

"Nice to hear. You know if he's married?"

"Nope. But just for you, I'll be sure to bring it up in conversation next time I see him. Or at least check for a wedding ring."

"The lack of one wouldn't necessarily mean he's single."

"True, but he doesn't strike me as the cheating type if he was married."

"Good to know." She looked around to see if he might be coming. "But listen, don't be, you know, too obvious."

"What, you think I'm gonna say, *Hey Spence, some blonde babe wants to hook up with you. And how convenient, we're right near a hotel.* Give me some credit, will ya? I don't look it, but I can be subtle."

"Sorry. I appreciate any information you can get."

"Consider it done."

"And thank you for referring to me as a babe, but I'm not."

He rolled his eyes. "Oh, you're one of *those* women."

"What do you mean by that?"

"Offended by the term *babe*."

"That doesn't bother me. I've just never been called one."

"Then you're the other type, which you don't see too often from your generation."

"What other type?"

"Pretty woman who has no clue she's very attractive. Which is good, since I don't like women who are stuck on themselves."

"Well, thank you for the compliment, but I don't think I'm anything special."

"We'll have to see what Spence thinks, won't we? You just missed him, by the way."

Tish shook her head. "Damn."

"I hope that does not imply you've been wasting time talking to me in the hopes he might show up."

"Not at all. I've enjoyed meeting you."

He pointed at her t-shirt and cocked his head toward the hotel. "You staying there?"

"Till Christmas. My house caught on fire and a tree hit it, so that's where the insurance company put me up. It's close to my office." She stuck out her hand. "I'm Tish, by the way."

He shook it. "I'm Benny. Nice to meet you, Tish from the hotel. So, should I tell him you're looking for him?"

"I'd rather try to run into him. Less stalkerish, if you know what I mean."

"I got ya. But I can help you narrow things down. He's usually here between seven-thirty and eight."

"Thanks, Benny."

He flashed a wide grin. "See you tomorrow, Tish from the hotel."

"So that's what you're gonna call me?"

"Easier to keep track of people that way. So you're Tish from the hotel and he's Spence from the block. Some of my other regulars are garment district Julio and Broadway Jill. I think it's only fair since people call me Benny the soda guy."

"Anyone ever tell you that you're a character, Benny?"

He put his palms up and smiled. "Every day for the past thirty years when I get home to my wife."

"Benny, I have a feeling she's a very lucky woman."

"Nah. I'm the lucky guy."

Chapter Five

The light tap on his office door jolted Spencer out of deep thought. He looked up to see Ariel holding some newspapers. "Hey, Ariel, what's up?"

"You look like you're solving the world's problems."

"Nah, just thinking about stuff."

"Right. *Stuff.*" She walked in and took the chair in front of his desk. "Anything I can help with?"

He shook his head. "Nah. So what are you bringing me?"

"I'm going to need your help on a client I agreed to represent who is about to get sued." She handed him the one of the papers.

He quickly read the article on the front page, saw the name of the person in question, and shook his head as he tossed the paper on his desk. "No way. Ariel, we don't need a client like this."

She put up her hands. "Whoa, hold on. I told you I had a case coming up with a horrible person and you didn't care. I seem to remember you said *we're in business to make money.*"

"I know, but...Peter Brent? The guy is evil. And I thought we agreed not to take any more clients so we could slow down."

"I know, but I already told him I'd represent him after you didn't have a problem. Besides, he's a relative of mine so I'm kinda stuck."

"*You're* related to *him*?"

"Not something I want to shout from the rooftops, but he's a cousin. I can't say no."

"Sure you can. You pick up the phone and say we're too busy, which wouldn't be a lie. Then recommend the appropriate sleaze bag who won't mind getting in bed with him."

"I would but this is the guy who put me through law school. I never would have been able to afford it without him. I'm sorry, Spence, but I really do owe him despite the fact that he's turned into a creep."

"How did you ever get hooked up with someone who has this kind of reputation?"

"Like I said, he's a cousin and I see him every year at the family reunion. He's loaded. And back then he didn't have a reputation and simply wanted to help me out. He grew up with my mom and they're good friends. Look, I can certainly keep your name out of it but I may need your help with research and prep on this before I go to court. You've had a couple of cases like this one and you know how to win them."

"I'm not sure I'd wanna help him win anything. But that's not the problem. The problem is we can't keep our firm's name out of it. And you know the public is going to side with the plaintiff. He's the obvious bad guy here. Big corporate meanie screwing one of his employees out of a fortune. I'll help you behind the scenes with the research and prep but I can't be your second chair. Some of our clients would not be happy seeing me defending him."

"They won't be happy seeing me do it either."

"Yeah, but you have the legitimate excuse that you're related to the guy. Make one of his staff attorneys second chair."

"Okay, I see your point. Anyway, can you get some stuff together for me this afternoon since he wants to meet with me soon?"

"Sure. I'll dig out the old case files and write out some strategy for you." He looked at the newspaper again. "Ariel, is there any chance you can settle this?"

"Don't think so. My cousin is very stubborn even though a settlement would be pocket change to him. It's like he's got a vendetta against the woman. But I'll try like hell."

"Please do what you can. Tell him the negative publicity would be far costlier than any settlement. If he hasn't realized that after reading the papers. Speaking of which, don't give a damn thing to the media. Silent running and radio silence. The sooner we get this case off the calendar, the better."

"I will do my best. Hey, if nothing else, we'll make a fortune off him so we can take more *pro bono* stuff."

"I guess that's one way to look at it."

"And speaking of things on the calendar, don't forget you've got that charity auction tonight."

"It's on my to-do list though I'll be a little late. You wanna go with me?"

"Nah, I'd spend too much money. But I won't complain if you buy me something nice."

"I thought that was your boyfriend's job."

"It is, but you have really good taste. I've never returned a single thing you've given me. I must say, you really know how to shop for a woman."

He began to blush a bit. "Okay, I have a confession to make."

"What?"

"I, uh, don't actually pick out your gifts. I have, you know, help. From another woman. Don't be mad."

"I'm not. It's the gift that counts, not the thought, right?"

"Very funny. But you know how much I think of you."

"Just bustin' your chops, partner. Well, whoever your help is, keep her. She's doing a helluva job."

*

48

The well-heeled charity auction crowd applauded as Tish held up Socks at the end of her speech. "So thanks to this little furball, I'm here tonight. Socks would like to thank you all for supporting such a wonderful charity. It will save a lot of animals and really help raise awareness about pet adoptions. Now I'll turn things over to our auctioneer, and I hope those of you with deep pockets will empty them. I wanna see them turned inside out!"

The crowd laughed as she moved off the stage. She put Socks back in her carrier, then shook hands with all the volunteers from the charity as the auction commenced.

"Really nice of you to bring Socks," said one woman, poking her finger through the grate to touch her.

"Hey, she's a great spokes-cat. And she loves people. Can't get enough attention."

"Well, this should really help us raise a ton of money. That segment on the network Saturday morning really boosted our last-minute ticket sales. We've never had such a big turnout. And a lot of stores donated stuff for the auction after seeing the story."

"Glad to hear it. Yeah, that story has gone viral." She heard some big numbers being shouted out from the crowd as the auctioneer held up a beautiful statue. "And you've apparently got some expensive stuff to auction off."

"A few businesses were really generous. Especially one jewelry store."

Tish looked out at the crowd and saw some a group of men walk into the room and sit at the last table in the back as the auction was beginning.

What she saw made her stand up straight.

The white knight was among them.

Serendipity.

Her pulse quickened as she started to step off the stage to head in his direction. It would be great to pay him back while she was dressed in a new business outfit instead of exercise clothes.

Then a hand lightly grabbed her forearm. "Excuse me, Miss McKenna?".

She turned and found a young woman with a pad and a camera. "Yes?"

"Hi, I'm Jennie Stevens from *The New York Post*. Could you spare a little time? We'd love to do an interview about how your cat saved your life. I promise it won't take long."

Tish took a quick look out at the crowd just as she saw the white knight raise his hand and bid two hundred and fifty dollars to win a lunch at an exclusive restaurant. She turned back to the reporter. "Sure, be happy to talk to you."

Just her luck, the interview and photos had taken longer than she'd expected because the reporter couldn't get the camera to work. By the time she was done and returned to the stage the auction was over. She saw the crowd heading out the door.

The white knight was nowhere in sight.

Dammit!

She quickly headed over to the table where the volunteers were busy adding up the checks and cash. "How'd we do, guys?"

The woman counting the money looked up and smiled at her. "Fabulous. This is the most we've ever raised at an auction. We can't thank you enough."

"My pleasure. Hey, I thought I spotted someone I knew. He was the guy who bought the lunch at Harrison's."

"Yeah, got some serious money for that. Not too shabby for a lunch."

She pointed to the checks thinking there might be one of his with a last name and phone number. How many people named Spencer could there be at this auction? She could call him and thank him for supporting the charity, then...well, who knows. "Can I see if that's who I thought it was?"

"Oh, he paid in cash. And talk about nice...the winning bid

was two-fifty, so he gives me three hundred dollar bills and tells me to keep the change."

"Did he want a receipt for a tax write-off?"

"I offered and he said it wasn't necessary. Sorry, there's no paper trail on the guy. Does that sound like the person you know?"

"Yeah, actually it does."

*

Spencer breathed in the cool autumn air as he headed toward the drink cart for his morning coffee. Benny spotted him and smiled. "Hey, Spence from the block, beautiful day. You should knock off early this afternoon."

"With weather like this I'd like to switch jobs with you, Benny."

Benny started to fix his coffee. "Seriously, you wanna sell soda?"

"If I could work outside today, I'd be happy to. I used to love helping my dad on days like these."

"Your dad still around?"

"Yeah, but he's retired. I got him a nice place in Florida. He couldn't deal with the cold anymore. He cracked a bottle of champagne when he sold his snow blower in a yard sale."

"That's my goal as well. Love the Sunshine State. And it's like the sixth borough of New York anyway."

"Very true. I always visit in the winter."

Benny stirred the sugar into the coffee and handed it to him, then pointed at his hand. "So, since we're on the subject of family, is there no Mrs. Spence? I don't see a ring."

Spencer shook his head. "I'm single."

"Never married?"

"Nope. Never even came close to finding Miss Right."

"Kids?"

"I've never been married."

"That doesn't stop your generation."

"True. I'm old-fashioned in that respect."

51

"Well, nice lookin' guy like you in an expensive suit must have women bangin' down the door. I can understand why you wouldn't wanna be attached when you can play the field."

"If only, Benny. Haven't had a decent girlfriend in years. I've, uh, been kinda married to my job. Which hasn't helped."

Benny sat on his stool and folded his arms. "Really? You don't seem like that type. I'm surprised. There's more to life than work, you know."

"Yeah, I'm starting to realize that. As for women, well, the stars never aligned. It seems the women I'm attracted to aren't interested in me, and vice versa."

"So what's your type? Blonde, brunette, or redhead?"

"Hair color doesn't matter. I like professional women who are incredibly smart and have a lot of spunk. I really don't like party girls." He pointed at Benny's hand which featured a nicked silver ring. "I see *you've* found Miss Right, and from the looks of that ring you found her a while ago."

"Thirty years. Best thing that ever happened to me."

Spencer leaned against a light pole as he sipped his coffee. "So what's the secret of staying married so long in this day and age?"

"Respect. Never take your wife for granted. And don't stop dating after you get married."

Spencer's eyes widened. "You have affairs, Benny?"

"Hell, no. I meant you still take your wife out on dates. We go out to dinner and a movie every Saturday night. I still open doors for her, bring her a rose now and then, little stuff that says *I love you* without the words. Just because you're spending the rest of your life together doesn't mean the courtship ends. Too many couples start out as lovers and end up as roommates. And a lot of couples from your generation end up divorced."

"You're a wise man, Benny." His cell rang and he pulled it from his pocket. "Well, excuse me, gotta go. Enjoy the beautiful day."

"You should take some time to do the same, Spence."

Tish jogged across the street and noted her watch read seven-twenty-nine. If the white knight was always there between seven-thirty and eight, she wanted to be early.

Benny shrugged at her and put his palms up as she walked toward the cart. "You just missed him again."

She shook her head. "You said he's here between seven-thirty and eight."

"He was early today, what can I say?"

"I'll keep trying."

"Well, Tish from the hotel, this is not to say your trip was totally in vain. I did manage to acquire some information about the gentleman that may interest you."

Her eyes widened as she perked up. "Really? What'd you get?"

"You want orange juice?"

"Yeah. So what'd you *get*?"

He handed her a bottle. "Not married. Never been married. So no baggage to check."

"Well, that's half the battle. You get anything else?"

"Do I look like an amateur?"

"No. C'mon, c'mon, what else you got?

Benny shot her a sly grin. "No girlfriend."

"And there's the other half of a perfect answer." She couldn't hold back a smile. "I'm honestly very surprised."

"I was too. He mentioned that the women he's interested in never feel the same about him. And something about the stars not aligning for him yet."

"So there's hope for me."

"Well, that depends."

"On what?"

"If your stars and his stars are in the same constellation."

"What, you're into astrology?"

"No, I meant if you're his type."

She nodded. "So you actually found out what kind of women he finds attractive?"

"Young lady, you give Benny a chance to play matchmaker, he will not disappoint. I'm better than a Jewish mother, even though I'm an Irish father. By the end of the week I'll have a complete dossier in your hands with all his likes and dislikes."

"Yeah, yeah, so what's he lookin' for? C'mon, dish."

"You're such an impatient little thing."

"I'm not exactly little."

"Well, you're a helluva lot better looking than that bag-o-bones supermodel who drops by every day and has Diet Coke and cigarettes for lunch."

"Thank you, but we're getting off track, Benny. So what's his type?"

"I started by asking him if he liked blondes, brunettes or redheads and he said hair color didn't matter. He's a head man."

Her eyes went wide. "Excuse me? If he's looking for a girl to spend all her time on her knees—"

"I didn't mean *that*! Geez, your mind is in the gutter!" He tapped his head. "I meant he wants a woman with a great head on her shoulders. A guy might be a leg man, a boob man…or in this case a head man. You get what I'm sayin'?"

"Never heard it put quite that way. You might want to retire that particular designation, especially when talking to a woman."

"Yeah, I guess you could take it the wrong way. Anyway, what Spence from the block wants is a professional woman who is really smart and spunky." Benny studied her face. "I don't know you well enough to tell if you fit the bill, but you seem like you have a good head on your shoulders. Already know you have an attitude."

"Very funny."

"I meant that as a compliment."

"Nice save, Mister. Anything else?"

"He got a call while we were talking and had to take off."

"That seems to happen with him. Well, you still cleared up a lot, Benny. Thank you. I appreciate it."

"So now that you know he's unattached, does that change your strategy?"

"It just gives me hope. I still need to meet the guy."

"I think you need a different approach."

"How so?"

"He said he likes professional women. So when you show up here, don't do it in a jogging outfit."

She nodded. "Point taken."

"What do you do for a living?"

"Lawyer."

"So you must have nice clothes."

"I do."

"So, see you tomorrow, Tish from the hotel? All dolled up?"

"Not dolled up, but professional."

Chapter Six

Tish enjoyed being one of the rotating guests for the weekly legal show on one of New York City's talk radio stations. Giving free legal advice to people who couldn't afford it was an easy way to give back. It was an hour every few weeks that had actually brought her a few paying clients over the years. It was a good strategy to get her name "out there" when she first got out of law school and also helped her develop a reputation as a lawyer who was on the side of good. The show had a sizable listening audience. She'd often said, on the air, that she turned down clients with whom her philosophy differed. Anyone looking up her track record would discover she wasn't kidding.

The studio was freezing cold as always, since broadcast equipment had to be kept from overheating. She adjusted her headset as the middle-aged host, James Berger, handed her a cup of hot chocolate and took a seat opposite her. "How's it going, Tish? I'm surprised to see you after the thing with your house."

She placed her hands around the mug to warm them. "Well, I'm lucky to be alive, so I'm counting my blessings. A house can be repaired. In the grand scheme of things, it's just a thing."

"Very true. But that was an incredible story about your cat."

"Yeah, she saved my life. I don't think I can feed her enough treats. Anyway, I'm living in a hotel during the week and with a friend on the weekend. I'll be back in my house in a couple of months. Though right now it's not my biggest problem."

"Really?"

She nodded. "My biggest client was Clint Davies."

"Oh, hell. I couldn't believe his company went under. Loved his products. I guess we'll have to find you some new business. You want me to say something today?"

"Nah, this show is for *pro bono* work. It would be tacky to solicit clients."

"That's the reason the callers love you. The rare ethical attorney. Tell you what, though, I could toss you a little work myself. Since I'm getting married I could use one of those pre-nups. It's not a big project but it might pay your light bill for a month or two."

"Pre-nup? You worried about your fiancée?"

"Twenty-three year old bikini model marrying an overweight, balding guy of fifty? The thought that she wants me for my money *has* crossed my mind a time or two. And my friends refer to her with the G-word."

"G-word?"

"Golddigger."

Tish shook her head. "Why do guys like you date women like that?"

He flashed a wicked grin as his eyebrows did a little jump. "Because we can."

"Very funny. Typical man."

"Anyway, if she refuses to sign it I'll know she's in it for the money."

"In other words, you won't have any trouble finding another young bikini model?"

"Fame is an incredible aphrodisiac. You'd be amazed at the women who approach me. And I know damn well they wouldn't give me the time of day if I worked at the post office."

"Well, best of luck with your marriage. And I appreciate the business but hope I will not have to handle your divorce proceedings. A new client is welcome right now. Though I will tell you it would be a lot cheaper for you to buy yourself a nice mid-life crisis convertible."

"Already got one of those. It's how I met her. The thing is a chick magnet."

"Well, so much for that theory. You sure you want legal advice from me?"

"Absolutely. Anyway, I'll come to your office this week and bring you a list of my assets."

"Sure. And I can't wait to meet her."

"You won't have much to talk about. She ain't exactly Stephen Hawking." He put on his headset and adjusted the microphone. "Here we go."

*

Spencer started eating the chicken parmigiana he'd brought back to the office for lunch. Usually he listened to the sports talk radio station whenever he ate at his desk, but last week he'd heard about a show featuring lawyers giving free legal advice and wanted to check it out. He took a bite of his meal as he flipped on the radio.

"*And welcome to Legal Briefs, I'm James Berger and our attorney in the house today is Tish McKenna—*"

His jaw dropped a bit, sending a bit of red sauce onto his red silk tie. Thankfully it matched pretty well. He quickly grabbed a napkin and wiped it off, then turned up the volume on the radio.

"*…amazing that you even showed up today after your house caught on fire. I know our audience appreciates it.*"

"*Well, in the grand scheme of things, a house is just a thing that can be repaired. As a lawyer it's more important to put lives back together when you can.*"

"Damn, I like that. Her stock just went up."

"And that's why Tish has always been a welcome guest on this show for so many years. Anyway, if you have a legal question, she will be here for the next hour to hopefully point you in the right direction. Our number is…"

Spencer took a sip of club soda as he grabbed a pen and wrote down the phone number.

Apparently Mrs. Spock was still a walking law library. Spencer sat in amazement at her ability to cite obscure cases without missing a beat while answering questions from the callers. The woman was much too fast to be looking stuff up on a computer while on the air.

She was still smarter than he was.

But what really surprised him was how she did it with such personality. The woman was a quick wit and very conversational on the air. Casual, almost, as she had a genuine rapport with the host and the callers as well. She'd obviously changed quite a bit. There was more to her than the cold, focused student he'd seen in law school.

Then again, he'd changed a lot since law school too…

And, of course, that voice of hers was mesmerizing. If she ever got tired of the law she had a real future as a narrator for erotic novels.

He finished his lunch, then paused a moment, wondering if this was the right thing to do. "Ah, what the hell." He grabbed the phone and called the number to the talk show.

Busy.

He hit the redial button.

Five tries later the phone began to ring and then the call connected. *"This is Big Apple talk radio, do you have a question for our attorney?"*

"Yes, I do."

"Need your first name and where you're calling from."

"This is Joe from Manhattan."

"What's your question, Joe?"

"I'd like to know…what should a client look for when choosing an attorney?"

"Okay, Joe, I've got two callers ahead of you and then you'll be up. Remember to turn your radio down when it's your turn."

"Got it, thanks."

"I'm going to put you on hold now but you'll be able to hear the show. Please, no profanity as we do have a seven second delay."

"Not a problem."

He turned off his radio as he heard her voice through the phone. Her answer to his question would tell him a lot.

Ten minutes and one commercial break later, it was his turn. *"Okay, we've got Joe from Manhattan. Joe, you're on live with Tish McKenna."*

"Hi, Ms. McKenna, thanks for taking my call."

"Sure thing, Joe. What's your question this afternoon?"

"This is pretty simple compared to what everyone else is asking. You mentioned earlier that you only choose a certain type of client. So let's reverse the point of view. Basically, what should someone look for when choosing a lawyer?"

"Well, Joe, that depends on the case and what kind of person you are. Some people are out for blood and will hire the biggest shark they can find. Others base the choice on money. Some people think an expensive lawyer will be better than one who charges less, and that's not true. My advice to you is to find a lawyer whose values are closest to yours. And you want a lawyer who honestly cares about you. If an attorney is simply in it for the money, you're not going to get the kind of representation you would from one who not only believes in your case, but you as well. I'm not saying you need to pick a lawyer like you'd choose a friend, but I will say that at least in my case, I fight a lot harder for someone who I care about. It's one reason I never take a case where I don't feel a client is in the right."

"That's very noble, Ms. McKenna."

"Well, if you saw me in court sometimes, you might not call me noble."

"Actually I did see you in court recently, and I will tell your audience that you owned the room and seriously kicked butt. The opposing lawyer didn't stand a chance. You wiped the floor with her star witness."

He heard Tish and the host laugh. *"Well, thank you for the compliment, and thanks for calling, Joe. Best of luck in your search for an attorney."*

The call ended and Spencer turned the radio back on.

"Well, there goes your reputation as a nice person," said the host. *"I guess I need to drop by the courthouse and see who I've been dealing with all these years."*

"James, you can still be nice, but you have to fight with all your heart for every client. The jury has to actually feel your passion, believe in your cause. If they think your heart's not in it, they'll be less likely to consider your argument. But once the trial starts, my gloves come off. You can be really tough as long as you're fair."

He heard Ariel return to the office and her heel clicks on the marble floor approaching his office. "I'm back!" she yelled.

"Come on in, you gotta hear this. Hurry up!"

"Okay, okay, I'm coming. What the hell is so urgent?" She entered his office, tossed her jacket on a chair and cocked her head at the radio. "That's not WFAN. Why aren't you listening to sports talk?"

"This is that legal call-in show we heard about the other day."

"Oh, yeah. Is it any good?"

He heard Tish's voice come through the speaker. "Recognize the voice?"

She listened a bit, then her eyes grew wide. "Oh my God, that's your courtroom crush!"

"Yep. And what a brilliant legal mind. The woman is amazing.

61

She can answer the most obscure questions off the top of her head."

"Still smarter than you, huh?"

"Yep."

"Does that bother you?"

"Just the opposite. Anyway…uh…I called her."

"You called a woman to ask her out on a radio show?"

"Jeez, Ariel, do you think I'm that clueless when it comes to women?"

Ariel stood up straight and folded her arms. "You really want me to answer that?"

"Counsel withdraws the question, your honor. Anyway, I called with a legal problem."

"You tried to stump her?"

"Nope. Don't think I could. I asked what a person should look for in a lawyer. And from the way she responded she sounds like one of the most ethical attorneys on the planet. Only takes good clients."

"I think the universe is trying to tell you something." Ariel listened to the radio for a moment and heard the woman crack a joke. "Also sounds like she's grown a personality. Does this sound like the gal you knew in college?"

"Not remotely."

"Interesting. So what's your strategy now?"

He shrugged. "Since you implied that I'm clueless about women, I will admit that I have no clue. But I *have* to meet her. You got any more ideas since she didn't show up at the class reunion thing?"

"Let me think about it. But perhaps we're approaching this the wrong way."

"What do you mean?"

"Maybe *I'm* the one who needs to meet her first."

"Huh?"

Socks, like every cat, had a world-class nose. Able to smell something good to eat from a hundred yards.

And something smelled really good coming through that vent. It reminded her of her days as a kitten, when the woman who'd saved her and her siblings shared dinner with friends, and the one with the dark hair brought food that smelled like this. And tasted really good.

All was quiet, even though it was the middle of the day. Her person was not around and neither was the other woman who shared the place.

Her dish was filled with treats, but something else smelled a lot better. Besides, the treats would still be there when she got back. There were no other cats around to eat them.

Socks jumped off the desk, headed into the vent, followed the scent and emerged in the other place, not finding the nice man there either.

But that wonderful smell was stronger.

She followed it, finding the source in a plastic container next to a trash can.

A few scraps were left. She took a little taste. Mmmm. Chicken and cheese and a lot of delicious red sauce.

She licked the container clean, then headed back home through the vent.

Tish walked back to her office from the conference room with Shelley close behind. The meeting had gone well, the prospective new client with deep pockets seemed impressed. Though he did say he was talking to two other firms. So while nothing was definite at least she was finding some prospects.

Tish found Socks at her usual spot on her desk, busy washing her face. She scratched the cat's head as she plopped down behind her desk while Shelley took the chair on the other side. "So, waddaya think?"

Shelley nodded. "I think we've got a good shot. And he's our kind of client. Seems like a decent human being and he's got a good argument."

"Yeah, I like the case. Sure hope we get it. Meanwhile—" She stopped and sniffed the air. "Did you have Italian for lunch?"

"No, why?"

"Because I'd swear you had something from my friend A.J.'s deli."

"I had a roast beef sandwich. And I do actually use mouthwash."

"Hmmm." She leaned toward the cat and sniffed. "Why does Socks smell like an Italian restaurant?"

"Beats the hell out of me. You feeding her ravioli from a can or something?"

"No, just cat food." She picked up Socks and held her close. "It's definitely her. They must put something in the food to make it smell attractive to the cat. Who knew?"

"Like I said before, cats have it better than us."

Chapter Seven

This time, Tish was determined to be early.

She strutted, and I do mean *strutted*, across the street in her new business suit, which happened to be the same shade of blue as her eyes. She'd never strayed from the traditional New York City black, grays, and earth tones that seemed appropriate for the courtroom, but Madison had told her that her clothes were boring and it was time to spruce up her wardrobe a bit. Well, more than a bit. She'd taken Tish shopping and forced her to buy stuff she never would have considered. Despite the primary color of her outfit, it was still very conservative while making a bold statement. And she noticed she had already turned a few heads in the hotel lobby.

She hopped the curb and arrived at Benny's cart just as he turned toward her and gave her the once-over. "Good morning, young lady. What can I get you?"

She noted that he didn't recognize her. "Benny, it's me."

"Me who?"

"Tish from the hotel."

He slid his glasses down on his nose and studied her face. His eyes widened. "Damn, woman, look at you. You sure clean up good. When I told you to get all dolled up I didn't expect this."

"Is it too much?"

He cocked his head toward the street. "You see cars slowing down to take a look?"

"I'm not remotely a traffic stopper, Benny."

"You're definitely getting guys below the speed limit. Anyway, you'll turn Spence's head."

"I assume that means I'm not too late this time?"

"Nope." Benny looked at his watch, then handed her a container of orange juice. "So hang with me awhile and I'm sure he'll show up." He flashed a smile. "This is exciting for me."

"Really?"

"Yeah. Beautiful woman taking time to talk with an old guy like me. And I'm not even rich."

"Very funny."

"Seriously, I'm excited to get you two together and see if there are sparks. Like I told you, I'm a hopeless romantic."

"No such thing, Benny. The term is backwards. You're a hope*ful* romantic. And so am I."

Ten minutes later Benny looked over her shoulder. "Hey, here he comes." Tish started to turn but he took her shoulders. "Don't look! It'll be too obvious. Let me handle the introductions."

For the first time since she was in high school her pulse spiked in anticipation of meeting a guy. *I'm not sixteen. What the hell is happening to me?*

Tish saw him in her peripheral vision as he arrived at the cart. "Morning, Benny," he said, then turned to face her. His jaw slightly dropped as his eyes widened a bit. "Uh…hello." He flashed a warm smile.

Her heart fluttered a bit as she locked eyes with him. "Hi."

"Well, how about that," said Benny. "Two of my favorite regulars here at the same time. Spence from the block, meet Tish from the hotel."

He extended his hand, still staring at her. "My pleasure, Tish."

"Nice to meet you, Spence."

Benny fixed a cup of coffee and held it out to Spence.

But he was still staring at Tish. Her face flushed a bit and she was powerless to stop it.

Benny tapped him on the arm. "Yo, Spence, your coffee's gettin' cold."

"Huh?" He turned to Benny and saw the cup. "Oh, yeah. Thanks." He paid him with a five dollar bill, then turned back to Tish. "So, you're one of his regulars, huh?"

"Yeah. And actually, I'm really glad to finally run into you because I owe you a dollar." She pulled a bill from her pocket and held it out. "Now I can sleep at night with my tab paid in full."

"Excuse me?"

"We've actually met before, but were not formally introduced."

"I, uh, think I would remember meeting someone like you."

"Well, at the time I was the sweaty jogger who forgot to bring cash and you bought me a cold drink."

His smile went wide as he raised his eyebrows. "That was you?"

"Yep. So now you've already seen me at my worst."

Benny laughed. "Don't feel bad, Spence, I didn't recognize her in the business outfit either. Though she's still cute in her workout clothes."

She was still holding out the dollar bill but he put up his hand. "You don't have to pay me back. It was my pleasure."

She took a deep breath, and then for the first time in her life she took the plunge. "Then…how about I buy you breakfast? Otherwise we can't call it even. And I do hate owing someone."

He looked at his watch. "I'd love to, but not enough time."

Aw, hell, that old excuse. He's not interested, despite the look he's giving me. "That's okay—"

"But I'm free for lunch if that works for you."

And we're…back in the game! "I can do lunch. My afternoon is pretty clear."

He pointed at the corner restaurant. "How about you meet me there at noon? They have good food."

"Sure, I've eaten there before. Sounds like a plan."

He reached in his pocket, pulled out a business card and handed it to her. "In case you get tied up or have to cancel, just give me a call."

"Okay, thanks."

"Uh…can I have one of your cards just in case?"

"Men don't cancel on me, Spence from the block. So you'd better show up." She cocked her head at Benny. "Or I know where to find you."

*

Spencer beamed as he entered his office. "Ariel, you're not going to believe this. I met her."

His partner looked up from her desk. "Met who?"

"Duh-uh. The woman I've been obsessing about. Tish McKenna. *Mrs. Spock* from law school. *Jaws* from the courtroom."

She leaned back and smiled. "Ah, so you finally worked up the nerve and stopped by her office."

"Nope. Ran into her at the little drink cart where I get my coffee every morning."

"Huh. Well, the stars must be aligning. So, tell me more. What's her story?"

"Don't know yet, but get this. We had met recently at the same place. She was out jogging and stopped to get something to drink. She had no money so I paid for her soda."

"And you didn't recognize her?"

"I was in the middle of a phone call and she was in workout clothes. I wasn't really paying attention."

"In other words, you were being a typical man not noticing when a woman who's your type is right under your nose."

"Stop it. So anyway, Benny the drink cart guy introduced us

since we're both regular customers. Then she tried to pay me back for the soda and I told her it wasn't necessary, so she asked me to breakfast and I told her I didn't have enough time so I asked her to lunch and then we agreed to meet at the restaurant near the cart and I gave her my business card but she wouldn't give me one saying I'd better not stand her up—"

"Slow down, Spence, you've gone into run-on sentence mode like you always do when you're excited. Need a little punctuation here and there. *Quietly beautiful woman* alert. Now sit down and breathe. Tell me again what happened because I lost you after she asked you to breakfast."

He took a deep breath and sat. "Sorry. Anyway, like I said I'm meeting her for lunch. So I gave her a card and told her to call me if she's late or has to cancel. Then I asked her for a card in case I have to cancel and she wouldn't give me one. Said I'd better not stand her up or she knows where to find me."

Ariel folded her arms and nodded. "I like this woman already. Though you realize she already has the upper hand with you."

"Hell, who cares?"

"So, did you have any chance to talk at all?"

"Not really. I had to go. But we can do that at lunch."

"So, did she seem interested in you?"

"She asked me, remember?"

"Oh, right. Quite different than the woman in college, huh?"

"I'd say so. And she looks damn good up close."

"Ah, the *eyes* have it."

"She had her glasses on, and they're pretty thick so I didn't get a good look. Funny, she's the girl that blew me off when I tried to bring her a cup of coffee in college and now she's inviting me out to eat."

"Just proves that people change, Spence. Well, you may as well give me all the work you had planned for this morning."

"Why?"

"Because I know how you are when you're smitten, and you won't be able to concentrate worth a damn."

He waved his hand like he was shooing a fly. "Pffft. I don't get smitten."

"Oh, what a load of crap. Go look in the mirror. You may as well have the word written on your forehead."

"Fine, you win. I'll admit I'm smitten. It's been a long time since I dated anyone interesting. Even if this is just lunch."

"Well, bring your A-game and there will be a dinner in the future."

"Enlighten me, counselor. What do you consider my A-game?"

"That boy-next-door thing you do with a judge. Trust me, it'll work."

*

Tish stood up from her seat in the TV network lobby as Madison quickly approached her. "Everything okay, Tish?"

"Yeah, very."

"When they said you were in the lobby I thought there was an emergency. By the way, you look great. That suit really brings out your eyes."

"Thank you. I can't argue with your good taste. I really love this outfit."

"So what brings you by?"

"I met the white knight this morning."

"No kidding. Where, at the courthouse?"

"No, at that soda cart I've been stalking. Anyway, I invited him out to eat."

Madison took her arms. "Hang on, I gotta call my producer. This is major breaking news."

"Oh, stop it."

"*You* asked a man out? This really is like seeing a unicorn."

"I tried to pay him back for the soda he bought me, and he

wouldn't take the dollar, so I asked him to join me for breakfast. He didn't have time, but he said he'd meet me for lunch."

"Well, look at Tish McKenna. High powered lawyer who's fearless in the courtroom finally takes the initiative with men."

"May I remind you of a certain redheaded kick-ass reporter who was equally as frightened of the male species until recently?"

"Fine, I used to see her in my mirror, and thank God she's gone or I wouldn't have Nick. But I'm really proud of you taking the big leap. So, what's he like?"

"We only had a minute to chat. But we had serious eye contact. And he said something that makes me think he finds me attractive. *I think I'd remember meeting someone like you.*"

"Oooh, that's a good sign. You definitely made an impression."

"Anyway, he gave me his card so I can call in case I'm late or have to cancel, but I didn't give him one. I told him he'd better show up."

"Oh. My. God. What has gotten into you?"

"I don't know." Tish put her hand over her chest. "My heart was pounding and it just came out." She flashed a big smile. "But it felt really good."

"Well, I'm happy for you. So what does he do for a living?"
"Don't know."

"Well, you shouldn't need an investigative reporter to find out. He gave you his business card, let's take a look." Tish pulled the card from her pocket and handed it to Madison. "Spencer Capshaw. Uh-oh. He's a lawyer. Well, given enough ointment, there's always a fly."

"What's the fly?"

"You do remember the last time you dated a lawyer."

"You would bring that up."

"Sorry. But that's why I never dated another person in the news business. Too much in common is often not good."

"Look, we've seen the guy do a really nice thing. Maybe he's different. Hell, he has to be." Tish took the card and looked at it. "Spencer Capshaw. Damn, that name sounds familiar."

"Maybe you had a case against him or saw him in court."

She shook her head. "Nah. I'd remember a guy who looked like that."

Madison started to laugh. "Funny. Didn't he just say something similar about you? You two are already on the same page."

*

It was clear his lunch date wasn't kidding about not showing up, and there was no way he was going to miss an opportunity with a woman like Tish, so Spencer arrived at the busy restaurant twenty minutes early. Fortunately he was a regular so they let him camp out at a corner table. He tried working on some research but couldn't concentrate. Being smitten trumped all. He pulled out a newspaper and started to read the sports page.

There was something about the look they'd shared at the drinks cart. Even though it was through her thick glasses.

She had obviously changed, personality-wise. The woman who'd blown him off in law school had asked him out to eat. And she actually smiled, unlike the valedictorian who was a sphinx in a previous life. But it was obvious she liked to be in charge, not giving him a business card or the chance to stand her up. Which he had no intention of doing. It was clear she had no tolerance for men who played games. Which was fine since he didn't do that anyway. So if he told her he'd call, he'd better not fail to do so.

He looked up each time the little bell above the restaurant door rang to announce a customer, his pulse spiking in anticipation each time. When it wasn't her he relaxed and tried to go back to the newspaper. Of course Ariel was right, he really couldn't concentrate, even on something mindless like the sports page. Was Tish one of those women who would be fashionably late, making him wait to show the upper hand?

His question was answered as he heard the bell ring, then looked up to see her enter the restaurant at exactly noon.

Spencer waved, caught her eye and stood up to greet her.

She wore a big smile as she power-walked in his direction, her shoulder length hair bouncing with every step. One of those women who moved with a purpose, like she had the world by the tail.

Damn, she's come a long way since law school.

She's quietly beautiful, all right.

She shook his hand as she arrived at the table. "See, I'm a good judge of character. I knew you didn't need a business card."

"Hey, when a woman like you asks me out to eat, I'm not missing that opportunity." He pulled out a chair for her.

"Why thank you, kind sir." She sat and adjusted her seat a bit as he sat opposite her. "And what do you mean, *a woman like me?*"

"Aw, hell, I've tipped my hand already. I meant to say I don't turn down a free lunch."

"Uh-*huh*."

"Can we look at the menu?"

"I'll let this one slide, Mister. But your comment is already on the record and I can have the court reporter read it back if you'd like."

"Damn, you're good. I concede round one to the young lady."

"Fine. So, is this gonna be a quick lunch or do you have to get back to work?"

"I'm good till two-thirty, so no hurry. How about you?"

"My calendar's pretty light for this afternoon. And as it turns out, I'm in the same line of work as you." She reached into her purse and handed him a card.

"I know." He didn't look at the card.

"How'd you know I'm a lawyer?"

"Besides what you just said about reading back my comments, I saw you in court on Judge Winston's first day. I was one of the attorneys in the back row making too much noise. Actually I was probably making the most noise talking to my partner."

"You remembered me from that?"

He nodded. "Pretty hard to forget what I considered to be an inquisition of a witness. I must say, you're really good. The Feds ought to send you to Guantanamo. You'd break those terrorists in no time. By the way, the chatter in the back of the room was about you, not the judge. You're an impressive attorney."

"Well, I'm flattered. And I've also seen you in action."

"Oh, really? What trial?"

"Not in court, at a restaurant awhile back. You saved a waitress from an obnoxious guy trying to get a free meal. Paid his check, tossed him two bucks for a hot dog and told him to get the hell out. A girl doesn't see white knights very often."

"It was no big deal. Any guy would have done the same."

"Oh, bull. You don't see guys sticking up for women like that anymore. Pretty hard to forget. That was incredibly nice of you, by the way."

"That was no way to treat a lady." He looked at her card. "And speaking of our paths crossing, we actually met a long time ago."

"I think I'd remember you."

"I had this scraggly beard and it was several years ago. At NYU law school."

She furrowed her brow. "You went to NYU? Y'know, I thought your name sounded familiar."

"Not only that, I was in your class."

"Really? So when did we meet?"

"First year, about a month in. I brought you a cup of coffee in the library and you told me you wanted to study alone, picked up your books and moved to another table."

Her eyes grew wide as she bit her lower lip. "Oh my God, that was you? I am so, so sorry."

"I was so devastated I couldn't sleep all night."

"I'm really sorry—"

"Turned out it was the extra caffeine from drinking two cups of coffee."

She laughed a bit. "Very funny."

"By the way, I was just trying to be friendly. I wasn't hitting on you or anything."

She smiled and shook her head. "Wouldn't have done any good. I wasn't interested in dating. And I wasn't the nicest person to be around back then. I didn't have a life other than law school. I'll admit I had a rather abrasive personality. But I only take good clients so I guess they rubbed off on me. You know that feeling you get when you help the good guys win?"

"Yeah." *Well, I used to…until…oh, hell, we've got Peter Brent as a client.*

"Gave me back my soul."

And the clients I took for money did the opposite for me. Okay, universe, I'm getting the message.

Dear God, if she knows we're representing Brent she'll walk out of here.

"Well, you're obviously better for it. Unless you're gonna pick up your menu and move to another table."

"Not a chance. I'm the one who invited you, remember?"

"By the way, if the name sounds familiar, it's because I'm the one you beat out for valedictorian. Though I will admit it wasn't even close." He smiled at her and got one in return.

Damn, I wish she'd take off her glasses.

Those eyes.

A waitress arrived at the table. "Hey, Spence, how's it going?"

He looked up at the fiftyish woman with the pencil in her dark hair. "Very well, Jeannie. You doing okay today?"

"Now that you're at one of my tables." She cocked her head at Tish. "So who's your friend?"

"That's Tish."

She turned and smiled. "Hi Tish, welcome to our restaurant."

"Thank you, but I've been here before. So, my dining companion is a regular, huh?"

"We fight to wait on him. Best tipper in the city. But also treats the staff like equals."

"I see."

She patted him on the shoulder. "I tell ya, if I were twenty years younger…"

He blushed a bit. "Oh, stop it, Jeannie, you're husband's a great guy. Be careful, he might hear you from the kitchen."

The waitress turned back to Tish. "Well, honey, if you're not attached, don't let this one go." She took their orders and headed back to the kitchen.

"So, the waitress has a crush on you?"

"I think it's more like moms who want me to date their daughters. I get that a lot."

"Ah. Well, that was a nice recommendation. Moms do know best."

*

Tish leaned back in her chair and sipped her coffee, fat and happy.

And relaxed. All the anxiety she'd had walking into the restaurant had been melted away by his smile and the way he looked right into her eyes.

And, unlike many men, he actually listened to her without giving her the vacant head bob.

The conversation was fresh and easy, like they'd been friends for years. Not too much about law, either, as it was clear Spence from the block had interests other than the law. She was totally comfortable with him and he seemed the same way with her.

She noticed the bus boys cleaning up the table next to them and looked around the restaurant. It was mostly empty. She looked at her watch and saw it was almost two. "Wow, I guess we've been here awhile. Looks like they're getting ready to close up the place to get ready for dinner."

He looked at his watch. "Geez, you're not kidding."

She noted he wore a silver watch that looked very old. "That's a cool watch. Is it an antique or some sort of reproduction?"

"Found it at a yard sale and had it fixed. The jeweler said it's about a hundred years old. I got hooked on old watches and have about five of them I wear. I know most people use cell phones to tell time but I like old-fashioned stuff."

"Well, you seem like an old fashioned guy, so it's appropriate."

"Speaking of time, you gotta get going?"

"Not really. Things are slow since I lost my biggest client. Clint Davies."

"Oh, no. I read about that. I loved his products. Are you working in a firm, by the way?"

"No, all by myself. Sort of my only option since I had alienated everyone in law school and wasn't exactly great at interviews. Actually I was a disaster at interviews. Every firm thought they wanted to hire me, until they actually met me. When you're the valedictorian and don't get a single job offer after fourteen interviews, it told me I needed to work on my people skills."

"Well, obviously you've changed. Y'know, speaking of job offers, my partner and I have been talking about adding another lawyer to our firm, and when we saw you in action—"

"I like working for myself, but thanks."

"Well, we are a little overloaded right now. I could throw you some work. How about that? Nothing major but might help you pick up the slack until you build your client list back up."

She nodded. "I'd appreciate that. But remember, I only take clients who are decent people."

Yeah, I used to represent them in the DA's office. Before I became money mad and took every client who walked in the door. "I've got some cases that would meet with your approval. Anyway, since we work in the same building, may I walk you back?"

"I'd like that." He grabbed the check and reached for his wallet but she waved her hand. "Uh, I asked *you* to lunch, remember?"

He whipped out a credit card and put it on top of the bill. "Sorry, not up for discussion. Besides, you said you lost your biggest client."

"I can afford lunch, Spence."

"You can get the next one." He flagged down the waitress and handed her the credit card.

"Does *next one* mean you'd like to see me again?"

"For someone who was a valedictorian, you should have figured that out. *You get the next one* means there will *be* a next one. Of course, if I'm not being presumptuous and that's okay with you?"

"Yeah, I'd like that."

The bright sunshine and comfortable fall temperatures let them take their time walking back to the Empire State Building. Tish was energized after two hours with a really nice guy who seemed as interested in her as she was in him.

They arrived at the building and he held the door for her, then walked her to the elevator. "Here's where I get off, Tish."

"I thought you were going back to your office."

"Gotta go to court."

"That's in the other direction."

"It was a clever ruse to walk you back."

"Well, I'm glad I fell for it. This was really nice."

"Yeah. Anyway, about that next time…I'd love to take you out on Saturday but I have a wedding to go to, so how about the following Saturday?"

"Small world, I've got a wedding this weekend as well. But yeah, next Saturday would be great."

"Maybe we can sneak in another lunch before then."

"That would be nice. Today was the best lunch I've ever had."

"Hey, if you really liked the chicken, you should try their shrimp diablo."

She locked eyes with him. "I wasn't talking about the food."

He gave her a soft smile. The bell on the elevator dinged and the door opened. "Tish from the hotel, it was a pleasure."

"See you soon, Spence from the block."

*

"Caught screwing off, again. And here I thought you were working late." Ariel stood in the doorway to Spencer's office shaking her head as he played with the cat from the vent, dangling a catnip mouse from a string.

"Hey, it relaxes me and I needed a break after two hours of research. And I figured she might be bored being an office cat. I mean, she could be stuck in some corporate firm with a bunch of stuffed shirts who ignore her all day."

"You really think someone like that would bring a cat to work every day?"

"I was just concerned for her well-being. I read that an indoor cat needs exercise that mirrors the wild. They're natural hunters." The cat jumped up and grabbed the mouse, so he let go of the string. "She is seriously fast and can really jump."

"So this is part of your duties now. Amusing the vent cat."

"Hey, she comes here often enough."

"And you want her to keep visiting you."

"Sure. She's a sweet cat."

"I cannot believe you went out and bought her toys. And you know what catnip does to them. It basically gets them drunk. She's going to stagger back to her owner looking like she spent a night in a bar."

"Oh, I'm just having fun with her. And she obviously wants to play."

"Here's a wild concept. Why don't you just go to a shelter and get your own cat?"

"I'm going to do that after we clear some of those big cases out of the way. But now that you mention it, she'd have someone to play with."

"Geez, Spence, I didn't mean *we* should have an office cat. I love them but not in a place of business. And from the looks of things you'd never get any work done. Go adopt one for your home, then you've got a cat at two convenient locations to serve you."

Suddenly the cat stopped playing. Her ears perked up and she dashed behind the bookcase into the vent. "Well, off she goes."

"Hope she can find her way back to her owner. You got that cat so loopy she might end up in the boiler room."

*

Tish entered her office with Shelley right behind her, surprised that Socks was not at her usual spot on the desk. "Socks, where are you? Kitty, kitty, kitty…c'mon out." She crouched down to look under the desk just as a flying ball of black and white fur sailed by her head. "Whoa. There you are, you devious little thing. Launching a sneak attack at your owner." She reached out for the cat but it did a sideways hop away from her, arching its back, fur all standing on end. "What the hell is wrong with you?"

Shelley started to laugh. "She wants to play with you. The poor thing is probably bored. This isn't exactly a natural environment for a cat. She needs more attention."

"You're probably right. She doesn't get much exercise in here. I brought her toys but I forget to play with her when I get busy."

"Poor neglected kitty."

Tish got up and pulled one of Socks' favorite toys from the box, a stuffed chipmunk on a string. She tossed it near the cat, then slowly pulled it back. Socks crouched down and started to stalk the toy, wiggled her hindquarters, then launched herself into a perfect jump, landing on the chipmunk. Tish released the string as the cat began to toss the thing in the air. "It's got catnip in it. It'll wear her out and she'll sleep the rest of the day."

Chapter Eight

"I really don't feel like going to a wedding," said Tish, as Madison worked on her makeup.

"Oh, stop it, you and A.J. will have fun. Now please hold still while I'm doing your eyes."

"Pretty sad that I have to take another woman as a *plus one*. Sure wish the white knight wasn't tied up."

"Well, from what you told me that situation is looking up. Who knows, maybe you won't need a *plus one* ever again. Too bad he won't see you tonight. You look terrific. Of course with these eyes it would be hard not to."

Tish heard the doorbell ring. "Ah, my date's here." She heard Nick answer the door and heel clicks heading toward the guest room.

A.J. poked her head in the door. "Hey guys. Tish, you look smokin' hot."

"I probably look like a streetwalker. I've never worn this much makeup before."

"It's not much at all," said Madison. "Besides, just getting you in practice for the white knight."

A.J. shook her head. "And here I'll be on a Saturday night while she's pining away for someone else."

Tish smiled at her. "A.J., I really can't thank you enough for coming with me. I couldn't go to one more wedding with my usual *plus one.*"

"I don't blame you. He's nice, but beyond boring. Dating him would be like reading the Wall Street Journal."

Madison pulled the tissues from Tish's collar. "Okay, young lady, you are done. I now pronounce you gorgeous."

"Very funny." She stood up and looked in the mirror, surprised at what Madison had done. "Wow. I mean, my eyes have never looked so good. Thanks, Madison."

"My pleasure. Like I said, it's just a little makeup."

"Well, let's hit the road," said A.J. They headed toward the door, passing Nick who was reading in a reclining chair.

He gave Tish an approving nod. "Whoa, babe alert."

Tish couldn't help but smile. "Nick, you are the world's sweetest man."

A.J. moved closer to him and folded her arms. "So what am I, chopped liver?"

"I was referring to all three of you."

"See," said Madison, "I've got him well trained."

*

Spencer knew bringing a blind date as a "plus one" was a bad idea the minute she'd opened the door and he'd gotten a good look at her. If only he'd met Tish before a lawyer buddy had set him up with this "nice girl named Jennifer" who had spent the entire ride to the reception looking in her compact mirror and talking about how drunk she got at her last wedding. All the while drinking a beer.

Nice girl, my ass.

And showing up with a party girl in a too-short red bandage dress, too-big peroxide blonde hair, and false eyelashes that could swat a fly would get him more than a few raised eyebrows from

82

the crowd of legal eagles. As his sister had once told him, "A woman shouldn't out-do the bride on her wedding day."

Too late now. If the bride wasn't such a good friend he would have feigned a sudden attack of food poisoning and driven his date home. Then again he worried the bride would never speak to him again after bringing such a bimbo along on her big day. He pulled into a parking spot and took a deep breath, knowing that every single one of the three hundred guests would think he'd showed up with a hooker.

He opened the car door for her and she stepped out onto the sidewalk, a five-foot-two extra from a porn movie teetering on five-inch platform heels.

Everyone else in the parking lot stopped to gawk as they headed toward the reception hall.

I want to dig a hole all the way to China and jump in it.

They started heading up the stairs. "So, everyone here is a lawyer?" she asked.

"Well, since the bride and groom are both attorneys, I'd say most of the people probably work in the legal profession."

"Wow." She took his arm as they walked through the front door. "Lotta people here. Lotta money, I'll bet. Hope there's not a line at the bar."

"I'm sure everyone will get a glass of champagne when the newlyweds arrive."

"That's it? No open bar? And how long do we have to wait for the bride and groom?"

He rolled his eyes. "I don't know, Jennifer. We'll find out soon enough."

"Well, we can always leave early if there isn't an open bar."

Yeah, I'd like to leave now and drop you at home.

But sadly, as they entered the hall his date spotted the bar. "You find out where we're sitting and I'll go get the drinks. You want anything?"

"I'm fine."

She made a bee line for the bar, leaving a batch of dropped jaws in her wake as Spencer stood in line to get his seat assignment.

An hour later that food poisoning idea was looking awfully good.

*

After a few glasses of champagne on an empty stomach, Tish had loosened up. And it helped that her usual plus one was not boring her to death with tales of his accounting business. Of course A.J.'s running commentary on the various inappropriate fashions worn by some of the guests had those at her table in stitches. It made for a warped kind of "red carpet" and helped that everyone at the table was a lawyer with a wicked sense of humor.

All's fair in love and fashion *faux pas.*

Tish got into the spirit of things, pointing out a young woman on the dance floor with royal blue hair and a black dress. "What about that one, A.J.?"

"*Costume de riguer* for a Smurf at a funeral."

Everyone laughed as one of the male guests singled out a guy wearing a bright green sport coat over a tie-dyed shirt. "How about the guy in the green, A.J.?"

"Looks like he won the Masters golf tournament in the sixties. At Woodstock." Then A.J.'s eyes widened. "Oh. My. God."

Tish looked around to see what had captured her attention. "What?"

"Target at twelve o'clock. Cheap bimbo at the bar who looks like she needs a bail bondsman and a public defender."

Tish's jaw dropped as she spotted the top-heavy woman spilling out of a very short candy apple red bandage dress that left little to the imagination. "Think she's a leftover from the bachelor party?"

84

"Sounds about right," said one of the guys. "I guess she forgot her stripper pole. Anybody got some dollar bills?"

A.J. laughed as she shook her head. "Who the hell brings a woman dressed like that to a wedding?"

"Hell, what kind of woman *dresses* like that for a wedding?" Tish watched the girl as she left the bar carrying two drinks. "We're about to find out who brought a date from Caligula's palace." The woman weaved her way through the crowd on the dance floor, nearly falling down as she was obviously drunk. Then took a seat next to—

Tish's face dropped along with her voice. "Oh, no. I don't believe it."

A.J. turned to her. "What?"

"She's with my white knight."

"You're kidding."

"Nope. Sonofabitch." Her heart sank as she grabbed her drink and threw it down. "Aw, shit. I guess I read him wrong."

A.J. grabbed her arm. "Hang on a minute. She might just be sitting next to him."

"She just handed him a drink. Dammit, if he likes that type then I'm really not—"

Suddenly Spencer turned and spotted her looking at him. He flashed a big smile and waved.

"Well, don't worry your pretty little head. I'll find out," said A.J.

"Huh? How are you going to find out?"

"Wave him over, dumbass. And smile."

Spencer leaned over to his date. "Hey, I'm going to go say hello to a friend."

The girl whipped her head around, looking in all directions. "Who?"

"A lawyer I know." He nodded in the direction of Tish. "She's sitting over there."

Jennifer looked around. "Which one? The brunette on the dance floor? She's fat."

He rolled his eyes as he shook his head, didn't answer and got up.

"Hey!"

He ignored her and headed toward Tish, laser locked on her. She smiled and got up to greet him. "Tish, we just keep running into each other."

She nodded. "Can't believe we're at the same wedding." She reached down and pulled A.J. out of her chair. "Spence, this is one of my dear friends, A.J."

He shook her hand and smiled. "Pleasure, A.J."

A.J sized him up. "You too. I'm her plus one since she wasn't interested in any of the other men who were free tonight. The one she wanted to go with was already *tied up.*"

Tish shot her a wide eyed look.

A.J. looked over his shoulder. "Uh, your *companion* over there doesn't look too happy."

Spencer rolled his eyes. "Last time I let a friend fix me up with a blind date for a wedding. I'll never hear the end of it next time I'm in the courthouse."

Tish smiled a bit. "Oh, so she's not your—"

"I'm not dressed like a pimp, am I?"

Tish couldn't help but laugh. "Uh, no. You look very nice."

"You both look terrific. Anyway, just met her two hours ago. At the rate she's throwing down scotch I'll be carrying her home." He noted the band finished a fast song and started a slow one. He took Tish's hands. "How about a dance, Tish from the hotel?"

Tish looked at the bimbo, then back at him. "I dunno, Spence, your date looks awfully steamed."

He turned to A.J. "I will give you a thousand dollars if you can find a guy to go hit on her."

A.J. laughed, gave Tish a wink and pushed her toward him.

"Go dance. I'll find some sucker who thinks with the wrong head. Oh, Tish, I'll hold your glasses."

"Huh?"

A.J reached up and removed her glasses, then gave her a wide-eyed look. "You don't want these flyin' off while you're dancing, do you? Like they *always* do when you dance?"

"Oh, right."

Tish turned back to him and he got a close up look at those eyes for the first time. His jaw dropped slightly. "Whoa."

"Whoa, what?"

"I've, uh…well, come on."

He led her to the dance floor, took one hand in his while resting the other lightly on her waist. She put her free hand on his shoulder as they began to sway to the music. He locked eyes with her. "Y'know, if I'd paid more attention to you the day I bought you a soda, I wouldn't be stuck with *her* tonight."

"Back up a minute. You didn't tell me what the *whoa* was for."

"Oh. Your eyes are such an amazing color. They're really spectacular. Hard to appreciate them with your glasses on."

"Why, thank you, kind sir. People do say it's my best feature."

"No argument here. If you didn't wear glasses I'd swear they were colored contacts. They're such a deep blue."

"I tried wearing contacts but they don't work for me. Really irritate my eyes. Besides, glasses make a woman look smarter, or so I've heard."

"I don't think you need any help in that department, Miss Valedictorian."

"By the way, you have gorgeous eyes as well. Such a beautiful olive green."

"Are we going to spend the evening complimenting each other?"

She shrugged. "I could live with that." Tish looked over his shoulder. "Oooh, speaking of eyes, your date is shooting daggers at me. Talk about a death stare."

"Good, maybe she'll get jealous and find someone else to take her home."

"A blonde in that dress and with that body…it shouldn't be hard."

"I dunno, some guys have a bad allergic reaction to silicone. And she's not a blonde unless she dyed her roots brown on purpose."

"You're funny, Spence."

"But speaking of blondes, you look fabulous."

"I thought we were done with the compliments. You trying to butter me up?"

"Oh, absolutely. So, was A.J. kidding about why she's your *plus one* tonight?"

"Nope. The available male choices were not remotely inspiring. Of course, she wouldn't be my date if you'd paid more attention when buying me a soda."

"Geez, I'll never live that down either. Though I would think men would be beating down your door."

"They don't, but I'm very particular anyway. And I have unfortunately discovered that a lot of men are intimidated by smart women and prefer…well, dates like yours. Also, I have an unlimited number of peremptory strikes."

"Ah. So since you're dancing with me I guess I am acceptable to this attorney."

"The jury is still out pending further cross-examination, but you seem to be a good fit for this case so far."

"So, you a friend of the bride or groom?"

"The groom. And you?"

"The blushing bride. So is he gonna treat her right?"

"Absolutely. He's a great guy. What about her?"

"Total sweetheart. Really decent person and smart as hell. We've been friends for years."

"Good to hear. Speaking of decent, you'd better do the right thing and get back to your table soon because your date looks

like she is about to make a scene, and you don't want that wedding reception."

He spun her around so that he was facing the woman, wh looked livid. He smiled at her and gave her a wave as the danc ended. "While I'd much rather spend the evening at your table and dancing with you, I think you're right."

"I'm always right. Now shake my hand, pat me on the shoulder and give me a wave."

"Huh?"

"Let her think I'm just a friend. Then get her drunk as fast as possible and get her outta here. I'll see you soon enough."

"Okay. Sounds like a plan."

"And if you don't want to dance with her, pretend to twist your ankle on the way back to the table."

"Excellent idea. Now I can see why you were the valedictorian."

"That stuff ain't in a book, Spence. Basically it's *bad dates 101.*"

He followed her instructions, shook her hand, patted her on the shoulder and gave her a wave, then turned and fell to the floor. He grimaced as he grabbed his ankle, then got up and hobbled back to the table.

"So who was that?" asked his date, arms folded, still glaring at Tish, not at all concerned with his fall.

"Like I said, a lawyer I know. Just a friend." He started to take off his shoe.

"Good." She took his hand and yanked. "C'mon, let's dance."

He shook his head. "Sorry, I really twisted my ankle when I fell. It hurts like hell." He flagged over a nearby waiter. "Hey, can I get a bag of ice? I think I sprained my ankle." The waiter nodded and headed to the kitchen.

"So, what's the deal, you can't dance with me?"

"Afraid not. I'm sure you can find someone as a partner. Plenty of single guys here." He pointed to the table where the friend who had fixed him up was seated. "I think you'd like the guy with the purple tie. He can't stay off the dance floor."

Payback.

She shook her head and threw her napkin on the table. "Fine. Sit here by yourself with your...ankle." She got up and headed to a table filled with men, grabbed his friend without asking and hauled his ass to the dance floor.

Spencer turned toward Tish's table, saw her laughing and mouthed a "thank you."

*

Spence had kept Tish and A.J. laughing as they had turned their chairs to watch the hilarious goings-on at his table. The party girl was giving him an earful and shaking her finger at him when she wasn't on the dance floor doing the bump-and-grind with any man she could find. Every time she left the table to get another drink he looked at Tish and did some hilarious pantomime, using his thumb and index finger to shoot himself with an imaginary gun or wrap an invisible rope around his neck to hang himself Tish pointed at the parade of empty glasses in front of her seat and mouthed "how many." He counted and held up eight fingers.

"Damn," said A.J. "How the hell does a woman that little drink that much? She can't be more than a hundred pounds."

"Most have a hollow leg. And about twenty of those pounds are silicone." The song ended and she saw the woman head back to the table, seriously unsteady this time. "Ah, this could be last call for our designated tramp. I think she's finally had one for the road. Wait for it..." The girl reached the table, swayed in a circle. "Going...going..." Then she practically collapsed on top of Spence. "Gone. And she is down for the count. Stick a fork in her, the party girl is done." She watched him pat her on the face, then shake her without any response. The woman was a passed-out drunk, mouth hanging open like a trophy bass. He looked at Tish, shrugged, stood her up, tossed her over his shoulder and carried her out of the hall.

90

Twenty minutes later Tish's cell phone beeped. She pulled it from her purse and saw a text. "Hey, it's from Spence."

A.J. leaned over to take a look. "Oooh, let me see."

Just dropped off comatose date. Thanks for saving me from dancing with her. You're brilliant. See you soon. Can't wait.

-Spence

A.J. pointed at the phone. "Reply with something fun."

She thought a minute, then tapped the keys on the phone.

You mean you didn't have your way with her?

-Tish

The reply came back fast.

Prefer women who are conscious and have a brain. I poured her through the mail slot.

They both laughed. "He's a quick wit," said A.J. "Keep it going."

Tish typed out a message but hesitated.

If you come back to the reception you can dance with a woman who's conscious. Band still here for two more hours.

Operators are standing by.

"Should I send it?"

A.J. shook her head, rolled her eyes, reached over and tapped the send button. "Damn, Tish, sometimes you're hopeless."

The reply came back in an instant.

Just made illegal U-Turn. No cops in sight. About to exceed speed limit.

Tish flashed a big smile. "Thank you, A.J. I don't know what I'd do without you."

A.J. pointed at the phone. "Tell him I wanna go home and ask if he can give you a ride."

"You want to go home? I thought you were having a good time."

"*Madonne*. Do I have to shoot you with the clue gun?"

"Oh. Right. I get it. You don't really—"

"Give me the damn phone!" A.J. grabbed it, wrote a text and hit the send button.

A.J. is feeling tired. Any chance you can run me home after the reception? I'm staying on Staten Island tonight. If it's too far out of the way, I understand.

Another quick response.

Change of venue not a problem. Appeal granted.

A.J. picked up her purse and stood up. "Okay, I'm gettin' out of the way."

"Thanks, A.J."

"I'll send you a bill for my services. And you'd better call Madison and tell her you'll be home late."

"Why?"

"Why? I saw the way he looked at you. And the way you looked at him. Trust me, you'll be gettin' home late. If you get home at all."

Chapter Nine

Tish shuffled out of the guest room preceded by Socks and saw her friends already seated at the dining room table for their regular Sunday brunch. She yawned and stretched, her eyes noting the clock which told her she'd slept past eleven.

"Well, look what the cat dragged in," said Madison. "Literally."

She covered another yawn, then held her head due to a slight hangover. "Morning, guys."

Rory studied her face. "She doesn't look too bad for someone who got in at seventeen minutes after one."

Tish's jaw dropped as she sat down. "What the hell, Rory, are you spying on me?"

Madison nodded. "She does that. You have to get used to it while you're living here. She thinks we find it endearing for some odd reason."

"I was up late reading and happened to see you," said Rory.

A.J. rolled her eyes. "Oh, what a crock. You've got the friggin' Hubble telescope across the street." She turned to Tish. "I already got them up to speed to the point I left. So, details about the white knight. C'mon, spill."

Tish grabbed a glass of orange juice and smiled. "We had a nice time. Could have talked all night."

"They pulled up in the driveway four minutes after twelve," said Rory.

Tish glared at her. "Yeah, and then we *talked*."

"Talking doesn't usually fog up the windows of a car."

"It was humid!"

"In October? Pffft. I hardly think so."

"Good God, Rory, you should work for the CIA. Fine, we talked and then we made out a little."

Rory leaned back and smiled at her. "Considering the kiss he planted on you when he walked you to the door, it looked like more than a little. Talk about a tonsillectomy."

Tish slapped her hands on the table. "Okay, stop it!"

Everyone laughed as Rory reached over and gave her a hug. "I'm just yankin' your chain, sweetie. We're all happy you met someone nice. Who is obviously attracted to you."

"Yeah, and amazingly he's unattached. That woman we saw him with in the restaurant turned out to be a partner at his law firm. By the way, Madison, he said my eyes are spectacular. So thanks for the makeup job."

"You didn't need makeup for that, I just brought them out. But I'm glad he noticed."

A.J. laughed. "You shoulda seen the guy when I took her glasses off. He got a good look at her eyes and it was like he got hit with Cupid's arrow. Bada bing. Though I must say, his are pretty spectacular as well and he's cute as hell up close. The boy is seriously doable."

"But they just *talked*, remember?" cracked Rory.

"The *plus one* he had at the wedding was very doable, and he didn't," said Tish.

A.J. laughed a bit. "I'd call her a *plus two* considering the fake boobs. I think if you pricked one with a pin she would have flown around the room like a deflated balloon."

Tish laughed. "She was rather top heavy. I'm surprised she

didn't tip over. Looked like every man's fantasy from a porn magazine."

"Yeah, I showed them a photo I took with my phone," said A.J. "But apparently she wasn't *his* fantasy. Give the guy credit for not thinking with the wrong head."

Rory flashed a sinister grin. "He didn't look like he was only interested in Tish's mind."

Tish looked at the ceiling. "Please, God, take me now."

A.J. patted her on the back. "Hey, I'm impressed that he ditched the cheap bimbo and came back for the classy chick. Gotta love a guy with priorities like that."

"So what's next?" asked Madison.

Tish started dishing out food onto her plate. "We're going to try to have lunch one day this week and then Saturday he's taking me out." Socks jumped into her lap and started to sniff her food. "Sorry, kitty, this stuff has salt in it. Not good for you. I'll get you some treats as soon as I'm back in my body."

Madison picked up her cat, Bumper and set him on her lap. "You find out if he likes cats?"

"The topic didn't come up."

"Surprising," said Rory, "considering all the *talking* you two did."

Tish rolled her eyes. "Next week I'll have him drop me off around the block."

"Don't know if it will do you any good," said A.J. "She's probably hacked into the city's traffic cams."

Rory shook her head. "I tried, but their security system is too good."

*

Spencer arrived at his office to find Ariel sitting at her desk. She bit her lip as she looked up at him, obviously trying not to laugh. "Okay, Ariel, what's so funny?"

"Oh, nothing. I, uh, read a funny joke on the internet." She snickered a bit.

He gave her face a closer look and knew she was lying. "C'mon, out with it."

"You had some...deliveries...this morning. They're in your office. On your desk."

"This oughta be good." He headed to his office and couldn't help but laugh at what he saw.

His desk, covered with dollar bills and condoms. A steel pole on a stand in the corner. A small wrapped package with a bow on it. "Very nice, very nice."

Ariel couldn't hold it in any longer and burst out laughing. "I heard about your *plus one*. Actually, I think *everyone* heard about her."

"Well, there were a couple hundred lawyers and a few judges at the wedding. I don't wanna go near the courthouse for a while. God knows what Judge Barrow thinks of me. And I'm gonna kill Chad for setting me up with her. I'm meeting him today for lunch and I *will* get even."

"I must say, as practical jokes go, it sounds like a good one. He showed me her picture when he came by this morning to drop all this off. Sorry I missed it. A guy like you on a date with a girl who looked like a stripper."

"Yeah, she was the polar opposite of *quietly beautiful*."

She pointed at the package. "So, you gonna open your gift?"

"You obviously already know what's in there, right?"

She shrugged and looked at the ceiling. "I can neither confirm nor deny the contents—"

"Yeah, right." He opened the package and found an assortment of porn movies. "Very funny. Ah, and such clever titles. *You've Got Male. Frisky Business. My Bare Lady.*" He started picking up the dollar bills. "I'm keeping the cash. I earned it. Consider it combat pay."

"So, she was that bad, huh?"

He shook his head. "I've never been more embarrassed to be with a woman in my life. However, the night actually ended very well."

"Oh my God, Spence, you slept with her?"

"Give me some credit, Ariel."

"Well, beneath the classy Boy Scout exterior lies the male of the species. She looked like every man's fantasy."

"She wasn't mine. Anyway, guess who else was at the wedding?"

"Hopefully not a photographer from *Page Six*."

"Nope. The object of my affections of late. Tish McKenna."

"Oh, shit. And she saw you with a cheap bimbo? Damn, Spence, I'm so sorry. Did she say anything?"

He laughed. "No, listen, she actually helped me out." He told her the story. "So the evening turned out well." He blushed a bit.

"Well, how about that. I know you never kiss and tell, but from the look on your face I can tell without you saying anything. So I'll just ask you if there were sparks?"

"Oh yeah. Enough chemistry to blow up a lab."

She took his chin in her hand and studied his face. "Yep. My sweetheart of a partner is definitely smitten."

He held out his wrists as if to be handcuffed. "Guilty as charged. It was all I could do not to call her yesterday to see if she wanted to spend the day together."

"Glad you didn't. Women like that don't want to be smothered and usually like to take things slow. I can tell you're excited about this one but do your best to play it cool. So, you're taking her out Saturday, right?"

"Yep."

"Where are you taking her?"

"No clue. Need your help on this."

"What, you can't come up with a place to have dinner and a good movie?"

"She's different, Ariel. I want to really make an impression on her. So give me some ideas that will really impress a smart woman."

She tapped one finger on her chin. "Hmmm. I just thought of something you have obviously overlooked."

*

Spencer shook his head at Chad as he headed toward the table where his friend was already seated. His tall, burly law school chum stood up to shake his hand. "I can tell from your look that you're plotting some revenge."

"I haven't started yet, but I wouldn't let my guard down if I were you. You never know when an Acme anvil might drop on your head. And you might want to get someone else to start your car for a while."

They both took their seats. Chad couldn't help but laugh. "You have to admit, she was not what you expected."

"That's putting it mildly. Where the hell did you find a girl like that?"

"A buddy of mine dated her a couple of times, which, as you can imagine, is about as much as anyone with a brain could stand since she has the IQ of a potted plant to go with a pickled liver. He said the girl should live on Coney Island because she qualifies as a carnival ride. And considering you came back to the reception, I assume you did not partake of that excursion."

"Didn't have a prescription for penicillin handy. Besides, she was out cold and I like my women conscious. So what possessed you to fix me up with her?"

"Oh, we all thought since you have such a thing for super classy women we'd set you up with someone who was the direct opposite. And I knew you would show up since you're such a good friend of the bride."

Spencer picked up the menu. "I was worried she'd be upset. I hope everyone knows it was a joke."

"Yep. Even the bride and groom. However, we did not foresee

the sprained ankle scenario and you sending her over to my table to dance. Very quick thinking on your part."

"Actually it was someone else's idea. So did you enjoy that bump and grind?"

"Actually, since she didn't talk it was not unpleasant. Hell, she offered to do me in the coat room. Hard to turn down a girl with a body like that, but I didn't have any antibiotics either."

"Gotta love old fashioned girls. By the way, you're paying today and I'm ordering the lobster."

"Fine, you deserve it. Meanwhile we all found it rather curious that you returned and spent the rest of the evening with a woman who *did* seem to be your type. So what's the story on the tall classy-looking blonde? She's kinda pretty. Nice body. Got some dangerous curves."

"Met her last week and had lunch. We really hit it off and I'm seeing her again this weekend. By the way, you've already met her."

Chad shook his head. "I don't think so."

"Don't feel bad, I didn't recognize her either. It was a long time ago. She was in our class at law school. I think you even sat next to her in the front row. Remember our valedictorian? *Mrs. Spock?*"

Chad's eyes widened. "*That's* the Vulcan attorney? Damn, she's changed. And if you like her she must have grown a personality."

He smiled as he nodded. "She has. And you should see the woman in court. She'd blow me away if I ever went up against her. Honestly, I've never seen anyone with her style. But it's devastating."

"Huh. How about that, number one and number two in our graduating class are dating. Anyway, back to the wedding reception, I saw you leave with her at closing time. Did you—"

"No, of course not. You know I don't do one-nighters."

"You must have hit it off if you're going to see her again."

"Yep. Actually I can't wait."

Chad studied his face. "This one's different, huh?"

"Yeah. She seems really special. I get a good feeling about her. But it's early."

"Knowing you as I do, you'll take your time."

*

Tish arrived at Benny's cart on Tuesday morning, not seeing Spence. "Hi, Benny."

He turned and smiled. "Hey, Tish from the hotel." He reached into the cooler and handed her a bottle of orange juice. "You missed him. He was here earlier. Had some meeting in the suburbs and got an early start."

"Well, I'm meeting him for lunch tomorrow anyway."

"So, I must assume that went well last week. Considering how long you guys were in the restaurant."

Tish shook her head. "Good God, is everyone spying on me?"

"Not spying. Look, I'm here all day and the restaurant is in my line of sight."

"Uh-huh. Maybe if you crane your neck around the utility pole."

"What can I say, matchmaking is fun. Besides, my two daughters are married and I miss looking out for a single woman."

"Nice save. But anyway, yeah, lunch was great, we're on the same page. Lot in common. He's really nice."

"And how was the wedding?"

"What, you following me too?"

"Geez, Tish, get with the program. Spence told me about it and how you saved him from some cheap floozy."

"He told you?" She stood up straight, eyes wide. "Really? What did he say?"

"Sorry, I'm not that kind of matchmaker and this isn't high school. Suffice it to say the interest you have in him…well, the feeling is mutual."

She couldn't hold back a smile. "That's all I get? No details?"

"Sorry, that's it. I will not share the other side's playbook. But at least you know I'm not giving him anything either. I simply bring two compatible souls together. It's up to you guys to make the connection. However…"

"Yeah?"

"I will say I feel very good about this one."

"*This one*? You've done this before?"

"Three times."

"And?"

"All couples still happily married."

"That's really impressive, Benny."

"I have a knack for knowing when two people go together."

"And you feel that about me and Spence?"

"Big time. Actually, more so than the previous three."

Chapter Ten

Madison and Nick had already gone out for Saturday night when Tish answered the door to find a smiling Spence. "You're early again. I'm impressed."

"Well, you did give me that warning when we met. I didn't want to risk showing up one minute late and you not being here."

"That directive only applied to the first meeting, counselor. However, should you ever stand me up there will be hell to pay. A.J. is Sicilian and I have her on retainer."

"I've never stood up a woman. Definitely not starting with you." He gave her outfit the once-over. "You look great, as usual."

She noted he filled out a dark gray windowpane suit perfectly. "So do you."

All of a sudden Socks and Bumper went flying through the room, chasing each other.

"What was that?"

"Cats. One's mine, one's Madison's. They're from the same litter so they like to play."

Then they raced by in the other direction. "Damn, they're fast. It was like a blur of fur."

"They're still young and have a lot of energy. Unlike me."

"Oh, stop it. What are you, twenty-eight?"

"Okay, now I know you're being silly. We graduated the same year so obviously we're about the same age."

He shrugged. "Not necessarily. You're so damn smart you could have graduated college at fifteen."

"Okay, Mister, enough. I already like you, so dial it down a notch."

"You like me! You really like me!"

"What are you, Sally Field?"

"Sorry, couldn't resist. But you do look a lot younger than the other people in our class. Anyway, you ready to roll?"

"Sure." She locked the door and they headed to his car. "So where are we going?"

"You'll see."

Tish saw the name of the place in neon as they pulled into the parking lot. "*The Magic Act*? I thought we were going to dinner."

"We are. It's a restaurant and the waiters are magicians."

"Really? Sounds pretty cool."

"This may be the most entertaining meal you've ever had. Hope you like magic."

"Who doesn't? I loved it when I was little. Haven't seen a good magic show in ages."

He led her to the box office where he paid for two tickets, then headed inside. A thin, middle-aged man in a tuxedo and a cape greeted them, then with a flourish produced a rose out of thin air, bowed, and handed it to Tish. "For the lovely lady."

"Why, thank you." She breathed in the beautiful fragrance.

Spence furrowed his brow. "Nothing for me?"

"Sir, may I remind you that you already have the company of the lovely lady, hence you are not in need of anything else. Be careful with that attitude or I will make you disappear, sweep her off her feet and carry her away!" He turned to Tish. "Of course, should you wish to retain your current escort, I would suggest you hold on tight to him."

She grabbed his arm.

"That is not tight enough! I may still steal you away!"

She wrapped her arms around his waist and pulled him close. The scent of his cologne made her pulse spike a bit. "How's this?"

"Excellent." He turned back to Spence. "Alas, I have demonstrated my magical abilities to make your date give you a hug!" He lowered his voice and leaned forward. "Buddy, this is the part of the performance when the gentleman tips me."

Spence wrapped one arm around Tish's shoulders, then pulled a bill from his pocket with his free hand and gave it to the magician. "Well worth it. Do you have anything so she won't let me go?"

"Yes, but I do not know how long the spell will last." He threw his hands at her and waved his fingers as if casting a spell. "Young lady, since your escort has tipped me generously, you will be unable to release him regardless of how hard you try."

"Fine with me."

"Excellent! I will be back later!" He did a quick about-face, his cape spinning in the air as he headed off to greet the other guests.

Tish laughed as she turned to Spence. "What a character. I already like this place."

"Good. They had a show like this out in Vegas but it's not there anymore, so a bunch of New York magicians started something similar here. The food is excellent as well. And they change the show every few months."

They were ushered with the rest of the crowd into a large round room. The magician who had greeted them entered and closed the door. "Welcome, honored guests. You are about to enter an alternate universe. Where nothing is as it seems, because it is a world ruled by magic." He pressed a button on the wall and suddenly the room began to move.

Tish grabbed Spence's arm. "Whoa. What is this, a giant elevator? Where are we going?"

"You'll see."

The magician crossed to the other side of the room as the motion stopped and the lights dimmed. "We have descended into the realm of the impossible. But seeing is believing!" He opened the double doors and the crowd moved into a large dining hall that looked like the inside of a castle.

"This is really cool." Tish took in the medieval setting as she and Spence took their seats at a round table for eight. "How did you find this?"

"I know a lot of cool places."

A young buxom brunette carrying a large pitcher arrived at their table and began filling their glasses with wine. "Good evening, I am your tavern wench Desdemona. Should you desire anything from the bar, please let me know and it will magically appear. Should you gentlemen desire me, know that I am not available unless you are fabulously wealthy."

Everyone laughed as a waiter arrived, dressed as the first magician they'd met. He handed out a small index card to each patron. "Good evening, everyone, my name is Robert and I will be your magical host tonight. There are four choices for dinner. Simply indicate your selection, put the cards in a stack and I will be back to gather them. It is not necessary that I take your order personally, as I will divine your selections and sort them through my magical powers. I will return shortly."

Tish looked at the choices, then grabbed a pencil that was part of her place setting and checked off her choices. Everyone at the table placed the cards in a pile in the center. "So how do they know who ordered what?"

Spence shrugged. "Beats me. It's magic. But they're never wrong."

The food arrived fifteen minutes later. The magician started to slide a steak in front of Tish, but as she was about to correct him, he stopped. "Ah, that's right. You ordered the salmon." He swapped out the plates much to her delight.

"How did you know?"

He simply tapped his forehead. "Magical powers."

"Ah." She turned back to her meal and then realized she was missing one utensil. "Excuse me, I don't have a fork. Could you bring one when you get a chance?"

The magician nodded and studied her face, then shook his finger at her. "Do not play games with me, young lady. Hiding things will not curry you any favor." He reached behind her head and pulled out a fork, then handed it to her. "We do not take kindly to the pilfering of silverware. I'd better not catch you with sterling in your hair again or I will slice you in half and not put you back together."

Everyone laughed as Tish said, "I'll behave."

"See that you do." He clapped his hands and spread them wide. "Everyone, please enjoy your dinner and I shall return soon."

She turned to her date. "Spence, this is a blast."

"Glad you're enjoying one of my favorite things."

After an excellent meal with a few magic tricks sprinkled in they were led into a theater for the main show. Tish grabbed his hand and led him toward the front. "I've always liked being in the first row for magic shows."

"Sure, but you should realize they do tend to single out people who sit up front."

"Hey, I want to see their tricks up close so I can try to figure them out."

"Have you ever figured out tricks before?"

She picked out seats in the first row, right in the middle. "No, but there's always a first time."

The lights dimmed and a tall, dark-haired magician who looked to be about thirty came out on stage and introduced himself. He gestured toward the side. "And please welcome my wonderful magician's assistant, Deborah!" The audience clapped but no one appeared. "Hold on a moment." He moved toward the side, listened to someone behind the curtain and shook his head. "Well, how am I supposed to perform without an assistant? All right, I suppose that will have to do as we have no other choice." He moved back toward the center. "It appears my assistant has quit and run off with one of our stagehands. Apparently the spell I had over her wore off. Must have been that knock-off love potion I bought off the street in Times Square. However, the show must go on so I will need a volunteer from the audience. Now don't be afraid, all the magician's assistant has to do is stand next to me and look pretty, thereby distracting you from what I'm doing. A little matter of misdirection." He scanned the crowd. "Let's see…who has a look that will distract the audience?" He pointed at an overweight old bald man in the second row. "How about you, Sir?"

The crowd laughed as the man shook his head.

"Probably just as well," said the magician. "The costume was not a good color for him." He looked around again, then locked onto Tish. "Ah, I see someone who would be perfect. Come on up, young lady."

She shook her head and put up her hands. "No, really—"

Spence put his hand on her shoulder. "Go, it'll be fun. Trust me."

"Well, okay." She got up to a round of applause.

The magician took her hand and led her on stage. "So, what's my new assistant's name?"

"Tish."

"Well, Tish, thank you for volunteering. Now if you'll go behind the curtain our stagehand will lead you to a dressing room where you can get into costume—"

A look of fear instantly washed over her face. She backed up a step and put her hands up. "Whoa, you didn't say anything about a costume."

"I most certainly did when I told the gentleman he would not look good in it."

"I thought you were making a joke."

"You must learn to pay attention if you are to assist me. You cannot simply stand there and look stunning. Your date may let you get away with that and be powerless to resist you, but that is not the case with me."

She blushed at the compliment, then looked at Spence. He nodded and gave her a thumbs up, then yelled, "He's right!"

The crowd roared, then egged her on. "Well, okay. But nothing too skimpy."

"Of course not. Now go change and I'll do a few tricks till you return."

The red rhinestone costume wasn't skimpy but it did show more leg than Tish ever had as the hemline ended six inches above the knee. She teetered across the stage atop four inch heels to a round of applause, noting Spence was wearing a big smile.

The magician took her hands. "Please welcome my assistant, the lovely Tish!" The crowd applauded as she smiled and curtsied. "Now, here's all you need to do. While I'm doing tricks, you need to stand nearby and simply wave your hands like a game show hostess and smile. Remember, all you have to do is distract the crowd. Got it?"

She nodded. "I'll try."

"Of course I will saw you in half later, and then you might not be smiling. Only kidding!" He started his first trick and gave her a nod, as she began doing her best impression of Vanna White.

Spence was looking at her, not the magician.

An hour later she emerged from the dressing room back in her own clothes, finding her date talking to the magician. Spence looked up and smiled. "Here she is. Hey, you were terrific."

The magician nodded. "Yes, you did a great job. Thank you for being part of the show tonight. You're a good sport."

She laughed a bit. "All I did was stand there, wave my hands and get sawed in half."

"But you did it very well," said the magician. He reached into his pocket, pulled out an envelope and handed it to her. "With our thanks."

"What's this?"

"Your invitation to come back for dinner and a show on us. I suggest you come during the Christmas season, as that's when we have all the new tricks."

"Thank you, we'd love to."

"Good, we look forward to seeing you again. Are you two married?"

"Just started dating," said Spence.

The magician shook their hands. "Ah. Well, you look like a couple. Enjoy the rest of your evening. And thanks again."

Tish pointed at the curb before they turned onto Madison's street. "Pull over here."

"Huh? Isn't your friend's house around the corner?"

"It is. Now don't laugh, but my other friend who lives across the street from Madison spied on us last time."

He pulled over and parked. "You gotta be kidding."

"Nope. It's one of her quirks."

"So…uh…what exactly did she see?"

Tish blushed a bit. "Let's just say she considered the goodnight kiss you gave me on the front porch a tonsillectomy."

Now it was his turn to blush. "Well, y'know, you started the whole thing in the car. What was I supposed to do? Walk you to the front door and shake your hand?"

"I'm not complaining. Just warning you that Big Sister is probably watching. And since I wanted to spend some time talking before we say goodnight I thought it best to park here."

He flashed a sly grin. "So you wanna *talk*?"

"For now. There was something I've been meaning to ask you."

"This sounds serious."

"Not really. I don't know that much about you yet. I wanted to know if you like cats."

"Cats? Sure, why?"

"As you saw earlier I have a cat and I know a lot of men hate them."

"Nah, they're cool and independent. Smart as hell. And there's a neighbor's cat that comes to visit me pretty often. I give her treats and play with her. Funny, my partner says I need to get my own cat, so once I get a few of my big cases out of the way I'm going to a shelter to adopt one. We always had cats when I was a kid and since I live alone it would be nice to have a furry companion."

"Well, good."

"So what's the deal, if I said I hated cats you wouldn't want to go out with me anymore?"

"Not at all. Just curious. But I am pretty attached to my cat and it would be nice if the guy I'm seeing liked her."

"Well, if you want proof…" He reached to the back seat and pulled out a bag from a pet store filled with cat treats. "Here you go."

"That's really sweet of you to buy stuff for someone else's pet."

He shrugged. "Hey, she's a nice cat. So, what else you want to know? Giants or Jets? Mets or Yankees?"

"Nah, that's it for now." She turned so she was facing him. "I really enjoyed tonight. A lot more fun than just dinner and a movie."

He turned as well. "And you got to be part of the show."

"Yeah, wasn't expecting that."

"Well, I did warn you about sitting in the front row."

"That you did."

"But you looked like you enjoyed the hell out of it. Being the magician's assistant."

"I did. Except for the costume."

"What was wrong with the costume?"

"I'm pretty modest, and as you probably noticed I dress very conservative. It was a bit…revealing."

He laughed a bit. "Compared to my date at the wedding, I don't think so."

"A string bikini would be modest compared to your date at the wedding."

"Very true. But I don't think the costume was revealing at all."

"You really don't think it was too skimpy?"

"Not at all. Though it did serve a purpose."

"Huh?"

"I found out you've got killer legs."

Her face flushed. "I'm nothing special."

"I strongly disagree. And you need to learn how to take a compliment, young lady. Damn, you blush every time I say something nice to you." He reached over and removed her glasses. "And speaking of compliments, *whoa*."

"Again with the *whoa*."

"Can't help it. Your eyes truly are amazing. I could get lost in them. They deserve a *whoa*."

"You're so sweet to me."

"Now if there's nothing else you need to know about me or cats or skimpy costumes and you're done with this line of questioning, I'd really like to kiss you."

An hour later their lips parted and Tish got a devilish look in her eyes. "Hey, you wanna have some fun?"

"Depends on what you have in mind. But I thought we were already having fun."

"We are, but this is something different. Pull around to the house, walk me to the door and shake my hand."

"Okay…why?"

"Because Rory is watching and I wanna yank her chain."

"You have a devious mind, Tish McKenna. But I like it."

He started the car, pulled around the corner and parked in front of Madison's house. He got out and opened the door for Tish. She stole a glance across the street and saw the curtains move. She lowered her voice to a whisper. "She's watching."

They turned and headed toward the house. "Seriously? She actually waits up for you like a parent?"

"Yep. Okay, remember, make a big to-do about the handshake. And speak up so she can hear. She's got the window open."

"You got it." They arrived at the front door and he turned to face her.

She raised her voice a bit. "I had a really nice time, Mister Capshaw."

"Me too. Well, good night Miss McKenna. It was pleasant dining with you this evening." He extended his hand and she shook it.

And then they heard Rory's voice. "Oh, give me a friggin' break." She looked over at Rory's house just in time to see the window slam shut and the curtains close.

They both laughed hysterically, then Spence reached into his pocket and pulled out a handkerchief. He twisted the porch light bulb until it went out, then took her in his arms. "Now, where were we?"

Chapter Eleven

Tish placed a legal pad filled with notes on the conference room table as she took a seat next to her client. "Okay, Cynthia, I'm going to file the lawsuit today."

"I think the word is already out."

"Yeah, it's been in the papers for a while and the negative publicity works in our favor. But from now on, I want you to be careful who you talk to. Don't say anything about this case to friends, neighbors, and especially your former co-workers. You may think you can trust them, but I assure you, when it comes to saving their own jobs, they're not siding with you. People will save their own skin and throw you under the bus."

"Sure, I understand. I didn't think the friend I told would have such a big mouth."

"Well, no harm done and actually you've gotten a lot of sympathy from the media on this. So, today I want you to tell me the entire story one more time to make sure I've got everything straight, starting with your history with the company and how you got the idea for the product. Because you will have to do it again in court." Tish noted her client's fists were clenched, so she reached over and took her hands. "Try to relax. I know it is very stressful re-living all this, but you're among friends here."

"Yeah, but I won't be among friends in court."

"But I'll always be there with you. And trust me, I won't let the other side take advantage of your good nature."

The woman exhaled. "Thank you. That makes me feel better."

"So tell me the story."

"Okay, I started at the company eighteen years ago as an intern, and when I got out of college I was hired full time as an assistant in the research and development department. I spent three years working directly for one of the senior researchers and then was promoted. Actually, I was promoted three times and when I left I was the director of the whole department. Well, until they reassigned me. I left after that."

"You *had* to leave, remember? Because of family obligations. That's what you told me earlier."

"Right. I know, it's important to include that."

Tish asked her several questions about her duties along the way, salary increases, and performance reviews. "Okay, your story is consistent so far. Now we get to the day you got the idea for the product."

"Right. Every year the CEO took employees who had performed well on a vacation down to the Bahamas. I was invited each year during my last twelve years with the company."

"Which is great because they can't possibly say you were incompetent. You wouldn't have been rewarded otherwise."

"Right. Anyway, one night we were all at this bar on the beach. I happened to be sitting next to him and that's when I got the idea."

"Did he say anything related to it? Anything that inspired it?"

"No, he didn't have anything to do with it. I saw something on the beach and it just hit me. Best idea I've ever had."

"No kidding, it's an amazing product. Did you tell the CEO about the idea at that time?"

"Yes, and I pointed out what I'd seen on the beach. He said it was a ridiculous idea and changed the subject."

"Okay. Now I assume you signed some sort of document when you were hired regarding anything you developed would be considered work product and would belong to the company."

"I did. But the thing here is that I got the idea when I was off the clock, he wasn't remotely interested, and I developed the thing at home on my own time."

"Did you use any company equipment? Work on it at all while at the office?"

She shook her head. "No to both questions. I spent my own money developing it. I was hoping he would be so impressed he'd want to buy it from me and market it or perhaps offer me a percentage of the profits. He was impressed, all right. Then he stole it and made a fortune because it became the company's signature product. He insisted it was, as you said, work product. Even though I came up with the idea on vacation and created it at home on my own time and using my own money."

Tish nodded. "Okay. Anyone else hear you at the bar when you talked to him about it?"

"Yes, a co-worker named Jeff Sanders. But he still works there and as you said he probably wants to keep his job. He later told me he thought the idea was brilliant and encouraged me to work on it on my own."

"And did the CEO ever mention it from the time at the bar until you brought it to his office?"

"Never."

"And what happened when you asked him for monetary compensation or a share of the profits?"

"He refused. And when I kept pressing the subject he transferred me to another division on the overnight shift. A huge demotion and salary cut. Basically making me miserable so I'd quit."

"But you weren't fired."

"No. I quit because the hours were killing me and I couldn't be a proper mom to my daughter. For years they had been letting me work flexible hours so I would be there when my child got home from school. And the work they gave me in the new position had nothing to do with my experience or training. A bunch of clerical stuff."

Tish asked questions for the next hour and then tossed her pen on the pad. "Okay, done for now. You were letter perfect. Your story didn't change at all. You want a glass of wine?"

The woman finally smiled. "I'll be okay. So what happens next?"

"I get this filed and we wait for the response. One of my best friends in the media gave me some contacts so hopefully there will be a lot of publicity on this. We may get a quick settlement offer to make this go away or they may want to play hardball."

"He's the hardball type. As stubborn as they come. Don't hold your breath waiting for a settlement."

"Should we get a settlement offer, do you have a figure in mind?"

"Well, considering I had to take a job and ended up making considerably less money, it would have to be several years' salary. Or maybe a share of the profits. Forever."

"Considering the value of his company, that might be doable."

"And in a perfect world I'd want the patent in my name. Do you know who his lawyer will be?"

"No clue. I'm guessing whoever heads up his corporate law department. But whoever it is will have an uphill battle. This is a classic David versus Goliath case, and we're the ones with the slingshot. My aim just has to be good enough to convince a jury."

The woman shook her head. "I dunno, Tish. The CEO can be awfully charming. You've seen him on TV, right?"

"Yeah."

"Well, in person he can make you feel like you're the only one in the room. Tall, dark and classically handsome."

"Well, looks sometimes deceive. I've known lots of good-looking devils who can be charming on the surface. We're going to peel back the layers to show his true colors."

*

Ariel stuck her head in the door to Spencer's office. "Hey, I gotta run. Our least favorite client just got officially sued."

He shook his head in disgust. "Aw, hell. I was hoping the bad press might make him offer a pre-emptive settlement."

"Trust me, I suggested it. But he feels he's in the right and he's digging in."

"Maybe so, but stealing an idea from a single mom and making millions from it sure doesn't make him look good."

"And I brought that up. Without using the term *stealing*. Anyway, I probably won't get back till late and the shit is going to hit the fan in the newspapers tomorrow."

"Yeah. Get ready for the phones to ring off the hook from the media. Get ready for me to not answer them."

"I think I'll be conveniently out of the office and refer everyone to his public relations department. Let them deal with the shit-storm." She reached in her pocket, pulled out a check and handed it to him. "He sent over the retainer."

His eyes grew wide at the check for a large amount of money. For an instant he felt his pulse quicken.

Then he thought of Tish, her penchant for only taking good clients.

A few weeks ago this would have excited me.

Now…

"This supposed to make me feel better about having him as a client?"

"If you see it as a way to cut our client list, yeah. If you see it as dirty money, then no."

"Then it's both, I suppose."

"You wouldn't have thought that a month ago."

117

"I know."

Ariel studied his face. "She's changing you."

"Who?"

"Your new love interest."

He slowly nodded.

"And I like what I see. Speaking of the girl with the eyes, I almost forgot...how was your date on Saturday night?"

He flashed a big smile. "Fantastic. She loved it and even got chosen to be the magician's assistant. Thank you for reminding me about that place."

"And I see your smitten-face hasn't gone away."

"We've really got some good chemistry, Ariel. This woman is very different than anyone I've ever dated."

"So when are you seeing her again?"

"Lunch, today."

"Wow, that was fast. Miss her already?"

"Well, I'm flying out later and won't be back till Sunday, so it was today or wait a week."

"Oh, right. I forgot about your trip. I was worried you were going into smother mode."

"Nope. She's the one who seems to be taking the initiative. She said she wanted to have lunch this week, I told her Monday was the only option and she said okay."

"Well, good. Just remember to keep your foot off the gas pedal. I don't want to have to tell you to cool your jets."

*

Tish handed her menu to the waitress and turned to Spence. "So, you're leaving me dateless this Saturday night."

"I know. And I'm really scared."

"Huh?"

"Well, some other guy could swoop in and steal you away. Then I'll come back and you'll be gone."

She reached over and patted his hand. "Trust me, I'll either be out with my girlfriends or home with a bottle of wine, a good book and my cat. However, I could worry about the same thing with you out of town, especially in a place like Vegas. Leggy showgirls and hookers on every corner."

"Prostitution is legal in Nevada, but not in Las Vegas."

"You really shouldn't admit you know that. Makes me wonder."

"I saw it on an episode of *CSI*."

"Uh-huh. Right."

"Oh, stop giving me a hard time. What happens in Vegas won't be terribly exciting in my case."

"Speaking of cases, I meant to thank you for sending me three new clients."

"No problem. They had been referred by a buddy of mine and I'm overloaded anyway. They looked like they wouldn't take a ton of your time and he assured me they're good people."

"Thanks, the income will really help."

"I'll send you more if anything else crosses my desk."

"I'd appreciate it." Tish looked up and noticed Madison entering the restaurant. "Hey, my friend Madison's here. You guys need to meet." She waved and got her friend's attention.

Madison saw her and headed over to their table. "Hi, Tish." She looked at Spence. "And I assume this is the guy I've heard so much about. Of course if you're not, I've gotten my friend in trouble."

"Well, I *hope* I'm the guy she's been talking about. If not, *I'm* the one who's in trouble." He stood up and shook her hand. "Hi, Spencer Capshaw. Call me Spence."

"Madison Shaw. Pleasure." Madison nodded and turned back to Tish. "So, you two didn't get enough of each other on Saturday night, huh?"

"Spence is flying out for the week today, so this is the only chance we'd get to see each other. Anyway, are you meeting someone here for lunch?"

Madison shook her head. "It's my research day. Being in the public eye I really can't eat alone in a restaurant. I was going to get takeout and eat at my desk."

Spence stood up again and pulled out a chair. "Don't be ridiculous. Please, join us."

"I don't want to be a third wheel."

Spence pointed at the chair. "Not up for discussion. You're not eating alone in the office."

"Well, okay. If you insist." Madison sat down, turned to Tish, raised her eyebrows and gave her a slight nod.

Tish got the message. *Wow, he's not the smothering type who won't share me with my friends.*

He waved the waiter over. "Can we have another menu, please?"

The waiter nodded, walked by and handed one to Madison. "Thank you." She opened the menu, quickly pointed to a selection and handed back the menu. "I knew what I wanted when I walked in."

"Excellent choice," the waiter said, then headed back to the kitchen.

Madison turned to Spence. "Y'know, the funniest thing happened to me last night at my house. I noticed the front porch light was out and when I went to replace it with a new bulb, I discovered it had somehow gotten disconnected. Someone had twisted it halfway out. I simply cannot imagine why anyone would do that."

"Guilty as charged," said Spence. "Tish gave me the lowdown on your friend across the street and I assumed she didn't have night vision goggles."

Madison shook her head. "Damn, I shoulda thought of that years ago. Though I wouldn't put anything past Rory's surveillance techniques. I like this guy, Tish."

Tish rested her chin on her hand while staring at Spence. "Yeah, me too."

Spence leaned back in his chair. "So Madison, I feel I already know you from TV and that amazing story with the kittens. How'd that turn out? I guess I missed the follow-up. You still have them all?"

"I kept one. Tish adopted one. Rory and A.J. have the other two."

"Tish told me she had a cat, I didn't know it was a famous one."

Madison laughed. "Yeah, she named her Socks Fifth Avenue because she has white socks and her office is on Fifth."

"Cute."

"You'll have to meet her some time," said Tish. "I know Socks would like you."

*

Ariel headed into the CEO's spectacular penthouse office and forced a smile at her new client. "Peter, good to see you again."

The fifty-five year old distinguished corporate executive moved forward and gave her a hug. "Sorry about all this. Wish we were just at those family reunions."

"Well, when you run a big company like this one you're going to have legal problems pop up from time to time."

"I appreciate you taking this. I realize I'm not the most popular guy with the public right now. I'm really getting hammered. So I'm glad you're representing me since you know the real me."

I used to, before you became a greedy sonofabitch. "Hey, after all you've done for me, least I could do. Though I'm curious as to why you don't have your legal department handling this."

"Because I fired the senior attorney right before all this hit the fan. Something totally unrelated. I was about to call you anyway to put your firm on retainer until I find a replacement."

"But don't you have more than one lawyer in that department?"

"A few others, but they're young and I know they're not as good as you will be. They're not litigators. They can help on the

121

case though. Great at research. And you've got carte blanche on this, so hire as many people to help as you need. I assume your partner will be second chair."

"No, he's tied up with some other clients but he did give me some notes since he's worked on a few cases similar to yours. But getting assistance from your legal department will really help with the work product issue."

"Okay, just remember money is no object. Spend whatever you need."

"Sure. Well, let's take a look at this." They sat down at a large glass table. She opened her briefcase and pulled out the legal document containing the lawsuit. She turned to the first page.

What she saw made her jaw drop.

"Something wrong?" asked her client.

"Uh…the, uh, lawyer who filed the suit. Oh no."

He looked at the document. "Tish McKenna? What, you know her?"

"Not personally, but I've seen her in court. My partner Spence went to law school with her. She was valedictorian and got the highest score on the bar exam in the entire state."

And, oh yeah, my partner who wants nothing to do with you is in love with her.

Hell, now I really gotta get out of this case.

"And?"

She kept staring at the document. "Honestly, Peter, she's the best I've ever seen. The woman is amazing and she almost never loses. She has an incredible rapport with juries." She turned to face him. "Without even looking at what they're asking for, I strongly suggest you consider settling this. Make it go away as quickly as possible since it's taking on a life of its own in the media. And the fallout for you and your company could be devastating. I know you're already taking a financial hit. Offering a great settlement will go a long way to rebuilding your image."

"We already went over this, Ariel. I don't want to settle and I don't care if you tie her up in court for years or how much I spend on legal fees. It's the principle of the thing."

"I know we discussed this, but that was before I found out we would be facing the attorney from hell. And sometimes principle has its price. Do you want to make your point or make your sale? The damage to your reputation could be severe. And you're the face of your company every time you roll out a product. Have you thought of what the reception will be like if this gets ugly in court?"

"If I settle it would set a precedent. Everyone in my company would be claiming they got ideas while off the clock and demand money. What's the deal, Ariel, you don't think you can beat her?"

"It's not that...it's...what she would do to you on the witness stand. You've already gotten bad press out of this and she would make it a lot worse. And Tish McKenna doesn't just question witnesses, she destroys them."

"I'm not in the wrong here, Ariel. This is nothing more than a shakedown from a woman with an axe to grind looking for a big payday. I'm not settling."

"But you—"

He suddenly turned from her cousin to a client as he waved his hand to cut her off. "End of discussion on that subject. Now, let's go over this thing and work out a strategy."

"Right."

And now I need a strategy about how to tell Spencer.

But I'll wait till he gets back in town.

Chapter Twelve

Ariel's phone rang just as she was about to leave the office. She looked at the clock, noting it was past seven and her stomach was begging for food. She saw Spence was calling and reminded herself not to say anything about Tish being involved in the lawsuit. "Hey, partner, you in Vegas already?"

"Layover in Dallas. Nobody has direct flights anymore."

"Yeah, that's why I hate flying."

"Just calling to see how your meeting went and if you had any luck getting him to settle."

"He's got his heels dug in on that, but I'm not giving up." *Dear God, please don't ask who the plaintiff's attorney is. And let me settle this before he gets back.*

"Well, start a file of newspaper clippings and maybe show him how bad the press is going to be if he goes to court. This will be a high profile case."

"No kidding. It already is. I had to turn the phones over to the answering service. Reporters were bombarding me with calls." *Change the subject.* "So, how was your lunch with Tish?"

"Great. And the friend she's staying with happened to be in the same restaurant, so I met her. Madison Shaw, that television reporter who saved the kittens."

124

"Right, I remember that story."

"Turns out Tish adopted one of them. Speaking of cats, did you remember to give some treats to our furry visitor?"

"She hasn't dropped by today."

"You've gotta shake the bag of treats near the vent so she can hear it. That's how she knows it's time for treats."

"Spence, I'm really tired. Can't I just leave some out—?"

"Just shake it and pet her a few times. She comes by for the attention as much as the treats."

"I think you worry more about that cat than me. And she's not even your cat."

"C'mon, Ariel, you don't have to stay long. The poor thing is probably all alone in some empty office all night—"

"Okay, enough with the guilt. But once I see her with those beautiful eyes you know damn well I'll have to play with her too. You've gotten her spoiled."

"So, does this mean you're warming to the thought of us getting an office cat?"

"No, but I'm definitely getting one for my apartment." Ariel walked to his office, grabbed the bag of treats from under his desk and shook it. She immediately heard the patter of little paws and a meow. "And here she comes, right on cue. Pavlov and the dog, meet Ariel and the cat."

"Give her my best. Oh, my flight is boarding. Gotta go. Call you tomorrow. Bye."

"Okay, enjoy a Vegas buffet for me. Bye."

The call ended just as the cat jumped out of the vent and moved toward her. She shook a handful of treats into the bowl and the cat immediately gobbled them up, then walked toward her and rubbed against her leg. Ariel shook her head and started to pet the cat. "So now I'm a cat butler." She picked the cat up and looked into its eyes. "Kitty, you know that guy you come to visit? I'm about to really screw up his life unless I can figure something out. What do I do?"

The cat meowed and gave her a lick.

"You're no help at all, you know that?"

*

By Wednesday night it was clear to Tish that her relationship with Spence was different than any she'd ever had. She already missed him and had resisted the urge to call him yesterday, but realized she wasn't in high school anymore and holding out waiting for the guy to call her first was immature. "I'm too old to play games, especially with someone I really like." She reached for the phone just as it beeped with a text.

Spence.

She beamed as she swiped her finger across the phone.

Do you have video chat? Want to show you the great view from my hotel room.

She quickly enabled the video chat app on her tablet and punched in his contact information. In a few seconds his smiling face filled the screen. "Well, hey there, Tish. That was fast."

"I was just about to call you. Good timing. We must be on the same frequency. You get to Vegas okay?"

"Yeah, fine. Gorged on pretzels during my flight."

"Win anything?"

"I plead the fifth."

"Well, you can write it off since it's a business conference."

"I like the way you think. However, slot machines don't give receipts. Anyway, you ever been to Vegas?"

"Once, but it's been awhile."

"Well, check this out…my room overlooks those cool dancing fountains at the Bellagio." She saw him walking, then flip the view around to show her the spectacular water show. "I could watch this all day. It's really relaxing somehow."

"That's gorgeous, Spence. So, you're not relaxing looking at showgirls tonight?"

"We're all going to a magic show, but sadly my favorite magician's assistant will not be performing."

"I'm sure there will be some gorgeous babe to distract you."

"Not as distracting as you."

"Stop it, or I'll get a cavity."

"Again, you started this line of questioning, counselor. You can't object when you're the one who raised the topic. Compliments are therefore admissible regarding the subject of magic shows and said gorgeous assistants."

"Objection withdrawn. However, I will require full discovery regarding the entertainment upon your return."

"So there's no attorney-Vegas privilege?"

"Not a chance."

*

Tish didn't bother with makeup and put her hair up as she got ready for a Saturday night with the girls. She headed out to the living room, finding Madison and A.J. on the couch while Nick was on the phone. "Sure, Rory, I'll give them a head's up that it's about to start." He hung up the phone and turned to Madison. "Rory wants all of us to meet her in the back yard in ten minutes."

"What for?"

"This." He picked up the phone again and dialed a number. "Jimmy, it's Nick from the Main Street precinct. Look, my neighbor is about to have a small bonfire so if you get a call about some smoke at this address, don't roll on it." He gave his friend Rory's address. "Yeah, I'll keep an eye on it. Some sort of celebration my fiancée and her friends are having." He nodded a minute and smiled. "Thanks, buddy." He hung up and turned back to Madison. "Okay, we can tell Rory she's good to go."

"Good to go on what? We're not celebrating anything."

"She's setting fire to some stuff in the back yard."

"What stuff?"

"Don't know, I'm just the messenger. She said she's celebrating something and wanted all of us there. Anyway, I promised the fire department I'd keep an eye on things. So let's go. But I'm bringing a fire extinguisher."

They all headed across the street, then made their way down the driveway to Rory's back yard, where they found her next to a can of lighter fluid, some matches and a grocery bag, while holding a bottle of wine.

She was standing in front of a pile of clothing and other men's stuff.

Tish put her hands up. "Rory, what the hell is all this?"

Rory took a drink from the bottle. "I found out Brian is cheating on me. So while he's away with some floozy for the weekend, I thought it might be a good opportunity to thin out his wardrobe. And some other stuff."

Nick shook his head and laughed. "Damn, Rory, I'd better never get on your bad side."

Madison, her best friend, quickly moved to give her a hug. "Sweetie, I'm so sorry."

Rory, obviously buzzed a bit from the wine, blew it off. "Pffft. I'm over it. He was too controlling anyway. Nobody puts Rory in a corner." She reached into the grocery bag, pulled out a bag of marshmallows and some skewers, then handed them to Madison. "They were out of hot dogs."

A.J. took a closer look at the pile of clothes. "Wow, he had all this at your house? I didn't know he'd practically moved in."

"He didn't. I had a key to his place, went over and got this stuff."

Nick was now doubled over in laughter. "I didn't hear any of that! But damn. And I thought we Italians got even. You've raised it to an art form."

Rory bent down, grabbed the matches, lit one and tossed it into the pile. It went up like a torch and she wrinkled her nose. "Ewww. Cashmere doesn't smell very good when it burns."

Tish backed up a bit, the heat from the fire getting a bit much. "Geez, Rory, did you leave the guy anything to wear?"

"Oh, sure. A few outfits. But I soaked his underwear in *Heet*."

"What the hell is *Heet*?"

Nick's face tightened. "It's stuff you rub on sore muscles. Burns like hell. Like Ben-Gay to the tenth power."

"Yeah," said Rory. "Since he's hot for this bimbo, I figured it would be appropriate to keep him that way."

Tish admired Rory's ability to move on. Her friend was laughing it up at the restaurant, clearly enjoying the revenge she had taken on her ex. "Rory, you're amazing. You're not the least bit broken up about this."

"Hey, infidelity is a deal-breaker. No loss. Other than the time I spent dating him. Remember, a man is like a bus. If you miss one another will be along in twenty minutes."

Madison laughed. "She'll have men beating down her door in no time once guys find out she's back on the market. It's like ringing the dating dinner bell."

Rory shook her head. "Nah, I need a break. For the time being I'll live vicariously through you guys. Speaking of which, Tish, how are things going with your new guy?"

"Ah, you really *don't* have night vision goggles."

"Very funny. So what's the deal, why aren't you with him tonight?"

"He's out of town. Las Vegas for a law conference."

"Uh-oh," said A.J. "Vegas."

Tish turned to her. "What, *uh-oh*?"

A.J. shrugged. "Land of temptation. Prostitution is legal in Nevada."

Madison shook her head. "Nah, don't think he's the type. I finally met him the other day. Ran into the two of them at lunch.

129

Seems like a really good guy. I didn't catch any red flags. And he's got it bad for her."

"Hell," said Tish, "I've got it bad for him."

"Well, I'm happy for you," said Rory. "And if it doesn't work out, I've still got lighter fluid and half a bottle of *Heet* left over."

*

Spencer staggered back into his apartment late on Sunday night, tired and jet lagged from a day in various airports. He dropped his suitcase near the door and headed for the kitchen to get a cold drink. His maid had thoughtfully piled up his stack of newspapers on the kitchen table. He grabbed a cold root beer from the fridge, twisted open the bottle and sat down at the table, noting the large headline on the Sunday issue.

CHEAP SUIT

Multi-millionaire won't pay single mom for invention

He rolled his eyes, knowing Ariel's lawsuit was about to become a major watercooler topic all over town, if not the entire country. Anything that made the front page of *The Post* was sure to get New Yorkers talking. And no one would be on her side. "Aw, hell. I knew this would happen." He picked up the paper, turned the page and began reading.

More than fifty million Americans carry around one of Cynthia Riggs' inventions. But you haven't heard of her because the single mother never made a dime from it.

The former Research and Development executive at Brent Industries is suing her former boss, claiming she got the idea while on vacation and developed it at home with her own money after CEO Peter Brent laughed off the concept. Riggs claims that Brent then loved the idea when she showed him a working prototype, but considered it "work product" and therefore the property of the company. When she asked for a share of the profits, she was demoted and put on the overnight shift, making her unable to provide the hands-on childcare for her daughter that she had enjoyed with her previous flex-time schedule.

Her product catapulted Brent Industries to new heights, while Brent's net worth reached more than half a billion dollars.

In a news conference, Brent said he would not make a settlement offer since he believes the law is clear about the invention being work product. "She got the idea while on a company junket paid for by the company. So without me, the idea never would have crossed her mind. It doesn't matter that she was not sitting behind a desk when she thought of it." Asked why a man of Brent's wealth wouldn't want to share a bit of it, he said that such action would set a precedent. "Anyone at Brent industries who invents anything in the future could simply claim they got the idea while off the clock. It would open up a major can of worms for every company in America that develops new products."

Riggs' attorney, Tish McKenna—

Spencer dropped the newspaper. The color drained from his face and he went cold. "Dear God, no."

Chapter Thirteen

Spencer was waiting in the office, drumming his fingers on Ariel's desk when she arrived on Monday morning. "So when were you going to tell me?"

She shook her head and dropped her purse on a chair. "Today. I'm so sorry. I wanted to tell you but I didn't want to ruin your trip. Besides, I still haven't figured out how we're going to handle this."

"I know one thing *we* are not going to do. *I'm* not getting involved in this case anymore."

"Spence, I know you don't want to, but I still need your help. You've done work product cases before and I haven't."

He shook his head. "No. Brent has deep pockets, hire someone else and bill your client. Hire a bunch of people. He can afford it."

"You know damn well no one else is as good as you when it comes to what I need. And we wouldn't be partners if we weren't such a great team. Y'know, the sum of the parts…"

He exhaled and ran his hands through his hair as he leaned back and looked up at the ceiling. "No way he'll go for a settlement?"

"Trust me, I tried. Even the negative publicity didn't help. The man is beyond stubborn. I think he wouldn't care if he destroyed his company as long as he could prove a point." She sat on the edge of the desk and patted his hand. "Why don't you think about it for a while?"

"Because I already thought about it all night since I couldn't sleep. It will destroy my relationship with Tish and if you win the case it will really hurt her financially, maybe put her out of business. I'm not going to be a party to that. She already lost her biggest client and took this one on a contingency. She's hanging on as it is. How do you think she'd feel knowing the guy she's dating helped ruin her? It's bad enough that I already did some work on the case."

"Well, she's going to find out that we're partners eventually. When are you going to tell her?"

"I don't know. And I don't even know *how* I'm going to tell her."

"Look at it this way...if we were part of a large firm there would always be a lawyer working on a case for a bad client who might be going up against her. I'm just another lawyer in your firm."

"But there's just the two of us, Ariel, which makes it a lot different." He shook his head and looked at the floor. "I need advice from someone I trust about this. But I do know two things...I can't help you on the case any longer and if she finds out before I tell her...well, I'll lose her."

"She's really special to you, huh?"

"Yeah. I'm starting to think she's the one. And if she is my soul mate, I'm not going to lose her over some lawsuit that shouldn't even go to court."

"Okay. Well, I'll go ahead and hire some people to assist me. Brent already asked if you would be helping me during the trial and I told him you're tied up with your own. While I wanted your help, I wasn't going to tell him about it. We don't need your name attached to the case."

He looked up at her. "Thanks, Ariel. Hopefully that will be enough." He stood up and grabbed his jacket. "I'll be back in an hour."

"Where are you going?"

"To get that advice I need."

*

Spence saw Benny reading the *New York Post* as he approached the cart. The guy looked up and smiled. "Little late for your morning coffee, aren't ya?"

"There was something I had to tell my partner first. And right now I might prefer morning bourbon."

Benny studied his face as he grabbed an empty cup. "You feeling okay, Spence?"

"I'm in a bind, Benny. I actually dropped by to get your advice on something."

"You want advice from me? You're a lawyer and I sell soda."

Spencer laughed. "Well, you can't learn about life in a law book. And right now you're the wisest man I know."

Benny started to fix the coffee. "Ah, this must be about Tish from the hotel. She was here this morning hoping you'd drop by. Everything okay with her?"

"Yeah, we get along great." He pointed at the newspaper, which again had a front page relating to the lawsuit. "*That's* the problem."

"Because Tish is representing the single mom?"

"No, because my partner is the attorney for Brent."

Benny finished the coffee and handed it to him. "Uh-oh. That's not good. How many lawyers in your firm?"

"Just the two of us. We usually work together on big cases but I already told her I can't do any more on this one."

"Yeah, that wouldn't be good. So you already did some work on it?"

"Unfortunately, yes."

134

"Uh-oh."

"Plus, Tish just lost her biggest client and she needs to win this one. She doesn't get paid if she loses."

"Oh, the contingency thing." Benny slowly nodded, obviously considering the options. "So, you wanna know what to do and you have come to the romance oracle."

"Right. You're the happily married guy and you already know both of us. I figured you'd have some good ideas."

"Well, I know you a helluva lot better than her. But first thing, you've gotta tell her right away. If she finds out before you tell her, she'll think she can't trust you. And without trust, you've got nothing."

"You're right about that."

"Look, no matter how you deal with this, she's going to be upset. How upset depends on how you react. Give her space if she needs it, don't push. When a woman wants to be left alone, leave her alone."

"Yeah, I learned that the hard way a while ago."

"Look, regardless of how things go, I'll be here in your corner. And I have her ear every morning even if you don't."

"Thanks, Benny."

"My pleasure. I'm rooting for you two. I've never seen a couple that looks like they go together as much as you guys."

"Really?"

Benny nodded. "Yeah, I mean, I've fixed people up before, but there's a visible chemistry between you two. You both light up when the other one's around. So, do you love her?"

"Headed in that direction. So far, she's everything I'm looking for."

*

Tish noted the opposing attorney in her big case was actually in the same building and on the same floor, so she decided to walk down the hall to introduce herself and hopefully build a professional relationship. She also wanted to feel out the competition as to the possibility of a settlement, though she wouldn't be the one to bring it up. That would give the early advantage to the competition. Never let them know you're ready to deal. Let the other side make the first move.

She found the office with a sign reading "Empire Law Associates" on the door, opened it and found an attractive brunette on the phone in the outer office, head down, writing on a legal pad. She stood in front of the desk and waited for her to finish the call. The woman put up one finger as she took down some notes. "Sure, I'll get back to you. Gotta go, I have someone in the office. Bye." She hung up and finished writing without looking up. "May I help you?"

"Yes, I'm here to see Ariel Nix if she's available."

The woman looked up and her eyes went wide. "Uh…yeah, that would be me."

Tish extended her hand. "I'm Tish McKenna, representing the plaintiff in the Brent Industries case."

The woman was still staring at her as she stood up. "Uh, right. Ariel Nix. Nice to meet you."

"I thought we might set up a schedule for depositions. Since I'm right down the hall it will be pretty convenient."

"That would be fine. Can you give me one minute? I forgot to send a text to someone."

"Sure, no problem."

The woman picked up her cell phone, tapped a few keys. "Okay. C'mon into the conference room and we can work things out. You want coffee or a soda?"

"Thanks, I'm good." Tish followed her, trying to hold back a grin because the woman looked scared.

*

Spencer reached into his pocket for his phone but came up empty. "Hell, left it at the office." He decided to go back and get it, then go directly to Tish's office. He felt better after his talk with Benny, but the anxiety was still there. How would she take it? He wanted to get it over with.

He entered his office and noticed Ariel was in the conference room with a woman who had her back to him. Ariel turned and locked eyes with him through the glass door, hers filled with worry.

He tapped on the door and cracked it open. "Ariel, I'll be right back. I'm going down the hall to see—"

The woman turned around.

"Tish."

She studied his face. "Spence, what are you doing here?"

"Uh…this is my office."

Tish looked at Ariel, then back at him. "Whoa, wait a minute. You guys are partners?"

He slowly nodded.

She stood up, moved toward him and folded her arms. "And exactly when were you going to tell me you were representing Brent?"

"I'm not, Ariel is. And I didn't find out you were on the case until yesterday."

"It was filed last week."

"I didn't tell him," said Ariel. "I didn't want to ruin his trip."

"Uh-*huh*."

Spence moved toward her. "I found out when I got back late last night and read the story in *The Post*. I already told Ariel I couldn't work on the case anymore and was on my way to tell you—"

"Sure you were, now that you got caught. Whoa, wait a minute…you're not working on the case *anymore*?"

"I had a couple of work product cases years ago and I gave Ariel my notes and the files."

"Well, so much for all your talk about liking good clients."

Ariel stood up. "Tish, Peter Brent is a relative of mine and actually paid my way through law school. And I'm hiring outside help to assist me since Spence refused to work on it anymore. Because he didn't want to hurt your relationship. I didn't have any choice but to take the case."

"A lawyer always has a choice."

"Trust me, I didn't want this case either. The bad press is off the charts. Look, I've been trying like hell to get him to settle but the guy is dug in. I was hoping to make it go away before Spence got back from Vegas. Please don't judge him because of one of my clients. You wanna be mad, be mad at me for not telling him last week. But honestly, I didn't tell him anything till this morning."

Spencer saw fire in Tish's eyes and remembered what Benny had told him. That she would be upset and possibly need space.

That look told him both were true.

He wanted to reach out and take her shoulders but forced himself not to do it. "Tish, go talk to Benny."

"Why do I need to talk with him?"

"Because I just did. I told him—"

She put up her hand. "I think I don't need to be here right now." She grabbed her briefcase and headed out the door.

Spencer started to go after her but Ariel grabbed his arm. "Let her go. She'll calm down."

"I dunno, Ariel, she looks pretty steamed."

"It hit her out of the blue. But if she's as sensible and decent as you say she is, she'll take a breath and realize this is going to work out. By the way, I tried to warn you. Didn't you read my text?"

"I left my phone in the office. Guess I had too much on my mind. And it just got worse." He bit his lower lip, his eyes worried.

Ariel moved forward and gave him a strong hug. "It'll be okay, sweetie. She's not going to throw away a guy like you. Trust me, a girl that smart can figure this out."

Tish stormed into her office, blew past Shelley and slammed her briefcase on a chair, startling Socks, who jumped up from her spot on the desk and ran underneath it. Seeing the cat scared put her anger on the back burner. She reached under the desk, picked up the cat and gave it a hug. The poor thing was shaking. "I'm sorry, kitty, I didn't mean to scare you."

Shelley followed her into the office. "You okay? What the hell happened?"

Tish sat down, putting Socks on her lap. She stroked the cat's head and it calmed down. "You're not going to believe it. Brent's attorney is Spence's partner."

"Oh, shit. You gotta be kidding me."

"Nope. We were setting up a schedule for depositions and he walked in. Said he was on his way to tell me that she was his partner and he wasn't going to work on the case any longer. And *he claims* he didn't know I was representing the plaintiff till he read it in the paper last night when he got back from Vegas."

Shelley slowly nodded. "Well…do you believe him?"

Tish shook her head. "I don't know. I mean…geez, Shelley, how the hell can I keep seeing a guy whose partner represents a sleazeball like Brent? She claimed he's a relative and paid her way through law school and that she had no choice but to take the case, but I don't know if that's true either."

Shelley sat on the edge of the desk. "You want me to find out? Should be easy enough."

"How will that change anything?"

"We would at least know if his partner is telling the truth. That should be worth something."

She shrugged, staring at the cat as she was now purring. "What the hell, knock yourself out."

"So, what about Spence?"

"I don't know. Things were going so well…" Her eyes welled up. "Dammit! If I hadn't taken this case—"

"I wouldn't be working for you."

"Huh?"

"I could work for any attorney in town. I work for you not because you're a great lawyer but because you're a great lawyer with a big heart. You couldn't turn down a case like this because you actually care about clients who need help and that woman is desperate. You always do the right thing, Tish. When I came here it was a job, but now it's a cause. I admire you more than anyone I know. You're my role model and you have made me a much better person."

A single tear rolled down her cheek as she looked up and locked eyes with Shelley. "Thank you." Her voice cracked and then the waterworks started to flow.

Shelley leaned over and gave her a hug. "It'll work out, sweetie. Trust me."

Chapter Fourteen

Shelley poked her head through the door to Tish's office. "Hey, it's almost seven. I'm heading home. You should do the same."

"Thanks for staying late. I'll give you the overtime."

"Don't worry about it. I'll take half a day off sometime when we're not too busy. Why don't you go home?"

"Because I live in a hotel which is not remotely a home and if I stay here and keep working it will keep my mind off..."

"You hear from him?"

"No. I'll give him this, he's smart enough to leave a woman alone when she's mad. Every time the door opened I figured it would be him."

"I've been thinking about this. You have friends who work for big firms that sometimes take on sleazy clients. What exactly is the difference with this situation?"

"His is a two-person firm."

"What difference does it make? If he's not working the case it should not be a factor in your relationship."

"The whole thing about him supposedly not knowing until last night...I dunno, it doesn't sound right. By the way, I looked up his cases in the law database. He's represented some pretty shady corporations in the past. So I need time to think."

"Well, don't think about it too long. Guys like that don't grow on trees."

"Yeah, I know that too."

"Hey, I could use a glass of wine. Wanna join me?"

Tish was about to answer when she heard a faint rattling noise.

Then Socks jumped off her desk and ran behind the bookcase.

"Socks, don't go back there—" Her eyes went wide and her pulse spiked as she saw the cat disappear into the air vent. "Socks! Oh my God!"

"What?"

Tish craned her neck to get a closer look. "Sonofabitch! Those idiots that built the bookcases forgot to put the covers back on the air vents! Socks is in there!" Tish called the cat but there was no response.

Then they both heard a voice.

"Hey, there you are. I missed you last week. You want some treats?"

"What the hell?" Tish whipped her head at Shelley. "She's in somebody's office."

"C'mon, let's see who's still here." They headed to the hallway. "I'll go this way, you take the other end of the hall."

Tish quickly walked down the hall, noting only one of the glass doors had light behind it.

Spence's law firm.

"Oh, you gotta be kidding." She opened the door and heard something in a back room. She followed the sound and then saw Spence on the floor petting Socks while the cat ate some treats out of his hand. "What are you doing with my cat?"

He looked up, startled. "Whoa, Tish, you scared me."

She pointed at Socks. "So what are you doing with my cat?"

"Seriously? She's yours?"

"Yeah. Her name is Socks."

The cat finished the treats and nuzzled him on the arm. "Tish, she's been dropping by most evenings for the past few weeks. I had no idea she was yours."

"So this is the stray you were telling me about? I thought you were talking about a cat coming by your home."

"And I thought that's where you kept your cat. At Madison's place."

"On the weekends she's with me at Madison's. During the week I keep her at the office since she can't stay in the hotel. So what's the deal, you lure her through the air vent and feed her treats?"

"Yep. Shake the bag and she comes running. When she showed up the first time we were worried she was hungry so Ariel gave her a can of tuna, then I went out and bought some stuff for her in case she came by again. Which she does every night." He pulled a catnip mouse from a box and tossed it to Socks, who immediately grabbed it. "She likes to play. She's probably just bored at night. They are nocturnal creatures, you know."

"Are you implying I don't give my cat enough attention?"

"I'm just saying she's alone in the office after you go home and obviously she's a very social cat. At least now I know her name and who she belongs to. You really should put a tag on the collar."

"I'll take it under advisement." Her eyes widened as Socks crawled in his lap and licked his hand. "By the way, did you ever feed her Italian food?"

"No, but I had chicken parm takeout one day for lunch and later I noticed the container was licked clean."

"You shouldn't leave stuff out like that where she can get it."

"I don't think chicken with a little tomato sauce on it is going to hurt her."

Tish folded her arms and put one foot in front of her like a ticked off parent. "She's not your cat, I'll decide what she can and cannot eat."

He held up the bag of treats. "Are these acceptable?"

"They're fine, but...she's my cat!"

He got up, picked up the cat and handed it to her. "I under-stand that, Tish. I was just being nice to her and we like her."

"Ariel plays with her too?"

"Yeah, she loves cats. And I guess this proves I love cats." He gave her a smile that softened her a bit.

"I cannot believe you bought her toys."

"Like I said, she likes to play. She had a field day with one of my neckties so I figured I'd better get something else."

"Oh, I'm sorry. I can buy you a new one."

"Don't be ridiculous. And it was an old tie."

"Well...thank you for being nice to her."

"You're very welcome."

"I'm...sorry I got upset with you. About the cat."

"Nothing to apologize for, Tish. You obviously care a great deal about her."

She locked eyes with him for a moment. Neither said a word for what seemed like an eternity.

"Look, Tish—"

"I have a lot of work to do."

He nodded, his eyes suddenly sad. "Sure. Anyway, I'm glad to know she has such a loving owner."

The words hit her in the soul as her eyes welled up, the words thick in her throat. "I'd better go."

She turned and left the office, just before the tears began to flow.

Shelley spotted her from the other end of the hall. "You found Socks!" She started running toward Tish. "Where was she?"

"In another office."

Shelley noted Tish was crying. "Awww, look at you...tears of joy for finding your cat. You were worried that you lost the little dickens, huh?"

"Yeah, but that's not the only reason...She was in Spence's office."

"Oh, wow."

"She's been going there every night after I leave for weeks. He…feeds her treats…and…" Her voice cracked and she lost it. "He bought cat toys for her." She broke down in a flood of tears. "And he plays with her because…because…he thinks she's lonely at night."

Shelley took her by the arms. "Honey, you're in emotional free fall. Pull the ripcord."

"Sorry." She wiped her eyes with her free hand as she tried to compose herself. "I didn't expect the cat to be in his office…or for him to be taking care of her. He works late and he shakes the bag of treats and when she hears it she goes to his office through the vent. And then he plays with her."

"Yeah, I can certainly see why you're mad at the guy. He sounds like such a horrible person."

"The cat and the trial are…two different things."

"Right, he's Socks' surrogate by night, evil attorney from hell by day. Sure, let's go with that."

"It's too much to process, Shelley."

"C'mon, put Socks to bed and let's go get that glass of wine. Someone needs to get her head on straight. Because that's one hell of a boyfriend you're throwing away."

Chapter Fifteen

Two days later, Tish still didn't know what to do.

She simply couldn't dismiss the fact that Spence's partner would be going up against her, representing a client that the entire city of New York seemed to hate with a passion. And that he might possibly be helping her with the case. Which, if she lost, would really hurt both her client and her financially. She'd even stopped going to Benny's cart in the morning, not wanting to run into Spence.

Because she didn't know what she would say if she did. Every time she tried to get mad the image of him playing with Socks put her anger on the back burner.

One thing she did know.

She missed him terribly. Which made no sense since they'd only been out a few times and she'd never gotten attached this quickly. And there was another question.

Did he miss her?

He hadn't called, emailed, texted or dropped by her office. Was he giving up or giving her space?

He had to be giving up. Men didn't know about the space thing. And even if they did they wouldn't do it.

Her friends assured her it would all work out. But she'd heard that before and it hadn't.

Dating another lawyer was truly filled with land mines she hadn't anticipated.

She headed across the hotel lobby when a clerk at the front desk called her. "Ms. McKenna?"

She stopped and turned to him. "Yes?"

"I have a delivery for you."

She headed to the desk, half expecting some legal documents. Instead the young clerk handed her a bottle of orange juice with a yellow sticky note attached. He laughed. "We do have room service here, you know."

She read the note and couldn't help but smile.

Breakfast without Tish from the hotel is like a day without sunshine.

"It's from a friend who is reminding me of something."

"Ah. Well, you have a nice day."

"You too." She headed out the door and across the street to Benny's cart.

He looked up and smiled as he spotted her. "Well, look who finally showed up. She never calls, she never writes."

"I got your *message*." She held up the bottle of OJ. "So stop with the guilt. I wasn't avoiding *you*, Benny."

"Good, 'cause I woulda been deeply hurt. Anyway, I know the whole story, kiddo. You and I need to talk."

"Uh-oh. This sounds like a lecture from Dad coming my way."

"I've had a lot of practice with my own daughters. By the way, what is Tish short for?"

"Patricia."

"And your middle name is?"

"Megan. Why?"

"Patricia Megan McKenna, you are going to listen to some advice, young lady."

"Ah, the full name thing, I know it well. Go ahead, Dad. Hit me."

"Spence really *was* coming to tell you about his partner on

Monday morning. I know that because he was here asking me for advice about what to do. He'd only found out you were on the case the night before when he got back from Vegas because his partner never told him. He went to his office before he came to see you because he forgot his cell phone."

She studied his face. "He tell you to say that?"

"You're a lawyer, you know when someone's lying. Do I have that look?"

Tish locked eyes with him. "No, of course not. But I know you have an ulterior motive to get us back together."

"Because I'm an excellent judge of character and I think you guys belong together."

"Maybe, maybe not."

"Well since you're off to such a good start you owe it to yourself to find out. And I am batting a thousand when it comes to fix-ups."

"I dunno, Benny, I can't get past the fact that he already helped with the Peter Brent case against my client. She really got screwed."

"Yeah, I've been reading about that. What a cheap bastard. He'd better not show up at my cart. He'll get a soda shaken, not stirred. So, no chance of settling, huh?"

"Apparently not. And a million bucks would be pocket change to that guy."

"Hell, you should be able to win if public opinion is any indicator. Everybody hates Brent. A lot of people are boycotting his products."

"Yeah, but you know what they say about juries, Benny."

"What?"

"They're made up of people too stupid to get out of jury duty."

He laughed a bit. "Yeah, guess so. Anyway, how long you gonna give Spence the silent treatment?"

"Uh, it's a two-way street. He hasn't called me either."

"He's not going to because you're the one who is mad and therefore the ball is in your court. And I told him that when a woman is angry, you give her space."

"It figures you would know that. I'm impressed. I had not run into a man with that sort of knowledge before."

"Basic life skill. Most men learn the hard way, so I try to save the younger guys the trouble. This is why we invented man caves. When the woman in your life needs to be left alone, you don't badger her, you go shoot pool or watch football. Or, ya know, play with the woman's cat."

"Just what I need, more guilt."

"Not many guys would do that. But you're a smart woman, you probably know that already."

She sipped her juice. "You're a very wise man, you know that, Benny?"

"Then perhaps you should accept my wisdom and go talk to him. And even though you're mad at him, he's not mad at you. Not even close. I'm not sure the man is capable of being angry."

"Yeah, he seems really very calm about everything. The most easy-going man I've ever met. He's a good balance for me. In case you hadn't noticed, I have a tendency to get a bit emotional."

"And I shouldn't say this, but he misses you like you wouldn't believe."

"I shouldn't say this either, but I miss him a lot too."

Benny put his palms up and shrugged. "So what's your praablem?"

*

Tish had been on the fence about talking to Spence, but after her chat with Benny she was leaning over to his side. However, she still had no idea how to do it. She entered her office and found Shelley already sorting through the mail. Her assistant looked up and studied her face. "Ah, no morning scowl. Is the great wall of Tish breaking down?"

"Just had a long talk about the Spence situation with someone I trust."

149

"What am I, chopped liver?"

"No, but you're not an older married guy."

"Nor do I aspire to be one. So what's the advice you got?"

"That I should go talk to him."

Shelley nodded. "Sounds like the old married guy has a good head on his shoulders. Oh, speaking of Spence, his partner sent over some stuff for the Brent case. It's on your desk under the furry paperweight."

"Did she come by personally?"

"Nope. Her intern delivered it."

Tish nodded and headed into her office where she saw Socks curled up atop a stack of files. The cat spotted her, sat up and meowed.

And then she noticed the red, heart-shaped metal tag on the cat's collar. "What the hell? Shelley, come in here a minute."

Her assistant poked her head in the doorway. "What?"

She picked up Socks. "Did you put this on her collar?"

Shelley moved closer. "Nope. What is that?"

They took a close look at the embossed tag.

My name is Socks
If found, call Tish McKenna
212-555-0101

Shelley smiled as she read it. "Well, looks like *someone* put an ID tag on her. Good idea considering she likes to wander through air vents and could easily get lost."

"And it wasn't you?"

She rolled her eyes. "No, it was the cat fairy who shows up in the middle of the night. Of course it wasn't me. Tish, if you use the process of elimination, you know damn well who put it on her."

Tish sat down putting the cat in her lap. "Why would he do that?"

150

"Do I have to shoot you with the clue gun? It's an olive branch."

"You think?"

"Oh for God's sake, Tish, enough! Get your ass down the hall and talk to the guy. I can't take another day with you moping around here. You miss him so bad it shows. And I saw him in the elevator today. Poor guy looks like he's in mourning."

"What would I say?"

"Well, for an ice-breaker I'd start by thanking him for the tag he put on Socks. Then you might segue into an apology for not being understanding."

"You think I was wrong, don't you?"

"Yes. There's no question."

"So you don't think I was understanding?"

"Asked and answered, counselor. And you're in danger of being in contempt of your assistant." She pointed to the door. "Down the hall. Now."

She looked down at the cat. Socks offered a loud purr and a lick of her hand. "He is really sweet to my cat."

"And he's been really sweet to you. Of course, if you're going to throw him away I might take a shot at him. He's awfully cute. I'd do him in a New York minute."

Tish whipped her head up at Shelley. "Excuse me?"

"Awww, is Tish jealous that some other woman might scoop up Spence? I *have* learned a few lawyer tricks from you."

"That wasn't fair."

"Objection overruled. All's fair in love, my dear boss. Now either walk down the hall or I'm going to crack open the wine right now, because I'm the one who's gonna need it."

*

Tish gently tapped on the door and entered Spence's office. She saw Ariel and a young guy who looked to be an intern at the copy machine. Ariel turned around and was taken aback. "Oh, hello. I, uh, wasn't expecting you. Is there a problem with the files I sent over?"

"Not here about the case. I…well…was wondering if I could talk to Spence."

"He's in court today. And I think it will be an all-day affair."

Tish looked down at the floor. "Oh. Well—"

"He's in that new judge's courtroom. What's her name? Rebecca Winston. And, you know, I'm pretty sure they *will* recess for lunch."

Tish looked up and saw Ariel smiling at her. "Lunch."

"Right. Y'know, that meal in the middle of the day? I would venture to guess you can catch him then."

"Yeah, I guess I could."

Ariel moved toward her. "Look, Tish, I'm really sorry to have put both of you in this situation. If I could have found a way out of this—"

She put up her hand. "You don't owe me an apology. I'm the one who's sorry about the way I acted. I'm usually very professional."

"I probably would have reacted the same way. Don't worry about it."

"Thank you. You're as understanding as Spence."

"No one's as understanding as Spence." Ariel offered a warm smile. "And somehow when you really like someone, when true emotions are involved, being professional can go out the window, ya know?"

Tish laughed. "I didn't. First time for me."

"Welcome to the club. By the way, in regard to our case from hell, I tried to get my client to settle again yesterday." She shook her head. "He won't budge."

"Thanks for trying."

"I'll keep at it. The negative publicity has got to be wearing on him."

"We can only hope."

"And it's not doing our firm any good either. Trust me, Tish, I wanna make this go away as much as you do. Maybe more. By the way, did Spence ever tell you why we started this firm and took some of the clients we did?"

"No."

"Have a seat. I have a story to tell you."

*

Tish watched from the back row of the courtroom as Spence systematically destroyed the star witness for the opposing side. It was clear he was winning, as she noted the other attorney shake his head in disgust while Spence got the witness to paint himself into a corner.

Spence was good, really good.

And then she felt something she hadn't expected.

Pride.

That's my guy up there.

Wait, hold on. You threw him away, remember?

He's not yours right now.

Shelley's right. If I don't do something, another woman is going steal a great guy.

She looked at the clock, noting it was close to noon. The judge would call for a recess shortly.

C'mon, judge, hurry up.

The second hand on the clock seemed to be moving in slow motion.

Spence wrapped up his questioning. "I have nothing further for this…*witness*." The jury smiled as the judge looked at her watch.

"And with that," she said, "I believe it's a good place to break for lunch. Court is in recess till one-thirty." She swung the gavel and left the bench.

Tish's heartbeat kicked up a notch. She took a deep breath

and headed toward the front of the room, weaving her way through the crowd going the other way. She noted Spence didn't get up from his table, instead pulling out a pack of crackers from his briefcase. Another attorney came up to him and asked him to lunch. Spence shook his head, telling the guy he had work to do.

She stopped at the rail right behind him. "Surely that's not all you're gonna have for lunch?"

He turned around. "Tish. Uh, hi. What are you doing here?"

"I would have brought Socks to thank you for the ID tag, but I didn't think the judge would approve of cats in the courtroom."

He smiled a bit as he stood up. "My buddy is a veterinarian and he knocked that out for me. I was worried she might go through the vent and end up in the wrong office."

"Not likely. I think Socks knows a good thing when she sees it."

"So do I when it comes to women. Now, does that mean her owner knows a good thing when she sees it?"

"Most times she does. Occasionally she acts like a complete idiot. But luckily she has advisers who remind her of said idiocy. So I throw myself on the mercy of the court." She pointed at the crackers. "That's not a healthy meal for a growing boy."

He shrugged. "I figured I'd get some work done."

"Is it work that can wait?"

"Depends on the alternative."

"Well, since I never did get *the next one* after our first lunch, I was thinking this might be a good way to even things up. I mean, if you're willing to forgive me for—"

"No reason to forgive you for anything, Tish. I completely understand your point of view."

"So…does that mean you want to have lunch with me?"

He laughed a bit. "You know, for a woman who is so off-the-charts brilliant, you continue to ask a lot of stupid questions. C'mon, I'm starving."

*

Spencer handed the menu to the waiter and turned to Tish, who was wringing her hands. "For God's sake, will you relax?"

She exhaled. "Sorry. I was wondering how you'd react to me just showing up."

"We're here, aren't we?"

Finally, she smiled. "Yeah."

"But I think we need to set some ground rules for the immediate future."

Her face dropped. "Spence, if you want to see other people, I certainly understand—"

"Again with the stupid comment. Why the hell would I want to see other people when I just had this terrific woman ask me to lunch? Of course, your comment could imply that *you* want to see other people."

Her eyes widened. "No! I didn't mean   "

"Kidding!" He reached across the table, took her hands and locked eyes with her. "We're okay, you and me. I have absolutely no desire to date anyone else. We. Are. Okay. Got it?"

"Yeah. Sorry. I was really nervous coming to see you."

"When I said we need to set ground rules, I meant regarding the upcoming Brent trial. We don't ever need to discuss it until it's over. At all."

"I'll agree with you on that."

"So here's the deal. Ariel has hired outside help to do what I usually do. Hell, Brent can afford a team of lawyers, so he doesn't care. I'm not going to have anything more to do with the case. I may sit in the courtroom from time to time to watch my two favorite women work, though."

"Is this some version of a catfight that appeals to male lawyers?"

"Of course not. To be honest, I knew when I saw you in action I could learn from you. So I'll be picking up a few tricks. I already got one the first time."

"Really? What was that?"

"You turned to the jury, took off your glasses to supposedly clean them and gave the jurors a world class eye roll with your back to the judge."

"Oh. That. Luckily I haven't been caught yet. Thankfully there aren't any mirrors in the back of the courtroom."

"Anyway, I'd love to try that little maneuver. Can I see it again so I can get it right?"

She shrugged. "Sure. You take off your glasses as you turn." She removed her glasses. "Then—"

"Whoa."

"Excuse me?"

"I had missed those eyes. Forgive the lawyer's trick."

She laughed and shook her head. "Naughty boy. And it just hit me that you don't wear glasses. I am totally clueless today."

"Hey, I got you to laugh. Tish, please stop beating yourself up. This isn't law school where you have to be perfect. Real life isn't perfect and it's not something in a book. You're too hard on yourself. You don't have to be the valedictorian of life. You get an A-plus with me, that's all that matters."

"Thank you. I'm simply wired to win at everything. Though I still feel like I deserve the blame for everything. Benny and my assistant both let me have it this morning."

"Seriously?"

"Sometimes I need different points of view when I'm being an idiot. And Ariel told me the story about your dad and why you took on the clients you did. Why didn't you ever tell me?"

Spence shrugged. "I guess I'm not too proud of some of my work. It was great that I could help my father but think I lost part of my soul along the way. You helped me find it again and reminded me who I really am."

She bit her lower lip as she locked eyes with him. "I'm glad."

He grabbed his glass of water and leaned back. "Tish, there's one more thing we need to agree on."

156

"What's that?"

"The time machine rule."

"Huh?"

"We pick up where we left off. This past week never happened. Okay?"

She nodded. "Yeah, I'd like that."

"Good. Now what are you doing Friday night?"

Chapter Sixteen

Tish knocked on the door to Spence's apartment, her heart beating a little faster than it should. She shook her head, frustrated with her anxiety.

Relax. He wants you back.

She took a deep breath as the door opened and his smile instantly drained her tension. "Hey there, welcome to my humble abode. C'mon in."

She entered the apartment, expecting the usual Spartan bachelor decor, instead finding it tastefully decorated. Burgundy leather sofa, antiques, a Monet print on the wall, a beautifully set dining room table with candles already lit. "Wow. Nice place."

He shut the door. "Thanks. You can blame Ariel. She's the one with the good taste. If I'd decorated the place there would be nothing but a recliner, a giant flat screen, a popcorn popper and a beer cooler."

"So you admit the place needed a woman's touch."

He moved closer and took her shoulders. "The apartment isn't the only thing that needs a woman's touch."

She blushed. "I can see what's on your mind."

"I was really afraid I'd never get to see those eyes and kiss you again."

"Well, worry not counselor. As you said at lunch, we're here aren't we?" She sniffed the air. "And I smell something good. Ariel take care of that too?"

"Nope, I actually know how to cook. I'm not a typical bachelor in that sense."

"Good to know."

"Want some wine?"

"Now *you're* the smart one asking stupid questions. Hit me, barkeep."

Dinner had been terrific, and the two (or was it three?) glasses of wine had lowered her inhibitions. She'd leaned against him and melted into his shoulder during the movie, his arm wrapped around her the whole time.

She was finally relaxed. The time machine thing was working.

As usual, Spence had been the perfect gentleman.

The credits rolled as the movie ended. Spence grabbed the remote and turned off the TV. "Did you like it?"

"Yeah. You?"

"I thought it was well done." He pointed at her empty glass. "You want more wine?"

She looked up at him, keeping her head on his shoulder. "I think I've reached my limit."

"What happens if you go over it?"

"Don't know. I've never gone that far. I'm a pretty conservative girl."

"Big part of your attraction."

"Well, you seem to be a conservative guy. That's a big part of your attraction as well."

"That said, do I need to get you back to your hotel, or can you stay awhile?"

"It's only eleven and it's not a school night. And Benny said I could stay up late." He laughed as she sat up straight, then swung one leg over him, straddling him on his lap. She pulled out her

159

hair clip, shaking out her shoulder length hair, then took off her glasses and locked eyes with him.

"Whoa."

She smiled as she ran her hand across his cheek. "Am I always going to get that reaction from you when I take off my glasses?"

"Yeah, but I think this time it has a little to do with the fact the wine may have left the conservative girl on my lap in the dust."

She felt his hands rest lightly on her waist. "No, I'm not over the limit. I should have clarified that the conservative girl exhibits that persona in public. In private, well—"

"So you're kinda like a comic book hero with two identities. Same deal as Superman."

"Huh?"

"You both take off your glasses before the special powers kick in."

She slid closer to him, their lips inches apart. "First of all, a female superhero is a superheroine."

"Ah, you're right. Forgive me."

"That said, I hope my other identity meets with your approval."

"Let's just say that like a typical superheroine, you seem to have special powers over me."

"Actually, you might have that backwards, Mister." She tilted his chin up and gave him a long soft kiss. "But I'll never admit it."

Tish looped her hand around Spence's elbow, resting it on his forearm as he walked her back to the hotel. The night air was chilly and she hunched up her shoulders. He noticed, took off his sport jacket and put it on her. "Thank you."

"You looked cold, Tish."

"Well, it is autumn. Listen, I really enjoyed tonight, Spence. And I really needed it."

"Yeah, me too."

"I'm so impressed with you."

"You liked the pasta that much, huh?"

"I wasn't talking about your cooking, which is amazing. I meant how you handled the whole situation of the past several days. You're so laid back, so understanding. It's like nothing upsets you."

"It's not that big of a deal, Tish."

"Yeah, it is. Most guys would have told me to get lost. Or badgered me to come back. You didn't do either and gave me time to figure things out."

"You can thank Benny for that."

"Yeah, we're lucky to have him. He set me straight as well. But back to what I was saying…you're so…different."

"How so?"

"You're such an old fashioned gentleman. You're sweet to me. You're even nice to my cat. You stand up for waitresses in distress. I practically attack you on the couch and you *don't* ask me to spend the night."

He stopped walking and turned to face her wearing a worried look. "I'm sorry if I offended you—"

"No, you've got it backwards. I'm impressed that you didn't."

"Really?"

"Really."

"Don't get me wrong, Tish, I'm really attracted to you physically and there's nothing I'd like better than to wake up next to you, but we haven't known each other that long and sex is a big step for me. Besides, even if I did ask I know you're not ready to spend the night with me either."

"See, that's what I mean about you being so different. It's like you can read my mind."

He tapped his forehead. "Maybe I picked up some stuff from the magic show."

"Whatever it is, don't lose it." They started walking again.

"Although if I'd had another glass of wine and you'd asked me to stay…"

They both laughed as they reached the hotel. "Well, here we are. Home sweet home."

She rolled her eyes. "More like room boring room. I am so sick of this place already. I can't ever feel comfortable here."

"How are the repairs going at your house?"

"They assure me I will be back home before Christmas. Luckily A.J.'s cousin is the contractor or I wouldn't believe that for a minute. They've got the roof done so weather is no longer a factor. But if I'm not home by the holidays, I'll be really depressed being stuck in a hotel. I love Christmas. Kinda go wild decorating the house. The holiday sorta turns me into a little girl."

"I look forward to seeing what you do. Well, keep singing *I'll be Home for Christmas* and you probably will be."

"Maybe so. Funny, Socks has adjusted to the office a lot better than I have to the hotel."

"Well, she does have an extra outlet for treats." He led her into the hotel. "C'mon, I'll walk you to your room. Even superheroines need someone to watch over them."

"I think that's *your* superpower, Spence. Honestly, I have never felt so safe on a date in my life."

"I'm not sure how to take that."

"Sorry, that didn't come out quite right. I meant that when we're out in public you'll be the perfect gentleman and protect me. But in private, let's put it this way…you might not be so safe with *me*."

"Something tells me you like being in charge."

"Just figured that out, huh?"

"Nah, kinda got the clue when you pinned me to the couch for about an hour."

"You didn't seem like you were trying to get away."

"I may be a gentleman, but I'm not stupid. You don't argue with a hot woman on your lap."

She blushed a bit. "I'm not hot."

He shook his head and smiled. "Again, she's brilliant in the courtroom, clueless about the obvious. I'm getting you a mirror for Christmas."

Chapter Seventeen

Tish picked up Socks on Saturday morning, loaded her into the carrier and drove to the local fire station that had responded the night her house went up in flames. They'd asked her to bring the cat by for a fundraiser since Socks was, after all, a kitty who had saved her owner.

She had to park a few blocks away since there was apparently a really big crowd, so she walked a few blocks with Socks meowing the entire way. "Can't wait to get back home either, huh? I know you hate cars. And apparently going for a walk as well." Madison, A.J. and Rory were already there when she arrived, sitting in the front row with a seat saved for her. Hundreds of chairs had been set up and were already taken. Tish put the pet carrier on her lap as she took a seat. "Wow. I never expected a crowd. I thought this was the usual fireman on the street corner holding a boot collecting loose change."

Madison shook her head. "Didn't they tell you what was going on?"

"They said it was a fundraiser and it would be nice for people to see a famous cat. Why, what am I missing?"

A.J. pointed at the stage without turning to face her. "That."

She looked up as *It's Raining Men* blasted from a couple of speakers and twelve shirtless firemen paraded on stage to huge cheers. "What the hell is this?"

Rory sipped a soda from a straw as she stared at the hunks. "It's the annual release of their firefighters' calendar. Hubba hubba. Bring on the new year."

Tish turned around and noted almost all of the people in the crowd were women who were screaming at the firemen. She shook her head as she turned back to the show. "So, you guys aren't really here to see my cat having a photo-op."

"Well, *some* people think we are," said Madison, flashing a sly smile. "I told Nick you're shy and needed moral support."

"Uh-*huh*. May I remind you that you are engaged to a wonderful man who's pretty hot in his own right?"

"I can look at the menu and work up an appetite as long as I have dinner at home."

"It'll probably save Nick the trouble of foreplay," cracked Rory. "Poor guy won't know what hit him."

A.J. was busy snapping pictures. "Hell, I want to have one of them for dinner."

The song finished and one of the firemen moved to the microphone. "Thank you very much. What a great turnout to see a famous cat!" The crowd laughed as he motioned for Tish to come on stage. "Seriously, we appreciate your support and hope you'll buy lots of calendars as stocking stuffers."

A.J. licked her lips. "He can stuff my stocking anytime."

The fireman put his arm around Tish as she looked up at this tower of muscle who had to be six-foot-five. "Now a few weeks ago this young lady's house caught fire during that big electrical storm. She's such a heavy sleeper and the smoke alarm didn't go off, but her cat woke her up and they got out in the nick of time. So we thought you'd like to meet a furry lifesaver. Please welcome Tish McKenna and this year's honorary firefighter, Socks the cat!"

The crowd cheered as Tish pulled Socks from the carrier and held her up. Amazingly, the cat was calm despite the noise. The fireman then placed a miniature firefighter's helmet on the cat, which got a big laugh. Socks, like most cats who do not wish to wear any additional attire, did not look pleased, but Tish stroked her under the chin and her frown disappeared. She put Socks on a table and a few newspaper photographers moved forward to take some pictures.

The fireman put his hand up. "Hang on a minute, guys. At least show how *we* rescue people." With that he effortlessly scooped Tish into his arms, cradling her.

"Oh, my." She couldn't help but blush as she wrapped her arms around the neck of this Greek god. "What are you doing?"

"Getting publicity," he said. "Smile for the camera."

"Well, okay." She faced the camera and smiled as the sounds of camera clicks filled the air. She noted her friends were snapping photos as well.

"Thanks," said one of the photographers, as they all moved off.

Tish looked up at the fireman. "You can put me down now."

"If you give me your phone number I'll be happy to rescue you tonight."

"I'm already spoken for, but I think you've got a few hundred takers out there. And see those two girls next to the redhead in the front row who are drooling over you? They're available."

The fireman looked at Rory and A.J., then put her down and patted her on the shoulder. "Thanks, you're a good sport. C'mon over to our autograph table. We're signing calendars and people can meet you and the cat. She can do paw prints."

*

Tish headed into the kitchen on Sunday morning to find Madison already fixing a cup of coffee. "You're up before me. That's a switch."

"Cat alarm. Bumper thinks he's a rooster on occasion and

166

howls for the hell of it. Unfortunately, cats have no snooze button. If they want you to get up, you have no choice. Want coffee?"

"Stupid question."

"Right." Madison pointed at the Sunday paper sitting on the kitchen table as she poured another cup. "You're in *The Post.*"

Tish rolled her eyes. "I'm already sick of this trial coverage and it hasn't even started. I cannot wait for it to be over."

"It's not about the trial." Madison carried two cups of coffee to the table and sat down. "Cute little article about that fundraiser at the firehouse."

"Oh, well, that's nice."

"You might not think so when you see the photo. Hope Spence isn't the jealous type. You're on *Page Six.*"

Tish sat and flipped the paper open to the city's most famous gossip page.

There she was in the arms of the hunky fireman, looking up at him like she wanted to be carried away. "Oh, geez. This looks like the cover of a romance novel."

"Is it gonna be a problem?"

"I don't think so. Spence is so easy going. And I did tell the fireman I was attached."

"Yeah. Just be glad he wasn't there to see the guy pick you up. Anyway, I told you things would work out with him."

"So far, so good."

A quick knock at the door preceded Rory and A.J. carrying bags from the deli for brunch. "Sorry we're late," said Rory. "We were, uh, out a little late last night."

Tish gave Rory a sinister grin. "Yeah. Getting home at one-thirty-four is definitely past your bedtime."

Rory's eyes widened. "What the hell, are you spying on me?"

"Payback's a bitch, huh? You don't like it when the shoe's on the other foot, do you?"

A.J. laughed as she started pulling the food from the bags.

"Glad I don't live on this street. It's like Ground Zero for Big Brother."

Tish started to pour the mimosas from a pitcher. "So you guys got dates with firemen, huh? Which ones?"

"Tom," they said in unison.

Madison furrowed her brow. "Which two guys were those?"

"Same one," said A.J., flashing a devilish grin. "The one built like Thor who scooped up Tish."

Tish's eyes widened. "You both went out with the same guy?"

Rory leaned back with her drink. "He's big enough to handle two women. I don't mind sharing. And A.J. isn't greedy."

Madison's jaw dropped. "Since when are you guys into three-ways?"

A.J. laughed. "Awww, we're kidding. I went out with Tom and Rory was with one of his buddies. I've never dated a fireman before."

"So how was your date?" asked Tish.

A.J. smiled. "You know what they say. Firemen carry big hoses."

Madison waved her hands. "Okay, enough."

Rory turned to Tish. "So, speaking of firemen and the fact that you weren't interested in that hunk of muscle who picked you up, am I to assume you are exclusive with Spence now that you're back together?"

"You know damn well I can't date more than one guy at a time."

"Still can't believe you're the one who broke down and went to see him," said A.J. "It's like the planet going off its axis."

Tish shrugged. "I finally realized that I was the one who was wrong, so I apologized. And then he told me there was no reason for me to be sorry about anything. He wasn't the slightest bit upset. We had this great date on Friday night. He cooked dinner for me and then we had this wonderful slow walk back to my hotel. He's so sweet…it was cold and he gave me his jacket."

A.J. leaned forward. "And…"

"And what?"

"Was he still there Saturday morning or did he just leave after—"

"We didn't sleep together!"

A.J. shook her head. "Woman leads man to hotel room, then sends him home. What is wrong with this picture?"

"I'm not ready yet. Neither is he."

Rory waved her hand like she was shooing a fly. "Pffft. Men are always ready, despite what they say."

Tish stuck her nose in the air. "Spence is different. He's old fashioned. Likes to take things slow."

Madison nodded. "That's probably because he's picked up on the fact that you like to take things slow and he doesn't want to lose you by making a move too fast."

Tish shook her head. "No, I think we're generally alike when it comes to that. Besides, I sorta…attacked him in his apartment."

Rory dropped her fork. "Madison, major breaking news again, call the network."

"So let me get this straight," said A.J. "You take the initiative at his place, you don't sleep there, then the guy walks you back *to a hotel* and you send him home with a bag of ice?"

Tish furrowed her brow as she put up her palms. "Why in the world would I give him a bag of ice?"

Rory rolled her eyes. "Oh for goodness sake. She means the guy needed a cold shower."

"Oh. Well then don't say *bag of ice*, say *cold shower*."

"Let's put it in a way even *you* can understand," said A.J. "Yesterday this hot, shirtless fireman whose muscles have muscles picked you up like he was going to carry you off to the bedroom. How did you feel when he was holding you and you had your arms wrapped around his neck?"

Tish blushed. "It was, uh, not unpleasant."

"Yeah, right. Then you spend the afternoon sitting next to eleven other hot shirtless firemen. How'd you feel when you left?

More importantly, what would you have done to Spence had your date been last night instead of Friday night?"

Madison shrugged. "She probably would have done the same thing I did to Nick."

"Where is your darling fiancée, anyway?" asked Rory.

"Still in bed. He's basically an invalid right now. I drained him of all bodily fluids."

Tish turned beet red. "Can we please change the subject?"

"No!" came the answer in unison, followed by a lot of laughs.

Madison reached over and patted Tish on the hand. "We're happy for you, sweetie. But I want you to know one thing."

"What?"

"As long as you're staying in my guest room, feel free to have a guest spend the night with you."

Tish shook her head. "I couldn't do that to Rory."

Rory furrowed her brow. "Huh?"

"You'd never get to sleep waiting for him to go home."

Chapter Eighteen

Two weeks later...

Tish readied herself for the first deposition with Peter Brent, confident that, if nothing else, her examples of the massive public outcry against him along with the financial losses he'd taken would finally force him to cave and offer a decent settlement. Still, she had plenty of ammunition up her sleeve if he didn't.

While she wasn't thrilled about doing the whole thing in Spence's office, at least he wouldn't be in the room. He'd kept his promise, staying completely out of the process and not having a single thing to do with the case. And they'd not spoken about it when they were together.

Still, with the ton of publicity the case was getting, she wanted it over and done with.

Of course, if she didn't win, her practice might be over and done with as well.

*

Spence wanted the case out of the way. Ariel had tried her best to get Brent to settle, but he was beyond stubborn and didn't care about the hit his company's reputation and bottom line was taking. His personal reputation was pretty much in the dumpster at this point. Good luck finding an objective jury in New York City.

Of course he secretly wanted Tish to win, knowing how desperately she needed the victory and knowing Brent was in the wrong.

While their relationship had returned to a smooth one and discussing the case was forbidden, the damn thing was always lurking overhead and impossible to ignore since it seemed to be front page news every day. This morning one of the New York tabloids had put cartoon horns on Brent with the headline *Devil May Care…When His Company Goes Bankrupt.*

He heard Tish's voice in the reception area, but didn't go out to greet her as Peter Brent was there as well and he had no desire to shake hands with that creep. The sounds of footsteps told him Ariel was no doubt leading everyone to the conference room. He heard the door shut and then muffled voices.

He turned back to working on his own case, but it was really hard to concentrate knowing what was going on in the room next door.

Twenty minutes later his curiosity got the best of him. He got up and quietly opened the air vent that connected with the conference room. Tish's voice poured through. But not with the tone he'd gotten used to on their dates.

Jaws was in the house. *Mrs. Spock* was destroying Brent with pure logic.

He pulled his chair up to the vent and listened.

"So, Mr. Brent, isn't it true that your company's stock nearly tripled within one year after the rollout of my client's product?"

"Objection to the characterization of the product as belonging to the plaintiff," said Ariel. *"It is the property of Mr. Brent's company."*

"I'll rephrase," said Tish. *"Since the rollout of the product that*

was the invention of my client, did the company stock nearly triple within one year?"

"Yes," said Brent, "but that could have been be due to—"

"I just needed a yes or no, Mr. Brent, not an explanation. Please pay attention and listen to my questions before answering. Meanwhile, the opening price of the stock this morning was ninety-eight dollars, which is lower than the day before you rolled out the product. Market analysts trace the decline to the story breaking about this case, the following negative publicity and the massive loss in sales."

"That's because—"

"Please respond only when I ask a question and I'm not finished asking it. Isn't it true that within three days of this story breaking and the stock taking a major hit, that you dumped more than fifty percent of your own shares?"

"Yes, but I was simply taking profits—"

"Again, a yes or no answer will suffice. Mr. Brent, do you know how many shareholders have stock in your company?"

"I have no idea."

"Well I do. More than one hundred thousand. And lots of mutual funds invest in your company as well, so even more people have a vested interest in your success. Any idea how much of a loss they've had due to all the negative publicity?"

"Objection as to the cause of the stock price decline," said Ariel. "That's speculation."

"I'll rephrase again. Any idea how much of a loss your stockholders have suffered since the stock reached its high water mark?"

"No, but the stock market—"

"Taking this morning's opening price into account, nearly one billion dollars, Mr. Brent. Does that bother you, Sir?"

"Of course."

"Would you agree that the negative publicity surrounding this case has hurt your company's bottom line?"

"We'll come back. The public has a short memory and they are addicted to our products."

"I'll take that as a yes. So what exactly would your marketing campaign be to turn things around?"

"Rolling out new products always gives the stock a bump."

"I'm so glad you saved me the trouble of bringing that up. But are you referring to new products, or new versions of older products?"

"Both."

"And for the rest of this year, do you have any new products, or new versions of older products on the calendar to be released?"

A long pause. "This year, uh, just new versions."

"Actually it's just one upgrade, isn't that correct?"

"Yes."

"And it hits the stores on the day after Thanksgiving, Black Friday, the biggest shopping day of the year. I note you will release the new version of a specific product. Which product would that be?"

Silence.

Spencer leaned closer to the vent.

"Mr. Brent, I'll be happy to show you about a dozen articles from technology magazines talking about the product that will be out in time for the holidays and was supposed to be on the top of just about everyone's Christmas list. Do I need to refresh your memory?"

"No."

"So, would that product be version two-point-oh of the product my client invented?"

"Yes." Brent's voice was barely audible.

"And when you do introduce new products, your company lets people place orders months before the rollout, correct?"

"Yes."

"And stores that carry your products have been taking pre-orders since April, correct?"

"Yes."

"And since the story about this case broke, what percentage of pre-orders have canceled?"

"I have no idea."

"Well, Mr. Brent, lucky for you I did a little research on your behalf, though you probably read it in the newspaper the other day and suffer from selective memory."

"Is there a question in our future?" asked Ariel.

"Yes. According to a few of the stores that sell your company's product, they've had between forty and sixty percent cancellations. Are you familiar with the term…boycott?"

"People are entitled to change their mind—"

"Again, please answer the question. Do you know what a boycott is?"

"Of course."

"And you don't think all these cancellations are due to a boycott?"

"No."

"Do you have a Twitter account, Mr. Brent?"

"Yes."

"Are you familiar with the account that has your name preceded by a certain f-word and has more than a hundred thousand followers?"

*

Several hours later Ariel exhaled as she entered Spencer's office and slumped into the chair opposite his desk. "I'm totally fried. Damn, that was brutal. Tish destroyed him."

"I heard."

Her eyes widened. "You weren't supposed to listen in."

He shrugged. "I couldn't resist. And I was hoping to hear him cave. Interesting strategy that Tish had. She obviously doesn't want this to go to court either."

"Yeah, she was definitely going for the settlement making the guy admit that he's taken a huge hit in the wallet and his company's reputation has been seriously damaged. And he's playing the role of anti-Christ for the holidays."

"I'm sure. How was Brent's body language?"

"Not good. The charm you've seen on TV wasn't evident. I mean, the guy looked guilty and he really has no good response as to why sales of his product and the stock have both tanked. Everyone in the country knows why and the boycott is taking on a life of its own. I don't know how he'll sell his argument to a jury."

"Did you tell him that?"

"Yep."

"And what did he say?"

She shook her head. "He said he'll do better in front of a jury and reminded me of the O.J. Simpson trial telling me that juries are stupid. And he added that he'd been sued several times, juries loved him and he'd won every time. Then said that people are so obsessed with the product, they won't care if he comes off as greedy when the new version comes out for Christmas. The guy is one of those rare people who honestly doesn't give a damn that people hate him. Spence, this case is a total loser and being associated with him is really going to hurt us."

"I'm not sure a jury is going to love him this time."

"No kidding."

"You gotta get him to settle."

"I keep trying. But don't hold your breath."

"Maybe ask a family member to take a shot. You said he's close with your mom."

"Not a bad idea. I'll give her a call and maybe she can talk some sense into him."

"Well, one thing you *can* do. If it does go to court, stay out of the media. Don't give them a damn thing. You don't want your name and face on TV. No quotes in the paper either. Let him take the shots since he loves the sound of his own voice anyway."

"Agreed. And on your end, for God's sake, don't tell Tish you heard the whole deposition."

"I won't. We don't discuss the case anyway. But I must tell you, when this is over, we have to hire her. She's incredible."

Ariel smiled. "Awww, someone wants to work with his sweetheart."

Spencer blushed a bit. "Uh, no, she's y'know, a terrific lawyer and we need another partner."

Ariel nodded. "No argument here. The woman could kick my ass even if I had Mother Teresa as a client. But with Brent, it's going to be a slaughter. I've got no shot."

"Hopefully it won't get to that point."

"I'll go light a candle. Meanwhile, that girlfriend of yours is going to need a shoulder rub tonight. She leaves everything on the field. I've never seen someone so intense. She defines the word passionate. In a business sense, I mean. As for her personal life, I don't know how passionate—"

"Wipe that grin off your face."

"Sorry, couldn't resist. But I'm hungry for details and it figures that I end up with a partner who's the one guy I know who *doesn't* kiss and tell."

"A true gentleman doesn't."

"You're no fun, you damn Boy Scout."

"Well, I'm picking her up for dinner, so if she's as exhausted as you are, that gives me an idea."

*

Tish looked in the mirror and proclaimed herself presentable for dinner with Spence, even though she had no desire to go out.

Emotionally drained from the deposition, she wanted to curl up and go straight to bed.

But she also needed a friendly face after the day fighting a battle. Ariel was a formidable opponent, and played fair, but Tish could tell the woman was in an uncomfortable position.

But then again, so was she.

With poor Spence in the middle.

She heard a tap on the hotel room door and checked the time. Exactly six o'clock. "Right on schedule, as usual." But when she opened the door, she found herself looking at a tall brunette in her thirties carrying what looked like a large suitcase. "Oh, hello. I think you have the wrong room."

"Tish McKenna?"

"Yes."

"I'm Della Wade, Mr. Capshaw sent me over. I guess he didn't tell you."

"He sent you over…for what?"

She pointed at the suitcase. "A massage. I brought my portable table. Mr. Capshaw said he'd heard you had a very stressful day and that I might help you ease that tension before dinner."

Tish relaxed and smiled. "He sent me a massage-gram?"

"I guess you can call it that. May I come in and set up?"

"Absolutely. I'm not turning this down. I could sure use it after the day I've had."

"Excellent. I'll get you nice and relaxed and Mr. Capshaw will be along in about an hour to escort you to dinner."

*

An hour later Spencer tapped on the hotel room door and heard, "C'mon in." He entered and found the massage therapist working on Tish's shoulders. He couldn't help but notice her toned bare back with that porcelain skin, which spiked his heart rate a bit.

"How's the patient?"

Della turned to face him. "I think I got all the trigger points out. Poor girl was a Gordian knot. She really needed this."

Tish said something he didn't understand, so he knelt down on the floor and looked up at her peeking through the hole in the table. "I didn't get that."

178

She was smiling and her eyes were at half-mast as she slurred her words. "You are the world's most intuitive man. Mind reader."

"Did you start drinking without me, Tish?"

"Not me. Della's hands are the equivalent of a case of wine. She's amayyyy...zing."

"Glad you enjoyed it," said Della, as she finished. "All done. Now, Tish, I want you to drink lots of water tonight to wash out the toxins."

"Ohhhh-kay," said Tish, sounding half asleep and not getting up.

"Sweetie, I need my table back, I've got another client waiting. And Mr. Capshaw, if you'll wait outside while she gets dressed."

Ten minutes later the hotel room door opened and Tish smiled, then gave him a "come here" gesture with one finger. "I have something for you before we go to dinner."

"Oh. Okay." Spencer walked in, Tish took his shoulders and pinned him against the door, then planted a long, passionate kiss on him.

He stood there stunned as their lips parted. "I, uh, missed you too."

"That was for the massage, you incredibly thoughtful man. And there's more where that came from."

"A thank you would have been sufficient, but I'm not complaining." She still had him pressed against the door, her eyes locked on his like never before. He swallowed hard. "Did you, uh, still want to go to dinner?"

"Yep. I want to go to dinner with the most attractive man I know."

"Yeah, I kinda picked up on that." She didn't move, still staring at him. "You, uh, need to let me go if you want to go out."

"I'm not in a hurry, are you?"

"No."

"So shut up and take it like a man."

179

Tish felt a bit unsteady as Spence walked her back to the hotel. The massage, too much wine, the makeout session as an appetizer, and a romantic candlelight dinner with a man who she trusted more than any she'd ever met had her feeling incredibly relaxed. She leaned her head on his shoulder, breathing in his earthy cologne as they walked in step. He slipped his arm around her waist. "That was a wonderful dinner, Spence."

"Glad you liked it. I was wondering if we were going to make it to the restaurant."

"Oh, come on."

"Well, when a gorgeous woman has you pinned to the door—"

"You weren't *pinned*." He gave her an incredulous look. "Okay, so I had you pinned. But I didn't hear you complaining."

"Again, gorgeous woman pins man to door. Man has no desire to leave. Dating 101."

"Seriously, this has been a terrific evening. And the massage to start things off…How did you know I needed something like that?"

"I have my sources."

"Well, your sources were correct. Today's stress was off the charts. You might want to treat your source to a massage as well." She started to stagger as they walked through the hotel lobby. "Between the massage and the wine…and being with you…I've never felt so relaxed."

He steadied her as they headed into an elevator. "Luckily one of us isn't over the relaxation limit."

The elevator doors closed. Suddenly she felt her head spinning and saw spots. "Whoa." She reached for him as she started to fall but he caught her and scooped her up into his arms.

"You okay, Tish? You're pale as a ghost."

She wrapped her arms around his neck and lay her head on his chest. "I will be when I'm laying down. Sorry, I just got real dizzy." She closed her eyes and savored the touch of his toned muscles. "I guess we found out what happens when I go over my limit with wine."

"Well, let's get you tucked in." The elevator doors opened and he carried her down to her room. She pulled her key card from her pocket, reached out and opened the door. Spence brought her over to the bed and gently laid her on it, then sat on the edge. "You think you're okay?"

"I am now."

"You're getting your color back." He gently brushed her cheek.

She reached up and stroked his hair. "I didn't realize you were so strong. I'm a hundred and forty pounds and you carried me like I weighed nothing."

"Well, ya know, I'm not as strong as, say, oh, a shirtless fireman."

She instantly blushed as her eyes grew wide. "Oh my God, you *did* see that in *The Post*."

"I was saving it in my back pocket for the right blackmail moment."

"Spence, nothing happened—"

"Oh, stop it, I'm just playing with you. I'm the one who got to take you home tonight. Besides, when a man dates a woman like you, other guys can't help but take a shot."

"You're an incredibly sweet man, you know that?"

He shrugged. "I try. So, can I get you some water? Anything you want?"

Her eyebrows did a little jump as she licked her lips. "There *is* something I want…" She took off her glasses and placed them on the nightstand.

"Whoa."

"I never get tired of that."

"I never get tired of looking at those eyes."

She took his hand, entwined her fingers with his as she gave him the most soulful look she could muster. "As I said, there's something I want—"

He put one finger on her lips. "Tish, as much as I'd like to…I'd be taking advantage of you in your current condition. You do know that, don't you?"

She nodded in resignation. "Yeah. Dammit, why do you have to be so sensible and decent when you know you could have your way with me?"

"One of us has to behave when the other one is drunk. Every couple needs a designated lover."

"Very funny."

"Besides, I would assume you want a guy who's sensible and decent."

"He can be *indecent* once in a while."

"Don't worry, I'm fully capable of that. But, like I said, it's not that I wouldn't want to, Tish."

"Well, glad to hear you say that. I was worried that maybe the physical attraction wasn't…enough for you."

"I could have the court reporter read back the transcript when I called you the gorgeous woman who had me pinned to the door."

"That's right, you did say that. But were you under oath, or simply being a typical man trying to wear me down with compliments so you could get me in bed?"

He shrugged. "Well, you are in bed. So either way, it worked."

"Smartass. Answer my question."

"The compliment was sincere, as they all are. I would never perjure myself with you."

"Good. You'd be in contempt of Tish. And there are severe penalties for that." She stifled a yawn. "Oh my God, I'm so sorry. That was rude. I'm not bored—"

"No, you're exhausted, young lady. You were on the ropes from the day at work and the wine and massage have you down for the count." He took off her shoes, placed them at the foot of the bed, and tucked her in. "I think it's time for Sleeping Beauty to start counting sheep."

She put out her lower lip in a playful pout. "I guess. But dammit, I don't want this night to end. Can I at least get a good-night kiss from Prince Charming?"

"Absolutely." He leaned down and gave her a soft kiss. "That hold you for a while?"

"Not for long, but I'll take it. Thank you again, Spence, for a wonderful evening. This was really special and you have no idea how much I needed it."

"Glad I could be of service."

"You're not here to serve me. Considering the way you treat me it should be the other way around. And it will be once this trial is out of the way."

"Tish, I enjoy spoiling you. Alas, I patrol the streets of New York as it is my sworn duty to pamper damsels who have had a rough day. Pleasant dreams, fair lady."

"Good night."

He got up, blew her a kiss, and left the room.

Tish turned out the lights. Moonlight spilled into the room, giving it an ethereal look. She looked at the New York skyline and smiled. "I'm already living a pleasant dream."

Chapter Nineteen

TRIAL OF THE YEAR HAS INTERESTING SIDEBAR
By Janice Brewster

While the case between technology giant Peter Brent and the inventor of his signature product has already been tried in the court of public opinion, jury selection begins today. Unless you've been living under a rock (and that may be the only place to look for jurors who haven't heard about this case) you know that Brent is about as popular in this city as a case of the flu.

What you might not know is the lawyer for plaintiff Cynthia Riggs is only able to represent her due to her cat. Because without her fur baby, she'd probably be dead.

If the name of attorney Tish McKenna sounds familiar, it's because she is the woman who was saved from a house fire by her cat Socks, who woke her up when the smoke alarm didn't go off, a story that got national attention. And that cat is from the famous litter of orphaned kittens adopted by network TV reporter Madison Shaw, a longtime friend and one of McKenna's college roommates.

The attorney says her pet (full name: Socks Fifth Avenue, named since the black-and-white tuxedo cat has white socks and her office is on that street) helps keep things in perspective as she prepares for what is sure to be a very stressful trial. "No matter how wound up

I get over this case, having her jump in my lap and purr instantly calms me down. This cat seems to have a sixth sense about when I'm having a rough day."

Tish gathered up her notes and started to load her briefcase, trying in vain to keep her heart rate down. While she rarely felt anxiety at the beginning of a trial, there was way too much riding on this.

Shelley headed into her office carrying a bunch of copies. "Here you go." She studied Tish's face. "Hey, you don't look like yourself. You okay?"

"Yeah, just…nervous."

"You're never nervous when you go to trial. Where's the soulless gunslinger look all your clients love?"

Tish shook her head. "This case is so critical…for so many reasons. I feel like the whole thing is a house of cards that could fall if I don't win."

"I know. Hey, do me a favor. Sit down for five minutes, take a deep breath and hold your cat. Take the advice from that article about Socks in today's paper. She'll calm you down."

Tish nodded and smiled. "You're right." She plopped down in her leather swivel rocker, grabbed Socks from the corner of the desk and put the cat in her lap. She immediately got a lick and the loud purr she'd grown to love. "Y'know, we could get rich if we could somehow synthesize the purring of a cat into blood pressure medicine."

"Yeah, no kidding. Sometimes she's better than a bottle of wine." Shelley sat on the couch on the side wall. "So how are things with you and Spence?"

Tish's eyes took on a dreamy look. "I swear, Shelley, that man is about the nicest on the planet. I think he's the one. I mean, we haven't been going out that long and you know how careful I am about dating, but he seems to be everything I'm looking for."

"Do you think you love him?"

"I'm heading in that direction." Socks meowed and Tish realized she'd stopped petting the cat so she scratched her under the chin. "I already love *you*, kitty." She looked at the clock. "Well, I'd better get going. Jury selection should be really interesting."

*

Ariel picked up her briefcase just as Spencer arrived in the office. "Well, I'm off for a day in hell. I'd say wish me luck, but I know you have a rooting interest in this case, and it isn't me. Actually, I have a rooting interest, and it isn't me either."

"I'm sorry you're in the middle of my relationship with Tish."

"This truly is a no-win situation. Speaking of your quietly beautiful girlfriend, have you two finally—"

"No, and stop asking."

"Right, you don't kiss and tell. I'll be able to tell from your face anyway when it does happen."

"Huh?"

"You glow like a pregnant woman after you sleep with someone."

"Seriously?"

"I won't need a lie detector when you and Tish finally hook up. But your face already tells me one thing."

"What?"

"Whenever you talk about her, you light up like I've never seen you. You have moved beyond smitten. You're in love, dear partner."

"Not quite there yet, but close. She's an amazing woman."

Ariel patted him on the cheek. "Well, whatever this is, it's a good look for you. Ride the wave, sweetie. From what you've told me she's perfect for you. And even though I barely know her and her taste in men, I have a feeling you're perfect for her. Well, gotta

186

go and get a dozen jurors who will love Peter Brent, since he says all juries love him." She headed for the door.

"You'll have better luck finding Jimmy Hoffa."

"And Hoffa would be more likable." Ariel left as Spencer walked to his office.

And then it hit him.

Brent had won every lawsuit. And thought juries loved him.

It was time to find out why.

He pulled the wrinkled business card from his wallet and dialed the number.

He knew if anyone could find out, his friend from the old neighborhood could.

Chapter Twenty

One week later...

Spencer felt bored on Saturday night with Tish out of town for the whole weekend at a family reunion in Florida.

He missed her.

And then he remembered something a happily married friend had once told him.

Love isn't about finding someone you can live with, but someone you can't live without.

Right now, he was having a problem without Tish in his life, if even for a few days.

The phone rang, jolting him out of his deep thoughts. He looked at the caller ID, not recognizing the number, and decided to answer the call. "Hello?"

"This is Trooper Carpenter with the New York State Police calling for Spencer Capshaw."

He rolled his eyes. Damn, telemarketers don't even take the weekend off. He knew con artists loved collecting money in the name of police officers. "I don't donate money over the phone, just send me something in the mail—"

"Mr. Capshaw, I'm calling because you're listed as an emergency contact for Ariel Nix."

His eyes widened as he stood up. "Oh my God, is she okay?"

"There's been a bad accident."

A few hours later a doctor entered the hospital waiting room and looked out at the crowd. "Nix?"

Spencer jumped up and raised his hand. "Right here."

The doctor moved forward. "She's going to be okay. A broken leg, some bruising to her internal organs, whiplash and a collapsed lung, but she's out of danger. It will be awhile before she's able to get around on her own. She's going to need a lot of rest and support. But she will fully recover."

"Thank God. Can I see her?"

"She's being moved to a private room. Give us about an hour and then you can visit for a little while."

Spencer entered Ariel's room carrying some flowers he'd bought in the hospital gift shop. Her eyes were droopy but she managed a smile as she spotted him. "Hey."

He sat on the edge of her bed and took her hand. "Doctor says you'll be fine. How are you feeling?"

"Like I've been run over by a truck. Which I have."

"It was a drunk driver and he's locked up. I already called my friend in the District Attorney's office so they'll throw the book at him. The State Trooper said it was a miracle you weren't killed."

"Hey, I couldn't check out before finding out how you and Tish end up. Were you out with her? I'm sorry to ruin your weekend."

"She's out of town all weekend. And right now you're my top priority."

She squeezed his hand. "That's why you're such a good catch. You always take such good care of me."

Her eyes flickered a bit. "You're fading, kiddo. You need sleep. I'll come back first thing in the morning."

"Oh-kay…" Her eyes closed and she fell asleep.

189

Ariel was already up as Spence arrived the next morning. "Well, you're back among the living."

"Not quite, but better than last night. Sorry I nodded off while you were here."

"You needed it. Sleep well?"

"Yeah, the meds knocked me out. But I'm incredibly sore."

"Doctor been by to see you yet?"

"He said it will be a while before I'll be back in a courtroom." She reached for a container of orange juice on her tray. She grimaced as her hand shook.

"I'll get it." Spencer grabbed the container, put a straw in it and held it to her lips.

She took a long drink. "Thanks, you'll make a good wife."

"I can tell your personality has already recovered."

"You can't kill snark. Anyway, speaking of my returning to the courtroom, you'll need to go in for me tomorrow and ask Judge Winston for a continuance. Probably four months till I'm back to normal."

"I figured as much. Dammit, I was hoping all this would go away before Christmas."

"So was I."

"Y'know, maybe this is a way for Brent to use someone else. It's a legitimate excuse for you to get out of the case. Maybe we should tell him it will be longer than four months. How about a year?"

"Not a bad idea. The two attorneys from his legal department have been working with me and are familiar with the case. Either one of them could do it. Considering he wanted to make this all go away as quickly as possible, that's a great option."

"I'll try to sell it."

"Let me call him first. Oh, and you'd better tell Tish before she finds out in the courtroom, or she'll be ticked off like the last time. She needs to be the first to know."

"I'm heading to the airport to pick her up today anyway. I'll tell her then."

*

Tish spotted Spence at the security checkpoint holding a hand-written sign.

Girlfriend.

"Awww, how cute." She waved and he saw her, then she picked up the pace as she pulled her carry-on bag behind her.

Nice to have a boyfriend pick you up at the airport instead of getting a cab.

He gave her a warm smile as he waited, then extended his arms as she reached him and gave her a strong hug. "Welcome home. I missed you."

"Spence, I was only gone for the weekend."

"The correct response is *I missed you too.*"

"Sorry. I missed you too."

He looked up at the ceiling, nose in the air. "Too late, the moment has passed."

"Okay, I *really, really* missed you."

"Much better."

"Oh, I love your sign. Very sweet."

He glanced at his watch, then looked over her shoulder. "I think I got my wires crossed and my girlfriend must be on another flight."

"Smartass." She pointed at his wrist. "Another cool watch. I haven't seen that one."

"Forty bucks in a pawn shop. Best place to find stuff like this."

Hmmm...great idea for a Christmas present...

He reached for her bag and grabbed the handle. "C'mon. Baggage claim is that way."

"I didn't check anything. I'll be damned if I'm going to pay the airline fifty bucks when I can get everything I need in a carry-on."

"Oh my God, a woman who travels light. Every man's dream."

She playfully slapped him on the arm as they started walking toward the exit. "Hey, I'm a practical girl." She noted his face suddenly turned serious. "What's wrong?"

"Got some bad news this weekend. Ariel was in a traffic accident and is in the hospital."

"Oh my God, is she okay?"

"Broken leg, collapsed lung and internal bruising, among other things, but she'll be out of commission for several months."

"Poor thing. Anything I can do?"

"Well, right now you and I have to deal with the obvious."

The realization hit her and she slowed down. "Oh, shit. The trial starts tomorrow."

"I talked to her this morning and we have a plan. See what you think of this. Two attorneys from Brent's legal department have been assisting Ariel and are familiar with everything, so tomorrow I'm going before Judge Winston to ask for a continuance of a few days and then tell Brent he either has to use his own guys or wait till next year to resolve this."

Tish grabbed his forearm and stopped walking. "Suppose Brent doesn't go for it? Spence, my client can't wait any longer. She invented the thing more than two years ago. And she has serious health issues."

"I know, but Ariel thinks he'll want this to be over as much as your client. Who the hell knows, maybe without Ariel as his attorney he'll even offer to settle."

She started walking again. "That's a lot of variables."

"Well, Ariel is going to give Brent a call today, and then I'll talk to him, so hopefully he'll be on board. Thank goodness I haven't done any more work on this case or he'd want me to represent him."

She wrapped one arm around his waist. "Why is everything so difficult when it comes to this case? And why do we have to be caught in the middle?"

"I don't know. It's the opposite of stars aligning. But for right now, how about we take our minds off it and do something fun."

"Not sure if it's possible to get it out of my head, but let's take a shot."

*

It didn't work.

Tish crawled into bed in Madison's guest room and patted the mattress. "C'mere, Socks. Your person needs you." The cat jumped on the bed and lay down on her chest, giving Tish her usual look that went right into her soul.

She hadn't gotten the trial out of her head, and neither had Spence.

They'd tried. An afternoon matinee of what was supposed to be the funniest movie of the year only got a few chuckles, as they were unable to concentrate on anything else. A walk in Central Park and a casual dinner hadn't helped either. They'd ended the night with a strong hug, Spence stroking her hair, trying to assure her everything would be all right.

Still, she knew all sorts of things could go wrong.

Morning couldn't come fast enough.

Problem was, she couldn't sleep.

Chapter Twenty-One

Tish noted a pained expression on Spence's face as he entered the courtroom at a few minutes before nine, trailed by Peter Brent. She moved forward to meet him and lowered her voice. "What's wrong?"

He shook his head, jaw clenched. "You are *not* going to believe this."

"What?"

"Brent wants—"

"All rise! Court is now in session. The honorable Rebecca Winston presiding."

Spence lowered his voice. "You'll find out in a minute."

Her blood pressure spiked. A flood of anxiety washed over Tish in an instant.

The judge made her way to the bench. "Be seated." She turned toward Spence and furrowed her brow. "Good morning. I don't see Ms. Nix. Where is counsel for the defendant, Mr. Capshaw?"

Spence stood up. "Your honor, my partner was in a serious traffic accident this weekend and is currently hospitalized."

"Is she all right?"

"She suffered some bad injuries but she will recover. However, it will be several months before she will be back to work."

The judge shook her head. "I see. Please convey my wishes that she get well."

"I will, your honor."

"In the meantime, I assume you are here to ask for a continuance."

"Just a few days, your honor."

"I thought you said Ms. Nix would be out of commission for months."

Brent stood up. "Your honor, I would like Mr. Capshaw to represent me."

Tish's jaw dropped. *Oh dear God, no…*

The judge glared at the defendant. "Sit down, Mr. Brent. You may be the CEO of a major company, but you will speak when spoken to in my kingdom, and I'm the queen of this castle. Clear?"

"Yes, ma'am."

"And don't call me ma'am. I'm not that old."

"Yes…m…your honor."

She turned to Spence. "Are you prepared to represent the defendant, Mr. Capshaw?"

"No, your honor. My partner has been assisted by two attorneys from Mr. Brent's corporate law department, and she suggested that he would be well represented by either of them. Mr. Brent agreed that was the best course of action last night when he spoke with Ms. Nix."

"Did you know Mr. Brent actually wanted you to represent him?"

"No. He told me about five minutes ago, your honor. And other than giving Ms. Nix my files and notes from two similar cases, I haven't done any work on the case."

She turned to the defendant. "Mr. Brent, what's the deal? If you've got two attorneys from your company's legal department and they have been working on the case, it makes no sense that you would want Mr. Capshaw's representation."

"Your honor, it just hit me this morning that the lawyers from my legal department are not as experienced as Mr. Capshaw is as a litigator, and Ms. Nix has told me he is an excellent attorney."

"That may be true from what I've seen in my courtroom, but the fact remains he has not done any work on your case."

"I don't care. It's a simple case, he's handled two lawsuits involving work product before and his partner told me he had provided information to her. I will not agree to anyone else."

Spence glared at Brent.

The judge rolled her eyes. "Okay, I want both attorneys in my chambers, now."

Tish looked at Spence as they followed the judge and mouthed, "What should we do?"

He shrugged as they entered her chambers and shut the door.

Judge Winston took a seat behind her desk. "Okay, Mr. Capshaw, what the hell is going on?"

"As I said, your honor, I thought we had this all resolved yesterday. My partner and I called Brent from the hospital and suggested he use the attorneys from his legal department. I met with him earlier this morning and he was on board. I just came to ask you for a continuance of a few days so they could prepare. Then as we're walking into the courtroom he tells me he's changed his mind and wants me to take the lead. He said his staff attorneys don't have enough experience as litigators and he won't agree to them."

She slowly nodded. "And you really haven't done anything to help your partner with this case besides telling her about the cases you worked?"

Spence shook his head. "No, your honor. I had never even talked to Mister Brent until yesterday."

"Dammit. Jury selection took forever last week and I have no desire to go through that again. Trying to find people who hadn't heard about this case was nearly impossible." She turned to Tish. "Your thoughts, Ms. McKenna?"

"Your honor, I think this is obviously another stall tactic by Mr. Brent. My client has already waited a few years to bring this to trial. And she has personal issues."

"Can you be more specific?"

"She's dying, your honor, and she was hoping for either a settlement or to win this case before…so she can afford the medical care she needs to save her life. Either way, she wants it resolved. Making her wait several months until Ms. Nix is well would be a real hardship for her and the stress isn't doing her any good as she fights for her life. I'm not saying she's counting on winning—"

"I read the papers, Ms. McKenna. This case does look like a slam dunk for you."

"There won't be a case if Brent delays it long enough because she won't be alive to sue him."

The judge's eyes turned sad. "Okay, give me an hour to figure something out. Because I want this damn media circus off my docket as much as you guys, and this doesn't need to drag out past Christmas for the poor woman. In the meantime, you two use this time and see if you can work out a settlement to get us all off the hook."

*

Judge Winston returned and took a seat. "Will both attorneys please approach the bench."

Tish and Spence moved toward her as she put her hand over the microphone. "Were you able to work out a settlement?"

Spence shook his head. "Brent won't budge. And the amount Ms. McKenna asked for was very reasonable. He's dug in on not using his own attorneys as well."

She shook her head and exhaled. "I think Ms. McKenna is right. He's stalling. Unfortunate. Very well. Step back."

They headed back to their seats as the judge turned to Peter

Brent. "Mr. Brent, do you refuse to use your own staff attorneys to represent you?"

Brent stood up and nodded. "Yes, your honor."

"Do you fully understand that Mr. Capshaw has not done any work on your case other than giving notes and files to his partner?"

"Yes, your honor. But the attorneys from my legal department who have been working on it have very limited litigation experience and while they are brilliant researchers I do not believe they can provide the proper representation I need."

She nodded. "I checked, and you are correct about their trial experience. However, if this is some tactic to have me grant a long continuance until Ms. Nix is well, it is not going to work. This trial will proceed with only a slight delay. You may be seated."

Good. She's going to force him to use his attorneys.

The judge turned to Spence. "Mr. Capshaw, while you have not done any real work on this case, I checked and saw that you have been the attorney of record in two other work product trials, once representing the corporation and once representing the employee. And you won both cases."

Tish's eyes widened. *Oh, no, what is she doing? She can't possibly—*

Spence stood up. "Your honor, I don't see what that has to do with this case."

"Mr. Capshaw, this case centers on the exact same argument of your previous two cases. You know the playbook for both sides and are familiar with the laws regarding work product. This case is not at all complicated and has a very short witness list. Therefore, I will give you three days to go over the depositions and prepare yourself." She turned to the defendant. "Mr. Brent, nice try."

Tish's jaw dropped as Spence shook his head. "Your honor, if you say this is not a complicated case then Mr. Brent's staff attorneys can handle—"

"Mr. Capshaw, that point is moot since the defendant will not

agree to use his own attorneys and I'm not going to delay this case any longer than I have to. Sorry, but…tag, you're it. Court accepts Mr. Capshaw as attorney for the defendant. Trial to begin Friday morning at nine o'clock sharp." She swung her gavel. "Court is in recess."

Spence moved forward a few steps. "Your honor…"

The judge ignored him and quickly left the courtroom.

He turned to Tish. "We need to talk."

Chapter Twenty-Two

Spencer held the door for Tish, then closed it as they entered one of the meeting rooms across the hall from the courtroom. He threw his briefcase onto a chair. "I don't believe this."

"Neither do I."

He shook his head. "We've gotta tell her."

"Tell who?"

"Judge Winston."

"Tell her what?"

"That we're dating. I can't go up against a woman I'm in— I just can't."

"We can't tell her. No way."

"But Tish—"

"She'll take you off the case and since Brent won't agree to use his guys he gets the delay he obviously wanted. He wins. And my client doesn't have any more time to wait. He's using the classic strategy. Delay, deny and hope they die."

"I just met the guy and I already can't stand him. And everyone knows he's wrong. How the hell am I supposed to represent someone who I don't believe in…and against you?"

"You have to. If you don't, Brent gets exactly what he wanted. And you have to give it your best shot. If he even suspects you're tanking it he'll appeal and claim he didn't receive adequate representation."

He bit his lower lip as he looked at her. "Tish—"

"He can't even sense that we know each other. So don't you dare give this case anything but your best otherwise he wins. And don't you dare do anything to let me win."

He dropped his voice to a whisper. "I would never insult you like that, Tish. But I want you to win."

"You cannot even think that and for God's sake, don't ever say it again. Spence, I'm sorry we're stuck in this horrible no-win situation, but there's no way out of it."

He exhaled and shook his head. "We need to get away from here. Can we talk about this tonight at dinner? I've got reservations—"

"Spence, we can't see each other until this thing is over."

"Huh?"

"There's a media horde outside, probably following us when we leave. Do you have any idea what would happen if someone spotted us together in a restaurant?"

"Fine, come over to my place."

"Still too risky. Reporters were staking out my hotel this morning. I had to run through a gauntlet just to get out the front door."

"So, what, we're on some sort of dating hiatus?"

"Until this is over. I suggest you use the little time you have to read those depositions and get ready."

"I, uh, don't have to read them."

"Dammit, Spence, don't you dare phone it in!"

"I don't have to read them because I already heard them."

She furrowed her brow. "Excuse me?"

"My office shares an air vent with the conference room. I heard everything."

"We agreed not to talk about the case."

"And we didn't talk about it. I'm sorry, I couldn't resist listening in."

She glared at him and folded her arms. "You said you weren't going to do any more work on the case."

"I didn't do any work, I listened in. Tish, you were amazing."

"That's beside the point. So you *are* familiar with the case even though you haven't worked on it."

"Pretty much. And I actually have had two very similar cases involving work product."

"Anything else you aren't telling me?"

"No. Dammit, Tish, I can't believe Brent wanted me."

"He obviously came up with the plan after he found out about Ariel being hospitalized. But I'm sure he never expected the judge to actually stick you with the case. The only reasonable explanation is that he assumed he would get the long continuance."

"It doesn't matter, Tish. It's killing me that I have to fight my girlfriend in court."

She moved closer and locked eyes with him. "And you'd better bring your A-game, Mister, 'cause I'm bringing mine. We have to do this or Brent wins."

*

Tish stormed into her office, blowing past Shelley. "Tish, you're back already? What happened?"

She started to slam her briefcase but saw Socks on her desk and remembered how she'd scared the poor thing the last time she got angry. She placed it on the credenza and plopped down into the chair behind her desk. "Sonofabitch!"

"Why are you back so soon?"

"Since Ariel is in the hospital the trial hasn't started yet and won't start till Friday. And guess who is now representing Peter Brent?"

"Who?"

"Spence."

Shelley's jaw dropped as she sat opposite Tish. "How the hell did that happen?"

Tish picked up the cat, put Socks on her lap and told her the story. "So you see, there's no way out of this. I've gone over every possible scenario, and nothing works. Oh, and get this…Spence heard all the depositions through the air vent in his office."

"What is it about you two and air vents? Damn, Tish, what are you gonna do?"

"I've gotta win this case. But that's not what worries me."

"What then?"

"You know how ruthless I can be in court. I'm worried that going up against Spence I'll hurt him somehow and our relationship will never be the same."

*

Ariel was watching television from her hospital bed as Spence entered her room carrying a bag of snacks. She turned to him and shook her head. "What the hell happened? I just saw it on the court channel."

He sat on the edge of her bed. "Your *cousin* sandbagged me. And now I'm stuck going up against my girlfriend."

She took his hand and gave it a squeeze. "Damn, I am so sorry."

"It's not your fault that your relative is a conniving scumbag."

"Like I said, he didn't used to be that way. Money does strange things to people. I hate that you're in a no-win situation like this."

"Friggin' Kobayashi Maru."

"Who's that?"

"Not a *who*, it's a *what*. It's the no-win scenario in a Star Trek movie that they put the cadets through at Starfleet Academy. Captain Kirk re-programs the simulation computer so he can beat it."

"Oh, yeah, now I remember. But look, don't think of it that way. Focus on the fact that when the trial's over you and Tish can get back together and pick up where you left off."

"I'm just worried about the damage this trial will do to our relationship. We've been able to separate work and our personal lives so far. I mean, we never talk about the law or our cases. But now…we'll be in every newspaper in the country as adversaries."

"But you just said you've been able to separate work and personal stuff."

"That was before I was on the case. The problem is work could get personal this time. Ariel, you should have seen the look she gave me in the meeting room. She was not pleased when I told her I didn't need to read the depositions since I'd already heard them. Now I know why they call her *Jaws*. She looked at me like I was the prey."

"I think you're over-reacting."

"Maybe so. But that sweet woman who has me smitten was nowhere to be found. The girlfriend previously known as Tish has left the building."

"She's there, the woman is simply very passionate about her work. You've seen her in action, you know how important it is for her to win this case and how much she cares for her client. Let's face it, that woman got screwed big time and she's desperate."

"I sure hope that's all it is. Tish got upset when I said I wanted her to win."

"Spence, you shouldn't have said that. You can't give her the impression that you're letting her win."

"I know, and she raised a good point when she said Brent will appeal if I don't give him my best effort. Oh, and get this. We're leaving the courtroom and I'm assuming he's ticked off about his ploy to get a continuance not working. He grabs my arm and tells me not to worry, that juries love him. I've never met such an egomaniac. I don't think the guy realizes how much people dislike him right now."

"Yeah, they showed some video from his corporate headquarters. Lot of people protesting and the only things missing were torches and pitchforks."

"Hey, it's New York, it could happen. Give it time."

"Y'know, I can't believe Peter is the same person who put me through law school. He really changed when he started doing those TV presentations whenever he rolled out a new product. The fame went right to his head. He thinks he's the next Steve Jobs."

"I think he's closer to the next Lord Voldemort."

*

Shelley tapped on the door. "Why don't you go home, Tish, it's seven o'clock."

"Trial starts tomorrow. Just polishing up my opening statement."

"You were ready with that on Monday."

"That was before Spence became Brent's attorney. I've been going through the transcripts of his two work product cases. Damn, Shelley, he was incredible in both of them. He's gonna be a tough opponent and he did some things I didn't anticipate. At least now I know what he's probably going to throw at my client tomorrow."

"Well, don't stay up too late. It's been a long, stressful week and you need a good night's rest."

"I haven't had one all week. Going to bed early won't help."

"Then try wine."

"That hasn't worked either. Really could use that massage therapist Spence sent over."

"After you win a big settlement you can put her on retainer."

"Hell, I'd put her on staff."

"Well, for now you should concentrate on the fact that it will be over soon and you guys can pick things up where you left off. Just in time for Christmas. He's going to love the gift you got him."

She slowly nodded. "I just hope there are no hard feelings when it's over."

"You think you can handle going up against Spence?"

"I'm more worried about what he'll think of me. You know damn well I can't dial it down in a courtroom."

"He wouldn't expect you to, Tish. Remember, he's seen you in action before and in law school."

"I know, but I can get pretty vicious and go for the throat. And I'm already in great white shark mode. I hope he won't take it personally."

"He won't. And guess what? He's probably thinking the exact same thing. So make sure you don't take anything *he* might do personally."

Tish was almost finished reading by eight. Socks was curled up on her lap, fast asleep.

And then she heard it. Coming through the air vent.

The sound of Spence shaking the bag of cat treats.

Socks immediately woke up, ears trained toward the vent. She started to jump but Tish held her in place. "I've got treats for you here, kitty. Besides, I need you right now."

She went back to reading.

Then she heard it again.

Along with his voice.

"C'mon Socks, time for your treats. Kitty, kitty, kitty…"

This time Socks struggled to get away but Tish held her down.

"Socks, where are you?"

Tish shook her head and yelled toward the vent. "She's with me tonight."

Long pause. *"You shouldn't deprive her of her nightly treats."*

"She has treats right here."

He shook the bag again.

She rolled her eyes. "I don't *believe* this."

Socks narrowed her eyes at Tish and let out a low throaty growl.

Tish let the cat go. "Fine. Ditch me for food. I see you have

206

your priorities." Socks jumped from her lap and headed into the vent. Tish got up and moved toward the bookcase. "Send her right back."

"I'll try, but she doesn't understand English. Awww, there you are, pretty kitty. How are things in the cat world?"

"Why don't you get your own cat?"

"I can't help it if this one likes me. And I'm all alone here with my partner in the hospital."

And then a third voice came through the vent.

"I'm all alone here too trying to get work done and I gotta listen to two people have a conversation through a heating duct? Youse guys ever hear of a friggin' telephone?"

Chapter Twenty-Three

Tish stopped at her office door and took the hands of her client as they prepared to head to the courthouse. "Remember, head held high, show no fear. You did nothing wrong."

"I know, but inside I'm going to be a wreck. I've never been involved with anything like this. I'm worried I'm going to be terrified on the witness stand with all those people watching. At least there are no cameras in the courtroom."

"Well, keep in mind that most of the people there are reporters who are on our side. Here's one thing you can do... When I'm asking questions, pretend we're the only people in the room. Talk to me and not the crowd. Focus on me. And remember, you already know every question I'm going to ask you."

"What about when the other attorney asks questions? I don't know what those will be."

"Well, we went over a lot of stuff he is likely to ask. But it's the same deal, you're talking to him, not the whole room. Don't be afraid. He's a really decent human being. I seriously doubt he'll do anything that crosses the line."

"Let's hope so."

Tish looked at her watch. "Okay, time to go. Remember, I'm

in your corner and I will fight like hell for you. Nobody will stand in my way. Nobody."

Spencer entered the courtroom trailed by Peter Brent and saw that Tish and her client had already arrived. The courtroom was loaded with media people, so he tried to avoid eye contact as he made his way down the aisle.

Tish turned to face him as he arrived at his table. "Good morning, Mr. Capshaw."

He studied her face and didn't even see a glint of recognition. *Is she pretending that she doesn't know me at all so Brent won't suspect anything?*

Or has she actually turned into a blue-eyed gunslinger?

He decided it was best to play along. "Morning, Ms. McKenna."

"I trust you will keep things civil."

"I always do." He gave her a slight smile.

And received the death stare through her thick glasses. "Let's hope so. To do otherwise would not be advisable." She turned away and sat down next to her client.

Shit.

I'm in love with the female version of Dr. Jekyll and Mr. Hyde.

Tish noted her client looked terrified so she reached over and gave her hand a gentle squeeze. The crowd quieted down as Judge Rebecca Winston entered the courtroom, took her seat on the bench and gestured toward the crowd to be seated. "Good morning. Before we get started I want to set some ground rules as I realize this is a very high profile case that has basically been turned into a media circus, and I note many of those in the gallery are members of said circus. So let me say right off the bat that this court will not stand for any outbursts during the trial. No chatter either. If I hear a cell phone go off or see someone texting, your phone will be confiscated and dropped in this nice pitcher of water I have up here. So I want you all to behave like

you're in a 1950s Catholic school and I'm Sister Mary Hatchetface."
She turned toward the attorneys. "Okay, Ms. McKenna, are you
ready for trial?"

"Yes, your honor," Tish replied.

"Mr. Capshaw."

"Yes, Judge Winston."

"Excellent. I trust both of you will maintain a sense of decorum
during these proceedings and keep things moving as I know
everyone involved would like to have this wrapped up by
Christmas. Ms. McKenna, you may proceed with your opening
statement."

Tish stood up and headed toward the jury. "Thank you, your
honor." She reached the jury box and rested her hands on the
rail. "Good morning. My name is Tish McKenna and I'm representing the plaintiff in this case, Cynthia Riggs. As Judge Winston
just stated, this is a very high profile case and has attracted a ton
of media attention. I'm sure you have already heard both sides
of the story. And many of you know the defendant from his
appearances on television. But even if there were not a single
reporter in the courtroom today and this case had gotten no
media coverage, it still comes down to the facts, not what you've
read in the papers or seen on TV. And the facts I will present to
you are quite clear. The most important fact that the defense will
not be able to refute is that my client invented an amazing product
on her own time using her own money after pitching the idea
to Peter Brent and being laughed at. And then her former
employer, Brent Industries, stole it. The defendant, Peter Brent,
is nothing more than a white collar thief, no different than a
pickpocket in Manhattan who would steal your wallet and not
bat an eye. Upon first hearing of Cynthia's amazing idea, he told
her it was ridiculous and a waste of time. Since he obviously
didn't want it, she worked on it on her own because she believed
in the idea. Now, after developing the prototype she could have
patented the thing and tried to sell it to the highest bidder. Instead,

she demonstrated it for Mr. Brent, hoping for a share of the profits. But only after she showed it to him did he decide it was to his financial benefit to market it. He didn't offer to buy it or share in the profits. He simply classified it as work product and stole it. That's a phrase you'll hear a lot in this trial. Work product. It means that when you work for a company anything you might come up with on company time and using company resources belongs to the company. But in this case, Cynthia got the idea while on vacation, built it herself because the boss thought it was a stupid idea, and spent her own funds to develop it. Then, Mr. Brent, like the boy in high school who wasn't interested in the ugly girl until she got her braces off and turned into a swan, had to have it."

Tish then got an idea from the Judge's opening remarks. She reached into her pocket and pulled out the product. "This is one of the most popular technology products on the market today. My client invented it. I'm sure many of you have one. It has made Peter Brent almost a half billion dollars. To this day he has not shared one penny with the person who invented it. So I ask you, is that fair? Remember, while this case is about the facts, it is also about doing the right thing.

"As you entered the courthouse today you probably saw the large amount of protesters outside carrying some very unflattering signs about the defendant and shouting words that are not suitable for this courtroom. Nationally there is a huge boycott against Peter Brent's company. Thousands of people have canceled orders for the upgrade of this product, due out in a few days. Social media portrays him as Satan. That's because everyone knows he didn't do the right thing. He didn't play fair. And he's nothing more than a common thief."

She headed back to her table. "Judge Winston said if she heard a cell phone ring during this trial she'd have it confiscated and drop it in her water pitcher. Which makes me think, why do *I* want a stolen product made by a thief? The answer is, I don't.

Because if not one penny of what I spent for that product didn't go to its rightful creator, well…I'm sure I'm like you. I like to consider myself to be an honest citizen." She held the product over the pitcher on her table and dropped it in. "And it's against the law to be in possession of stolen merchandise."

*

Ariel was watching the court channel as Spence walked into her hospital room. "Hey, Ariel, how you feeling?"

"A little better, but still real sore."

"I'm real sore and I *didn't* get hit by a truck. I got run over by an attorney."

"You know, I never wanted cameras in the courtroom but this is one time I wish they were there. The commentators are going on and on about Tish dropping the thing in the water pitcher."

He sat on the edge of her bed. "Yeah, talk about taking the wind out of my sails. There was an audible hush in the room when she did that. And she left it in the pitcher all day. I saw a few reporters take a picture of it with their cell phones during a recess, so it will probably end up on every front page."

"So, beyond that little stunt, how do you think it went?"

"As for my opening argument, she blew me out of the water by sending the product for a swim. She had a lot of witnesses talking about how talented her client is and how she was great to work for before she got demoted. I couldn't really do much with any of them, but that was to be expected. What I didn't expect was how she treated me. I'm starting to get worried, Ariel."

"Why, what did she do?"

"The way she looked at me, like I was the enemy."

"In court, you are. Remember, she doesn't want Brent to know you guys are in a relationship."

"I sure hope so. But she's taking it kinda far."

Ariel reached over and patted his hand. "You guys will be okay."

*

Spencer heard the tap on the door and headed for the outer office.

Thankfully, it was not another reporter.

He unlocked the door and smiled at the tall, thirtysomething brunette. "Kayla, thanks for coming by at such a ridiculous hour."

She shrugged. "Hey, private investigators don't really punch a clock. Besides, I've got a cheating husband to tail later this evening at the Plaza."

"Sounds like fun. Anyway, I figured by this time all the reporters would be gone."

"Still a few in the lobby. I took the service elevator."

"Great." Spencer locked the door and led her to the conference room. "Got anything so far?"

She sat and pulled a manila envelope from her purse. "Not much. But I have a lot of leads to track down." She pulled several photos from the envelope. "These are the shots I could get from that company trip. You can see Cynthia Riggs sitting next to Peter Brent at a beach bar, but I'm not sure any of this is very useful. Most of them are people partying on the beach with him, playing golf, that sort of stuff."

Spencer flipped through the photos and didn't see anything that jumped out. "Probably not, but you never know what will come up during the trial."

"I'm still working that angle. Along with the other one you gave me."

"I'm sure you'll uncover something. You always do."

She leaned back and smiled. "You know, Spence, this is the first time you've had me investigate one of your own clients. Usually it's the person you're going up against."

"Well, as you know, this is an unusual situation. If you can find something that will force him to settle, I'll be the happiest man in New York."

213

"Yeah, I can see why you'd want to settle. The case is a total loser."

"Everyone can see that except Peter Brent. He really thinks he's going to win."

Chapter Twenty-Four

BRENT'S CASE IS ALL WET
By Jason Maddon

If you want a lawyer who can think on her feet, look no further than Tish McKenna.

The attorney for Cynthia Riggs took a comment made by Judge Rebecca Winston and turned it into what might be the signature moment of the Brent Industries trial. After the judge warned reporters that any cell phone which rang during the trial would end up in her water pitcher, McKenna wrapped up her opening argument by dropping Brent Industries' signature product into her own pitcher while calling it stolen merchandise.

And during day one of the most high profile trials of the year, the item remained underwater, like a wet elephant in the room.

While McKenna declined comment at the end of the day, legal analysts all agreed that her action set the tone for the trial. "It sucked the air out of the room," said law Professor Henry Jordan. "She basically created a visual for the national boycott, showing that Americans are throwing away Brent Industries as a company they support. Brilliant, absolutely brilliant. And what makes it more amazing is that she obviously came up with it on the fly."

Court Channel senior commentator Ed Harrison agreed.

"Nothing says you're disgusted with a technology product more than dropping a two hundred dollar device into water. Even more impressive than simply throwing it in a wastebasket. How she came up with that out of a throwaway line by the judge is incredible. That image is now seared into the brain of everyone who saw it. It will be hard for opposing counsel to get those optics out of the minds of the jurors."

The rest of the day was almost anti-climactic, as McKenna paraded a batch of witnesses who gave glowing testimonials of Riggs as a brilliant inventor, manager and a person. Peter Brent's attorney, Spencer Capshaw, had little to gain through cross examination, and is obviously saving his attacks for Ms. Riggs, scheduled to take the stand today. He also declined comment at the end of the day.

Notable was that Ms. McKenna fished the device out of the pitcher at the end of the day, dried it off, and put it in her purse. Will it return on day two? Inquiring minds want to know.

Spencer couldn't help but laugh as he passed the newsstand.

The front page of every newspaper featured a photo of the device sitting in the water pitcher. The headlines jumped out in bold type.

Splish, Splash. Brent's Takin' a Bath…in Court

Attorney Gives Brent Cold Shower

Brent's Case Takes a Dive

He headed for Benny's cart, not seeing Tish and wondering what she might say if she happened to show up. Then again, she seemed so terrified of the media catching them in the same place, it was doubtful she would drop by at all.

Benny spotted him and studied his face. "You okay, Spence?"

"Yeah. Day two in hell."

"So I read. Brilliant strategy on her part, droppin' the thing in the water."

"She's an incredible lawyer, Benny. Has she, uh, been by today?"

"Yeah, trailed by about a dozen reporters. So we didn't have a chance to talk."

"How did she act?"

"Not at all like the woman we know. Honestly, she had a look that made me want to call a priest."

"The woman is passionate about her work."

"You're worried this is going to be a problem, aren't you?"

"It already is. Just when the relationship was really rolling it has to come to a screeching halt. It's like getting an ice cold shower, then having to sit ten feet away from her all day and not be able to talk to her."

"You can pick up where you left off after the trial is over."

"I hope so, Benny. I keep thinking about a trial I had years ago when I went up against a good friend. Things got ugly in court and he hasn't spoken to me since."

"Guess he wasn't that good of a friend. Tish will be okay. Besides, I have her ear. Don't worry, this will all be over and you two can have a nice Christmas together. Speaking of which, you got a gift for her?"

"I have several but not sure which one to give her. Everything went on the back burner when I got stuck with this trial. And now I'm not even sure what to do as far as a present is concerned."

"What do you mean?"

"Well, you know, sometimes a woman can get scared off if the gift is too extravagant. I wouldn't want to give her anything that would be too much. Or seem like I'm moving too fast."

"I don't think that's possible, Spence. I think you're old enough to know if your feelings are real. And how she feels about you."

"It's how she'll feel about me after the trial that worries me."

*

Spencer glanced at the clock as he chatted with the bailiff, having already run the gauntlet of media people outside the courthouse and in the hallway. He'd also arrived early, not wishing to be seen walking in with Peter Brent. While guilt by association was inevitable, giving the television cameras a little less might soften the blow.

The bailiff suddenly looked over Spence's shoulder. "Buh-dum. Buh-dum."

Spencer furrowed his brow. "Excuse me?"

"Bum bum bum bum…buh da daaaaaahhhhhh!"

"What the hell are you talking about?"

He cocked his head toward the door. "Great white shark at twelve o'clock. *Jaws* has entered the building."

He turned and saw Tish power-walking side by side with her client, head held high as her heel clicks echoed off the ancient white marble floor. She locked eyes with him but did not offer a smile or even the slightest bit of recognition. He opened the gate for them. "Good morning, Ms. McKenna. Ms. Riggs."

She gave him a slight nod. "Morning, Mr. Capshaw." Her client said nothing and looked away.

Peter Brent gave Spencer a gentle elbow at one minute to nine. "She put the thing back in the water." He pointed at the pitcher in front of Tish.

Sure enough, Tish had brought the viral image back into the courtroom for a return engagement. Spencer shrugged. "Whatever. That trick is already played."

"It looks bad. Ask the judge to make her take it out."

"I'm not—"

"I'm paying your firm a fortune. I want you to ask for it to be removed. Either that or I'll stand up and do it myself."

"And you'll piss off the judge. She got no tolerance for that kind of stuff."

"I don't care. Either you do it or I will. And if you don't I'll tell the media that you're not adequately representing me."

Spencer exhaled and rolled his eyes. "Fine, I'll bring it up."

"Damn right you will. Remember, you work for me."

Judge Winston brought the room to order at precisely nine o'clock. "Good morning everyone. Let's get started. Ms. McKenna, call your next witness."

Spencer stood up. "Your honor, before we begin today, may I bring up one point of order."

"Yes, Mr. Capshaw?"

"It has been brought to my attention that opposing counsel has placed the product central to this case back in her water pitcher. I think she made her point yesterday as evidenced by the fact a photo is on the front page of just about every newspaper in America. I would respectfully ask the court to direct Ms. McKenna to remove it."

The judge turned, slid her glasses down to the end of her nose and looked at the pitcher, then Tish. "Ms. McKenna, I believe Mr. Capshaw has a point in that you've made yours. Either remove it from the pitcher, or I'd better see you drinking some water from said pitcher."

Tish nodded, reached into the pitcher with two fingers and removed the device. "No problem, your honor." She slightly turned her head and glared at Spencer.

Brent smiled and leaned toward Spencer, whispering in his ear. "See, it worked. Just do as you're told."

*

Tish took the entire morning with Cynthia Riggs on the witness stand telling her story. Since she finished up just before noon, Judge Winston called for the lunch recess till one-thirty.

Spencer spent his entire lunch hour in the courtroom going over his notes. But mostly because he didn't want to be anywhere near Peter Brent and had no desire to face the media, which Brent was happy to accommodate at every opportunity.

At one-thirty sharp the judge entered the courtroom as the witness returned to the stand. "Your turn, Mr. Capshaw."

"Thank you, your honor." He got up and approached the witness, noting she had a white knuckle grip on her chair while the color had drained from her face. "Ms. Riggs, are you okay?"

"I'm really nervous. I'm sorry, but I'm shy and this is the first time I've ever been a witness."

"Well, nothing to apologize for. Take a breath, try to relax and take a drink of water. We're just going to have a conversation, okay. I'm not going to attack you. You're not Jack Nicholson and I'm not Tom Cruise yelling at you. You're Cynthia and I'm Spencer and this is not a court-martial."

The room filled with chuckles as the woman smiled and relaxed a bit, then took a drink of water. "Thank you."

"Okay, since we've already established that you're the inventor of the product and the defendant does not dispute that, we don't need to go over all that again. So let's talk about the whole basis of this lawsuit, work product." He handed her the sheet of paper. "I just gave you a standard Brent Industries contract. Is that your signature at the bottom?"

She looked at it. "Yes."

He started walking around the courtroom, then leaned casually on Tish's desk. He saw her glare at him in his peripheral vision. "Would you please read paragraph four for the jury. Just the first line will be fine."

"Sure. It says, anything produced while under the employ of Brent Industries is the property of Brent Industries."

"And by signing that contract when you first started working there, you agreed to that, correct?"

"Yes, but—"

"A yes or no is fine, Cynthia."

"I'm so sorry. Yes."

"Again, you're new at this, so nothing to apologize for. We're just having a polite conversation."

"Sure."

"Okay. Now, would you agree that you were under the employ of Brent Industries when you came up with the idea for this product?"

"Yes, but—"

"I just need a yes or no, so the yes was fine. And would you agree that you were under the employ of Brent Industries during the time you developed the product. Just a yes or no will suffice, Cynthia."

"Objection!" Tish stood up.

Judge Winston furrowed her brow as she looked at Tish. "What exactly are you objecting to, Ms. McKenna?"

"I would appreciate it if Mr. Capshaw would refer to my client as Ms. Riggs instead of acting like her friend and calling her Cynthia. He represents Peter Brent, who is definitely *not* her friend."

Spence nodded. "I apologize, your honor, and Ms. Riggs. I was trying to put the witness at ease."

"And I would appreciate it if he would lean on something other than my desk," said Tish.

Spence stood up. "Not a problem." He moved toward the jury box and leaned on the rail. "How's this?" He turned to the jury. "Do you guys have a problem with me over here?" He smiled at the jury and a few of them laughed. The transit worker slapped his thigh, and Spence couldn't help but notice the guy wore a gorgeous watch. *Guess he blows all his salary on jewelry.*

"Okay," said the Judge, "now that we've gotten rid of first names and the leaning arrangements, continue, Mr. Capshaw."

*

Tish stormed past Shelley into her office, jaw clenched, eyes narrowed, as she put her briefcase on a chair and started stacking cardboard file boxes next to the bookcase.

Shelley followed her into the office. "Good God, Tish, what happened?"

"I'll tell you what happened!" She continued stacking boxes. "Spence happened. I cannot *believe* what he did to my client."

"So…you're remodeling?"

"No, I'm blocking access to the air vent so Socks can't get to him. If he thinks he's going to spend time with my cat after that stunt he pulled, he's got another thing coming."

Shelley moved forward and took her hands. "Hey, calm down. Now take a deep breath, sit down and tell me what happened."

Tish plopped into the chair behind her desk as she tried to exhale her tension, then picked up Socks and put the cat on her lap. "I spend three hours questioning my client and then after lunch he starts cross-examining her. But he's polite to her. Calls her Cynthia and gets her to relax. Questions her for about fifteen minutes, never once yelling or acting like a jerk."

"I guess I'm missing the point. You're upset because he was respectful to your client and didn't ask a lot of questions?"

"Any other lawyer would have badgered the hell out of her and worn her down for hours. But he manages to make his point in a very short time. Then, and get this, while he's questioning her he leans on my desk."

"Oh, how awful. I can see why you're so upset."

"So I object and tell the judge he needs to stop calling her by her first name and lean somewhere else. So he goes over to the jury box, leans on the rail, flashes those big green eyes at the jury and smiles at them. You should have seen the look on this gorgeous twenty-year-old size four sitting in the front row because this is the first time he's gotten so close to the jury box. She actually licked her lips and looked like she wanted to devour him. Oh, and get this. I put the device back in the water pitcher before we started and he objects first thing and the judge makes me take it out."

Shelley nodded as she sat across from Tish. "So, let me get this straight. You're basically upset that your boyfriend did not beat up your client who is already seen as a victim by the entire country. What a lowlife. Meanwhile, in order to punish him for this heinous act you're suspending visitation rights with your cat."

Tish sulked and put out her lower lip as she scratched Socks under the chin. "It wasn't fair. I was expecting him to go after her with both barrels and instead he comes off as sympathetic. The jury likes him more than me."

"I see. And you *really* don't like hot babe jurors lusting after him."

"You shouldn't be flirting with the jury."

"Was he flirting with her?"

"No, he wasn't looking directly at her, just the whole jury. He's so damn cute with those gorgeous eyes and that boy-next-door persona I guess she couldn't resist. And it's not only her, but all the women on the jury. Even the older ones. It's like watching a damn episode of *The Bachelor*."

"So, recapping for those not scoring at home…You're so ticked off at a guy who happens to be your boyfriend for being nice to your client and attractive to beautiful women that you are going to deprive your cat from seeing someone she likes."

Tish looked down at Socks and lowered her voice. "He can get his own cat."

And then she heard it.

Spence shaking the bag of treats.

Socks perked up and Tish released her. "Go ahead, kitty, but you're not leaving this office. I'll get you some treats." Socks jumped from her lap, ran to the bookcase and was stopped by the tower of boxes. She turned back to Tish and meowed. "Sorry, kitty."

Socks heard the bag shake again, turned, made an amazing leap to the top box, then jumped down and disappeared into the vent.

"Sonofabitch!"

Shelley couldn't help but laugh. "Well, cats can jump real high. Who knew?"

*

Spencer had bolted from the courtroom without saying a word to Peter Brent as soon as they had adjourned for the weekend. He sneaked out the back door of the courthouse to avoid the media gauntlet and made it back to his office without being spotted.

He flipped on the TV and saw a video of Brent holding his usual daily news conference as he fed treats to Socks and played with her awhile. The cat took off after twenty minutes so he grabbed his coat to head off to the hospital to visit Ariel.

And walked right into Peter Brent entering his office. Not looking happy.

"We need to talk," said Brent.

"We can do that before you testify. Right now I'm going to see Ariel and I need to get there before visiting hours are over." He started out the door.

Brent put his hand on Spencer's chest, stopping him. "No, we're going to talk now."

"Fine, but first take your damn hand off me." He locked eyes with Brent, giving him a death stare. The man dropped his hand. "What's your problem now?"

"The way you treated Cynthia Riggs. How the hell did you let her off the hook like that?"

"I didn't let her off the hook. I got exactly what I wanted from her."

"She's a shy, sensitive woman. You should have beat the hell out of her."

"Right, let's take cheap shots at a single mother everyone sees as a victim."

"*She's* the victim? *I'm* the victim!"

"I can think of half a billion reasons why you're not."

"I want you to recall her."

"There's nothing left to ask. And that's not your call."

"I'm paying you—"

Spencer got in his face. "You either back off and let me handle this case my way or your wife is going to know about your affair."

The color instantly drained from Brent's face and his eyes grew wide.

Spencer flashed him a sinister grin. "Yeah, how about that, I actually vet my clients. So unless you want your wife to end up with two hundred and fifty million dollars and your favorability ratings to sink even lower, you will get off my case, stop telling me how to be a lawyer, shut the hell up and *you* will do what *you're* told in that courtroom. Am I clear?"

Brent slowly nodded. "Very."

"And by the way, for what it's worth, you're about the sleaziest damn client I've ever had—and that's saying something. Now get the hell out of my office, be at the courthouse at eight and in the meantime don't even think about calling me tonight."

*

Ariel muted the TV as she saw Spencer walk into her room. "I already heard from him right after things recessed, so I don't need the recap."

"From who?"

"Your least favorite client. He's not happy."

"He's really not happy now."

"Why, what happened?"

"He was ticked off that I didn't go hard after Cynthia Riggs."

"Right, he talked my ear off about that."

"But he won't be any more trouble now. I'm basically blackmailing him to get him to shut up."

She leaned up on one elbow. "Okay, this oughta be good."

"I told him if he didn't let me handle the case without his interference that I would tell his wife about his affair."

Ariel's eyes widened. "No kidding, he's cheating on Martha?"

"No, I just took a shot that he was. You'd told me his wife was a shrew and Kayla brought me a whole bunch of photos from that corporate trip with him surrounded by bikinis, so I put two and two together. Shoulda seen his face when I told him. He went white as a ghost."

"Damn, remind me never to play poker with you."

"Hey, a guy who's nearly a billionaire with a wife he can't stand on vacation with a bunch of bimbos hanging all over him. It wasn't exactly a stretch." Spence shook his head. "Still, the guy acts like he's bulletproof. Something's not right. And I need to figure out what it is."

Chapter Twenty-Five

Tish loaded her notes into her briefcase, ready for the inquisition of Peter Brent. It would be like shooting fish in a barrel. She had everything she needed.

Along with an assist from her cat.

She threw on a bulky green sweater and gathered up her files as Shelley tapped on her door. "Tish, Cynthia's here."

"Great. Tell her I'll be ready in five minutes."

Shelley's face tightened. "Seriously, you're wearing *that*?"

"What?"

"That sweater. You have the most impeccable wardrobe of any lawyer, and that looks like something worn by a cat lady."

Tish flashed a smile. "Exactly."

Shelley folded her arms. "Enlighten me on the method to your madness."

"I happened to read a profile on Peter Brent in which he talked about the fact that he always wanted a pet but was severely allergic to cats and dogs. Cats, in particular, made him itch like crazy, and when I'm home taking a nap I wrap myself in this thing and Socks curls up on top of me. This sweater is so loaded with cat dander it will make the guy squirm on the witness stand. Which

I fully intend to lean on." She picked up Socks and hugged her. "Gimme a fresh dose, kitty."

Shelley chuckled a bit. "Incredible. Using your cat to win a case. I have to admit, this is pretty good. I'm coming down to the courthouse to see this."

"And I've got a little payback for Spence. He's not the only one who can flirt."

"Sweetie, don't take this the wrong way, but flirting is not one of your skill sets. I'm not sure the jury will pick up on it."

"Oh, honey, it's not for the jury."

*

Tish stood up after Judge Winston started the proceedings. "We call Peter Brent."

Brent got up, looking confident with head held high, and headed toward the witness stand. He smiled at the jury, the same charming grin he always exhibited during his TV presentations. The bailiff administered the oath and he took a seat.

Tish approached him carrying a few sheets of paper. All of which had been rubbed against her cat dander loaded sweater. She went through the usual preliminary questions, getting Brent to go over his history, that of his company and the development of the product, all the while standing close to him. After a few minutes he started to scratch his neck. She had him recap the story of how he'd laughed at the idea and then loved the proto-type. After an hour of basic questions, she handed him a sheet of paper. "Mister Brent, is this a personnel review form that you give to all your employees?"

He took the paper and looked at it. "Yes."

"And who is this a review for?"

"Your client, Cynthia Riggs."

"You rank your employees from one to ten on various catego-ries, with ten being the highest grade, correct?"

228

"That is correct."

"Things like attitude, punctuality, quality of work, ability to get along with co-workers."

"Right."

"And what was Ms. Riggs' score on her very first review that you're holding now?"

He looked at the paper. "All tens." He scratched his hand.

Tish handed him another sheet. "One year later, what were her scores?"

"All tens."

She went through this eight more times. "Okay, so far she's gotten nothing but perfect scores from you. Here's her last review. I'll save you the trouble of telling everyone she got all tens again. But I'd like you to read what you wrote on the bottom of the sheet."

He took the paper and suddenly his face started to twitch a bit. He scratched it as he read, his voice lowered to a whisper. "Cynthia continues to be a spectacular employee. She turns out—"

"I'm sorry Mr. Brent, we can't hear you. Speak up. And please start over."

He raised his voice to a normal level. "Cynthia continues to be a spectacular employee. She turns out incredible work and her staff has nothing but good things to say about her. The best department manager in the company."

Then he fidgeted in his seat, reached inside his jacket and scratched his chest. His eyes began to get watery.

"And then, after all those perfect reviews, calling her spectacular and the best manager you had, you demoted her."

"She suddenly became a problem employee."

"Why was that, Mr. Brent?"

"She kept bugging me because I wouldn't pay for her invention or give her a share of the profits."

"And you didn't just demote her, you put her on a shift that made it impossible for her to care for her child. You did know she was a single parent, correct?"

229

"Yes."

She handed him a bunch of greeting cards. "And you knew the age of her daughter, since these are birthday cards signed by you that you gave to her daughter. With personal notations in them. You gave these to her daughter when you attended her birthday parties, correct?"

He looked at the cards and nodded. "Yes."

"And you therefore knew that this change in her schedule to the overnight shift would really play havoc with her parenting"

"It was the only place to put her without firing her."

Tish nodded. "Ah, that's right, you didn't fire her. You made her miserable and impossible to be a good parent so she'd quit."

"Her resignation was her own decision." He shifted in his seat again and scratched his neck. His face began to twitch even more. "She could have continued working for us."

"Now, Mr. Gekko…"

"My name is Brent."

"Sorry. I was watching the movie *Wall Street* last night and you remind me of the Michael Douglas character."

"Objection!" Spence jumped up. "Your honor, she's comparing Mr. Brent to the villain in a famous movie."

"Sorry, your honor," said Tish. "*Wall Street* was on TV last night and I couldn't help but notice the similarities."

Spence threw up his hands. "She just did it again."

The judge turned to Tish. "Ms. McKenna, watch yourself. However, since you have been exemplary in my court in the past, I will cut you some slack on this since *Wall Street* was on channel eleven last night and I watched it."

Tish nodded. "I apologize, your honor." She turned back to Brent who again had his hand inside his jacket scratching his chest. "You okay, Mr. Brent? You look uncomfortable."

"New shirt. A little itchy."

"Sure, let's go with that. Now, Mr…*Brent*. How much money has your company made from Ms. Riggs' invention?"

"I don't—"

"Let me rephrase…how much has your own net worth increased since the invention hit the market."

"I don't have an exact number."

She handed him a bunch of clippings from various publications. "These newspaper and magazine articles estimate the increase in your bank account between three and four hundred million. Are we in the ballpark?"

At this point it was all she could do not to laugh since Brent was now squirming in his seat looking like he was covered in itching powder. "Sounds about right."

She pointed at his pants. "Guess that's a new pair of slacks too, huh?" The crowd chuckled a bit.

"Your honor, please," said Spence.

"Get back to your questioning, Ms. McKenna."

"Certainly, Judge Winston. Mr. Brent, how much money have you paid Cynthia Riggs for her invention?"

"I didn't owe her a dime. It was work product."

"In other words, you paid her *zero*. Not a penny. And you got a few hundred million dollars. As you would say, *sounds about right*." She turned to walk toward Spence, then pulled a handkerchief from her pocket and removed her glasses, at the same time using her thumb to knock her hair clip from her head. The clip fell off and hit the floor, sending her hair down to her shoulders. She crouched down in front of Spence to get it, tossing her hair a bit as she locked eyes with him.

He mouthed one word.

Whoa.

She shot him a slight smile from the floor that no one else could see, then got up, put her hair clip in her pocket and started to clean her glasses. "Your witness," she said to him, in the sultriest voice she could muster.

He sat there, staring at her, jaw hanging slightly open.

She headed back to her own table and took a seat.

231

Spence was still sitting there.

"Mr. Capshaw, you're up," said the judge.

He didn't move, still staring at Tish.

"Earth to Mr. Capshaw!"

He jolted back to reality. "Sorry, your honor, I was organizing my thoughts and didn't think Ms. McKenna would finish so quickly."

"Well, organize them on your own time. Tick tock, Mr. Capshaw. Let's rock."

An hour later she could see the frustration on his face. To the untrained eye he had done fine questioning Peter Brent, but she knew better having previously seen him in action. He had gotten flustered, off his game. That one little look with her eyes which were his Kryptonite had thrown him for a loop. At times he seemed to be lost searching for the right question.

And through it all she kept her glasses off. Every time Spence happened to look at her he turned into a lovesick puppy.

That should even out his flirting with the jury.

Brent was now squirming in his chair like crazy, looking uncomfortable in his own skin.

Thank you, Socks. You're now an associate in my law firm.

And as she thought of the cat, she got another idea just as Spence wrapped up his questioning of Peter Brent.

Tish stood up. "Re-direct, your honor."

"Proceed."

She walked toward Peter Brent. "So, Mr. Brent, bottom line, anything that your employees bring into your office belongs to you, does that about sum things up?"

He nodded. "Yes."

"Even if they are the personal property of the employee."

"The prototype was not her personal property."

"That's up to the jury to decide, Sir. Let me put it to you another way. Let's say you go home to your mansion one night—"

232

"Objection. We've already established that Mr. Brent is wealthy."

The judge nodded. "Sustained. Go ahead, Ms. McKenna."

"Let's say you go *home* one night and you're outside sitting on your porch when this stray cat walks up to you. It's a nice cat, rubs against your leg, purrs. Since you like animals you wonder if it's hungry. But you don't have your own cat and therefore no cat food, so you give it a can of tuna. The cat eats the food and goes on its merry way. The cat starts showing up every night so next time you're in the store you pick up a bag of cat treats, maybe even a catnip mouse so you can play with the cat."

Spence stood up. "Your honor, is there a question remotely in our future?"

The judge turned to Tish. "Move it along, Ms. McKenna. Though I have no clue where you're going with this."

"I'll get there shortly, your honor. Anyway, Mr. Brent, you start to think of it as your cat and all of a sudden realize it belongs to your neighbor. But you've been feeding it and playing with the little furball for weeks. So is it now your cat?"

Brent furrowed his brow. "I'm not sure what you're getting at."

"Does the cat now belong to you?"

"No, of course not."

"So, when Cynthia Riggs brings her *pet project* into your office, that's different."

"Of course. You can't compare an invention to a stray cat."

"But both the invention and cat are properties of the owner. Now, let's say the owner of the cat is getting upset that you're trying to steal the kitty by bribing it with treats—"

Spence got up again. "Objection! Giving someone else's cat a little food does not constitute stealing it. And treats are not a bribe. They are a reward for being a good cat."

Tish turned to him. "Oh, but they're high end expensive treats that the cat absolutely loves and now she's got someone else to pamper her and entertain her with a bunch of cat toys. He's luring her in."

He started moving toward her. "He's not *luring* her because he loves little animals. Maybe he happens to like this particular cat. And here's a wild concept…maybe the cat likes him as much as the owner."

Tish narrowed her eyes at Spence. "Maybe the guy should get his own damn cat."

"Maybe he would get his own damn cat if he weren't so damn busy. And I would think the cat's owner would be happy that someone else is being nice to her pet. Perhaps he might have even bought an ID tag for her collar in case she got lost since the owner forgot to do it."

She folded her arms. "Maybe the owner was too busy—"

Bang!

The sound of the judge's gavel brought the argument to a screeching halt. "Okay, enough with the cat metaphors or whatever the hell this is. Thirty minute recess and I want to see both attorneys in my chambers. Now."

*

Tish looked down at the ground as she stood next to Spence in the judge's chambers. Neither said a word as they waited for her. Finally, she entered the room, closed the door and took a seat behind her desk. "Okay, what the hell is going on with you two?"

Tish looked up at her. "Your honor, I'm just trying to do my best for my client—"

"Oh, bull." She leaned back and looked at the two of them. "It just hit me while you two were having your cat argument. You guys fight like a couple. You're in a relationship."

They both looked away for a moment.

"I'll take that as a yes." The judge rolled her eyes. "Good Lord, can this trial get any stranger? Why the hell didn't you tell me before we got started?"

"I wanted to," said Spence, "but Tish wouldn't let me."

Tish nodded. "Your honor, if I'd told you then you'd take him off the case and Brent would have gotten the delay he wanted. I couldn't do that to my client who, as you know, doesn't have any more time to wait. I didn't want to face the man I...my boyfriend in court. But I had no other choice."

Judge Winston shook her head. "Hell, talk about a no-win situation. But I need to know about this relationship. You two living together?"

Spence shook his head. "No, your honor. We've been dating a few months."

"So...have you two—"

"Not yet," came the response in unison.

The judge leaned back and smiled. "Interesting that you answered in stereo with a *yet* at the end. Which means you're going to."

Tish blushed like never before. "Your honor, we haven't seen each other socially since the trial started. We didn't want the media to know."

"Well, thank God you were both smart enough for that. Now what the hell is the deal with this argument about cats?"

Tish told her the story of Socks. "I thought using it would be a good way to illustrate how Brent stole the invention."

Spence turned to her. "You shouldn't bring our personal lives into the courtroom. If the judge picked up on it others might have as well. And *I'm* not trying to steal your cat."

"But *you're* not playing fair in this trial."

"This from the woman who compared my client to a movie villain. And what the hell did *I* do?"

She moved closer, hands on her hips. "You know damn well what you did." She turned to the judge and started waving her arms. "He acts like my client's friend, being nice to her. Then he leans on the jury box and uses that boy-next-door thing he's got going with the tousled hair, the beautiful olive green eyes and that sweet smile which makes your heart flutter, acting like the greatest guy in the world. And all the women melt." She looked sideways at Spence. "Especially that stacked brunette in the front row who is way too young for you but has been staring at you during the whole trial."

The judge laughed a bit. "Ms. McKenna, do you even hear yourself?"

Spence turned to Tish. "I would not have been leaning on the jury box if you hadn't complained about me leaning on your table. And I did not flirt with the jury, your honor."

"I agree," said the judge.

Tish rolled her eyes. "Oh, come on judge, he's damn cute with a killer personality, he knows it and he's using it against me."

Spence turned to her. "Oh, and I suppose that little trick you pulled on me this morning was fair?"

The judge furrowed her brow. "What little trick?"

"She took off her glasses!"

The judge threw up her hands. "Okay, now I'm totally confused. How the hell is that a trick?"

Spence pointed at Tish with both hands. "Look at her, your honor. She's got these spectacular eyes and she knows that I'm powerless against her when she takes off her glasses and gives me that seductive look. Then in that sultry voice of hers she says *your witness* sounding like a phone sex call. Then, and oh, this was *soooo* well done that *no one* in the courtroom could see it but me, her hair clip *conveniently* falls out when she takes off her glasses, so when she bends down to get it she shakes out her gorgeous honey blonde hair like she's in a damn shampoo commercial. I'm surprised she hadn't set up electric fans to blow it around and that it wasn't in slow motion."

The judge slowly nodded. "Ah, now I get it. Every man's fantasy with a woman like her."

Tish's face tightened. "What do you mean, *a woman like me?*"

"Totally professional look, all buttoned up, ultra conservative, like the cliché prim and proper librarian who takes off her glasses, lets her hair down and reveals herself to be gorgeous."

Tish wrinkled her nose. "You think I look like a librarian?"

"She didn't say that," said Spence. "You missed the whole point."

Tish whipped her head toward him. "I wasn't asking *you.*"

"The judge said you were gorgeous, if you'd bother to listen. Then again, you've never been able to take a compliment. It's your only fault."

The judge snickered a bit. "You guys should have your own reality show. The Kardashians have nothing on you two."

Tish stood up straight and stuck her nose in the air. "Judge Winston, I would appreciate it if you would ask Mr. Capshaw not to flirt with the jury during closing arguments."

Spence shook his head. "Again, I didn't flirt. And Judge Winston agrees with me."

"Then stop being so damn attractive!"

"What would you like me to do, put a bag over my head? Blindfold the jury? Oh, how about this…I'll get a bullhorn and deliver my closing argument from the hall."

Tish turned back to the judge. "He's using his appeal with the women on the jury against me. He's beyond cute and he knows it."

Spence was still looking at her. "You're beyond beautiful and you *don't* know it. But the men on the jury sure do." He turned to the judge and pointed at her. "See, not even a smile. Can't take a compliment. I rest my case."

The judge waved her hands. "Okay, enough. I don't care that Mr. Capshaw is attractive to the female jurors and it doesn't matter if Ms. McKenna wants to leave her glasses off to distract her opponent. And by the way, Ms. McKenna, he's right, I have caught a few of the male jurors staring at you, so it's a two-way street."

"Men don't stare at me, your honor. They never have."

"There it is again," said Spence. "I think she must have one of those circus mirrors in her house that makes everyone look ugly. You should see her on a date, Judge. I tell her she looks beautiful and she disagrees with me, says she's nothing special."

The judge laughed a bit, leaned forward and folded her hands. "Okay, stop it. I do have a few last questions and I don't want to hear any arguing, and I only want to hear from one of you at a time. Now, Ms. McKenna, while you two were dating, did Mr. Capshaw treat you well?"

The question took the steam out of her and she exhaled some tension. She looked down at the floor and answered in a soft voice. "He treated me like a queen, your honor."

"Only because you deserve it," said Spence.

Tish bit her lower lip.

"And Mr. Capshaw, did she treat you well?"

He slowly nodded. "She's as classy as she looks, your honor. And it's kinda nice that she has no clue she's beautiful. The opposite of high maintenance."

"Every man's dream, huh? I guess along with the librarian thing you've got no shot, Mr. Capshaw. Anyway, back to the problem at hand. Here's what's going to happen, and so help me if either of you deviates from this you're both going to spend tonight in a cell, and not together. You two are going to take a deep breath, go back to the courtroom and Ms. McKenna will wrap up her cat question or whatever the hell it is in less than sixty seconds. Then we're going to adjourn for the day so you both can calm down before closing arguments."

"Yes, your honor," they said in unison.

The judge stood up. "Oh, since I was a lawyer before I was a judge, one last thing about attorneys dating other attorneys."

"You don't have to tell us it's a bad idea," said Tish.

The judge held up her left hand revealing a wedding band. "On the contrary. For me it's been the best fourteen years of my life."

She started to leave the room, then stopped. "Oh, Ms. McKenna?"

"Yes?"

"Mr. Capshaw said you wouldn't let him tell me you were in a relationship. Good job getting him trained to obey already. You're way ahead of the curve on that timeline."

*

Spencer simply wanted to get as comfortable as possible when he returned to his office after dinner. He swapped out his dress shirt for a sweatshirt, took off his watch, and kicked off his shoes. The closing argument needed some polish.

But he wanted to see Socks before he got going. He needed the cat for a little while after such a stressful day. The confrontation with Tish had worn him out emotionally. And the image of her taking off her glasses and shaking out her hair was burned into his brain, making it impossible to concentrate.

He shook the bag of treats, poured a few in a bowl and Socks appeared a minute later. She quickly devoured them and then made a leap onto his desk. Spence scratched her under the chin. "Your ears must have been burning today, kitty. We talked about you in court."

Socks suddenly spotted his antique watch sitting on the desk and took a swat at it. Spence quickly grabbed it and put it in a drawer. "Whoa, that's expensive. Not a cat toy."

And then it hit him.

What he'd seen when he leaned on the jury box.

The transit worker…

His eyes went wide as his jaw dropped. "I'll be a sonofabitch. The damn Kobayashi Maru. Brent is changing the rules of the game. He thinks he's Captain Kirk."

He picked up the phone to call the private investigator, then shook out a few more treats on his desk. "Socks, you're a genius. You may have just saved another life."

Chapter Twenty-Six

"Trust me, I guarantee you'll be sleeping in your own bed on Christmas Eve." Angelo the contractor smiled at Tish as he led her and her friends through the construction work of her new and improved house. "Actually, we're done with the living room and dining room so if you want to put up a tree and decorate we'll get our equipment out of the way."

Tish shook her head. "Not really in the mood this year."

Madison took her arm. "*You* don't want to decorate for Christmas? You live for this time of year."

"Really, Tish, we'll help," said A.J. "I realize it's just a week away but we can get it done. C'mon, let's put up your tree."

Rory agreed. "It will get you in a better mood."

Tish looked at the floor. "Somehow I don't feel like celebrating."

*

Spencer leaned back in the chair next to Ariel's hospital bed on Saturday night as they watched the movie while sharing a pastrami sandwich from the deli. "I think I'd almost like to switch places with you."

She took a sip of creme soda. "Trust me, one day of this hospital

240

food and you'd be begging to switch back. Thank you so much for smuggling this in."

"Got tiramisu for dessert."

"My kind of *get well* card." She studied his face. "You look like you need to be in bed yourself."

"I'm totally fried. Between the case being dumped on me at the last minute and all the stuff going on in the courtroom with Tish, I just want to curl up, go to sleep, and then wake up from this nightmare."

"Well, it's in the hands of the jury so it won't be long now. I cannot imagine they'll deliberate very long."

"They'd better come back with a verdict before Christmas."

"I'm sure they want it to be over as well. Speaking of the holidays, what are you going to do about the gifts you have for Tish? Or are you going to get something else in light of recent developments?"

"Sticking with the last one I bought. Going with my gut."

"I think she'll love it. And hopefully it will help her put all this behind you guys."

"I really miss being with her, Ariel."

"I'm sure she misses you. And I'm sorry I'm not the most exciting date for a Saturday night."

"Hey, you're important to me too."

"I know. And so are you." Ariel took another bite of her sandwich. "Oh, anything new from Kayla?"

He shook his head. "Not yet. And we're running out of time."

"Well, if there's anything to your suspicion, that woman will find it."

*

Tish poked at her food as Christmas carols filled the air of the restaurant.

A.J. elbowed her in the ribs. "Hey, Mrs. Grinch, you gonna sit

241

there all night looking like you got coal in your stocking?"

She looked up and smiled. "Sorry, guys, I don't mean to be a wet blanket. It just feels like this was going to be the perfect Christmas and this damn trial has ruined everything."

Madison looked at her from across the table. "How has it ruined everything? What's actually changed between you and Spence? He's still the same great guy."

"Working against him in court…he acts like I'm just another lawyer."

Rory took her arm. "Well, in court you are. And you guys can't let the media think otherwise or the whole thing will blow up in your face."

"He's done an amazing job defending Brent…It's just surprising to see him working for a sleazeball and presenting such a solid case. I dunno, it's sort of guilt by association. And when he objects to something I do, I take it personally. I can't help it that I get so focused. He's such a damn good lawyer."

"You have to separate your boyfriend from the lawyer," said Madison. "You know damn well Spence doesn't want to be involved in this case, so don't blame him. And you wouldn't want him to let you win."

"Well, beyond the fact that he's doing such a great job…the other problem is the jury absolutely loves him. Why does he have to be so damn charming and cute?"

"Because he *is* charming and cute," A.J. said. "Big part of the reason you love him."

"I haven't said I love him."

Madison rolled her eyes. "Yeah, big news flash. Sweetie, you've been in love with him for a while. Have you already forgotten what you engraved on his Christmas gift? And speaking of which, are you going to give it to him?"

"I haven't decided."

A.J. shook her head. "Grinch."

"I'm not a Grinch!"

"No tree, no decorations, maybe no gift for your boyfriend. You ain't exactly Kris Kringle, honey. Get off your ass and get in the Christmas spirit."

Chapter Twenty-Seven

Christmas Eve

Spencer handed Benny an envelope and a bottle of scotch with a red bow on it. "Merry Christmas, Benny."

"Hey, thanks." He looked at the bottle. "Oooh, the good stuff."

"I figured you deserved a little something extra for introducing me to Tish."

"Part of my job."

"Speaking of your job, I hope you're not here all day."

"Nah. Once I'm done with the morning coffee crowd I'm heading home. We do a big Christmas Eve dinner. I'm surprised you're working today."

"Well, one of the courthouse workers who takes food to the jurors told me it sounded like they might be close to a verdict, so I'm going to hang around. And the judge told me to be available just in case. It would be great to get this damn case out of the way for the holidays."

"No kidding. Speaking of which, you give Tish her present yet?"

"No. I was hoping to do it after the verdict but since we're out of time I'll give it to her tonight regardless."

"I thought you weren't going to see each other till the case was over?"

"It's Christmas Eve, Benny. And I've got a plan. Which involves a cat."

*

Tish headed across the street trailing a suitcase and a gift. Benny looked up and smiled. "You're finally outta there?"

"Yep. They finished up the work on my house yesterday. Just in time."

"You'll be home for Christmas, just like the song. What a nice gift."

She handed him a beautifully wrapped present. "A little something for you, Benny, for being such a good friend to me these past few weeks."

"You didn't have to do that, but I'll take it. So, I understand there might be a verdict today."

"Huh? Where did you hear that?"

"A certain source."

"Oh."

"Speaking of a certain source, you give him his gift yet?"

She shook her head. "No. Not sure what to do about that, Benny."

"Not much point in going through all the trouble you did and then not give it to him."

"It's complicated, Benny."

"No, Tish *formerly* from the hotel, it's not."

She looked down and didn't respond.

"Anyway, young lady, I hope you have a Merry Christmas. And you know how to make that happen."

*

Spencer shoved his way through the horde of media people without saying a word as he quickly headed to the courtroom.

245

The jury was back. Obviously they wanted to be home for Christmas Eve as well.

He found Brent already in the courtroom, smiling and shaking hands with some of the people who had come to support him.

Tish was seated at her table next to her client. She looked up as he arrived. "Morning, Mr. Capshaw."

"Morning, Ms. McKenna. Ms. Riggs."

She locked eyes with him for a brief moment, then turned back to her client.

The jury filed into the courtroom and took their seats. Judge Winston turned to face them. "Ladies and gentlemen of the jury, have you reached a verdict?"

The foreman stood up. "We have, your honor."

"What say you?"

Spencer closed his eyes and said a quick prayer.

*Please God, let me lose this one...it's all I want for Christmas...
Along with Tish...*

"In the matter of Cynthia Riggs versus Peter Brent and Brent Industries...we, the jury, find for the defendant, Peter Brent."

Spencer opened his eyes as his jaw dropped.

You gotta be kidding.

He looked at Tish, whose face went ashen. Her client's sobs filled the courtroom. He stood up, ready to head in her direction when Brent patted him on the shoulder and shook his hand.

"Great job, Spencer. I never should have doubted you."

"Uh-huh."

"Merry Christmas."

He was about to tell Brent to go to hell when he saw the man look toward the jury and smile.

He got several grins back in return.

The courtroom emptied quickly as the media people had

reports to file so they could get home for Christmas like everyone else.

Tish still sat there, stunned and seemingly in shock.

When the room had cleared out he walked over to her. "Tish… I—"

"Not now, Spence."

"Listen, I'm sorry—"

She turned to face him, those spectacular eyes filled with pain. "You should take Benny's advice right now."

He slowly nodded. "I understand. I'll be around the office all day if you want to talk."

She said nothing, wiped away a tear and turned away.

Spencer started to wish her a Merry Christmas but it didn't seem right. He headed toward the side door to avoid the reporters, then saw Kayla quickly walking in his direction, carrying a large manila envelope. "Spence, am I too late?"

"Verdict just came in. They ruled for Brent."

"Dammit."

"Why, waddaya got?"

"The proof you needed." She handed him the envelope.

Spencer opened it and took a look at the photos and documents. "Maybe it's not too late."

*

The bailiff walked out into the courtroom a few hours later. "Ms. McKenna, I thought you were still here."

"Sorry, I know I need to clear out. I'm still in shock over the verdict and I can't bear to face the media. I know they're still out there and they've got the back door covered. I needed a place to hide."

"Anyway, Judge Winston wants to see you."

"Huh?"

He shrugged. "She said it's important."

Tish gently tapped on Judge Winston's open door and saw she was on the phone. The judge pointed to a chair in front of her desk and she took a seat.

"Bill, I appreciate you doing this on Christmas Eve," said the judge. "I'll be around all day. I'm not gonna miss this. Talk later." She hung up and smiled at Tish. "That was the Manhattan District Attorney."

"Okay…"

"He's on his way to arrest Peter Brent."

"Excuse me?"

The judge handed her a manila envelope. "He bribed the jury, Ms. McKenna. And we've got proof."

Tish opened the envelope and saw photos of a man in a jewelry store along with a whole bunch of receipts. "I don't understand. Who is this?"

"Mr. Brent's executive assistant buying a bunch of Rolex watches and other ridiculously priced pieces of jewelry for the members of the jury. Then giving them out. Along with receipts."

"How did you get this?"

"You know that transit worker on the jury, the guy in the front row? Someone noticed he was wearing a twenty thousand dollar Rolex and did a little poking around."

"So where did these photos and documents come from?"

"Not exactly sure. Mr. Capshaw brought them to me. He said a woman handed the envelope to him after the trial."

"A woman?"

"He said he didn't know who she was, but she asked him to bring this to me."

"Mr. Capshaw did this."

"Yep."

"And he didn't know who she was?"

"That's what he said. And I don't care."

"Who spotted the juror with the expensive watch?"

"Beats me. I wouldn't know a real Rolex from one of those

248

fifty dollar knockoffs they sell on the street. Guess it was someone who knows things about watches."

"Yeah, you would have to know about watches."

"Anyway, a bunch of jurors were hanging around doing interviews with reporters. I gave this stuff to a detective and he got a few of them to flip on Brent."

"Too bad we didn't have this earlier."

"Well, all is not lost, Ms. McKenna. I've scheduled a news conference in an hour. I'm setting aside the verdict and giving the judgment to your client, in the amount of one hundred million dollars, and ordering the patent to be transferred to her name. So she's free to sell it to whatever company wants to buy it. You're welcome to join me. In fact, I'd appreciate it if you would. And bring your client. This is nothing short of a Christmas miracle."

Tish sat there, jaw hanging open, speechless.

"Well, Ms. McKenna, say something."

"I don't know what to say. I'm stunned."

"Well, then, go say something to your client and get her back down here. She just got the world's best Christmas gift."

Chapter Twenty-Eight

Spencer kept an eye on the television as he watched the live news conference with Tish, her client and Judge Winston taking questions.

Tish was positively beaming, back to the girlfriend he knew.

Kayla's investigative abilities had saved the day.

The video of Peter Brent being hauled away in handcuffs had made his day.

Now it was time for his plan to come together.

He attached the gold locket to Socks' collar and put the cat down next to the air vent. "Okay, go home. Don't fail me now, kitty."

*

Shelley greeted Tish with a strong hug as she returned to the office. "Congratulations! I can't believe it! I'm so happy for you."

"I can't believe it either. Talk about a gift from out of the blue."

"Well, it is Christmas."

"What are you still doing here, Shelley? Go home, enjoy the holidays."

"I was waiting for you. Also waiting for you is your cat, who apparently has picked up some bling."

"Huh?"

Shelley cocked her head toward Tish's office. "Go take a look."

Tish headed into the office finding Socks at her usual post on the desk. She noticed an old, worn, gold heart-shaped charm hanging from the cat's collar. "What the heck is this?"

Shelley smiled at her. "It's one of those old fashioned lockets."

"Did you put it on her?"

"Nope."

"Where did it come from?"

Shelley folded her arms and rolled her eyes. "Where do you think?"

Tish examined the locket. "It's got a little clasp." She pressed it and the locket opened. A small slip of paper fell out. Tish unfolded it as Shelley looked over her shoulder.

Observation Deck. 6pm. I will wait 15 minutes.

-Spence

Tish turned to Shelley. "Did he come by and put this on the cat?"

"Nope."

"Are you in on this?"

"Tish, why do you have to analyze everything to death? Just go to the observation deck at six. And claim the Christmas gift you really want more than anything."

The bitter cold air smacked Tish in the face as the elevator doors opened. The Empire State Building observation deck was closed earlier than usual for Christmas Eve, but the building super had taken her up to the top. She pulled her coat tight as she stepped out and saw Spence, looking out at the skyline. "Hey."

He turned and smiled at her. "Tish. You came."

She headed toward him. "Of course I came. I guess the media can't see us up here."

"Not why I chose this as a meeting place."

"I, uh, can't thank you enough for what you did today. I guess I'll never be able to thank you enough."

"What did I do?"

"Oh, a certain person who knows about watches brings a big envelope of evidence to a judge given to him by a woman he didn't know. Right, that couldn't be you."

"The point is justice was done and you saved your client."

"I think *you* saved my client. I lost, remember?"

"The jury was rigged. You kicked my ass in court."

"I wouldn't say that. I think we were even." She looked out at the skyline, so beautiful under a full moon on a crystal clear night. "So thank you for the incredible Christmas present. And you have no idea how Cynthia feels. You saved her life."

"Now *that* makes my day. Anyway, I have a little something else for you. But I wanted to ask you something first."

"Go ahead."

"When Judge Winston figured out we were in a relationship and asked why you didn't tell her, you said, *I didn't want to face the man I…*and then you stopped and said *my boyfriend*. I was curious as to how you were going to finish your original thought."

She moved closer, locked eyes with him. "I could ask you the same question."

"Huh?"

"When the Judge first assigned you to the case you pulled me into a meeting room across the hall and said *I can't go up against a woman I'm in…*then you stopped and said *I just can't*. What was *your* original thought?"

"I asked you first."

"But I've already got you trained, according to the judge. So answer me or I'll take off my glasses."

He slowly nodded. "Okay, well, I might have intended to say I can't go up against a woman I'm in…a relationship with."

"Is that what you were going to say?"

"I said *might*. But that was not what I was thinking. Your turn."

"Well, I might have intended to say I didn't want to face the man I…have been dating for a while."

"Is that what you were going to say?"

"I said *might*. However, that was not what I was thinking either."

"I see. Tell you what, how about I give you your Christmas present first and then we *might* be able to resolve these two mysteries." He pulled a small box from his pocket, then dropped it. "Aw, hell." He knelt down to get it, then opened the box and held it up to her. "That answer your question?"

Her eyes bugged out at the diamond ring, a gorgeous emerald cut in a silver antique setting. "Whoa."

"That's *my* line."

"I mean…*whoa*. My God, Spence, it's gorgeous."

"Matches the woman I want to wear it."

"I'm not gor—"

"Stop! For once in your life, will you *please* simply say *thank you* when I give you a compliment?"

She kept staring at the ring.

"So, Tish from the hotel, how about you give me an answer by finishing your sentence? And do it quick, because I'm down here on ice cold concrete and my knee is about to lock up."

Her eyes welled up as she looked at him. The words grew thick in her throat. "I was going to tell the judge…I didn't want to face the man I loved."

"Funny, I was going to finish my sentence in a similar fashion."

"You really love me, Spence?"

"No, I was saving this for the woman on the jury who's too young for me." He stood up, slipped the ring on her finger, took off her glasses and gave her a long, soft kiss. "Again, she's brilliant in the courtroom, clueless outside of it."

Tish held out her hand, admiring the sparkles as it reflected the beams of the moon and the lights from the skyline. He couldn't have picked a more romantic spot. "I'm not clueless. I'm going to marry the man I love." She slid one arm around his waist and led him to the elevator. "C'mon, my dear fiancé, much as I love the current setting and having it all to ourselves, it's freezing up here. Let's go home and warm up by the fire."

"My apartment doesn't have a fireplace. I guess we can turn the heat up and watch the Yule Log on TV."

"Oh, that's right, you don't know. My house is ready. I checked out of the hotel this morning. So let's go get Socks and head home. *Our* home."

Epilogue

Tish's heart rate kicked up as she and Spence turned onto her street. She poked her finger through the grate on the pet carrier sitting on her lap. "Almost home for good, kitty." She smiled at Spence. "Applies to you too, if you want to live here instead of an apartment."

"Sounds good to me. Which house is yours?"

"That's right, you've never been here. Turn right. Last house on the left. Number 479."

"Okay. Now close your eyes."

"Huh?"

"Just cover your eyes for a minute till we get there."

"Okay." She put her hands over her eyes and felt the car move, then slow down a minute later. "Can I look now?"

"Yep."

She took her hands away and what she saw filled her with joy. Her house was fully decorated for Christmas. "Oh my God, did you do this?"

"I cannot take credit. Madison, A.J. and Rory said you loved Christmas and wouldn't decorate, so they did it for you."

"It looks spectacular. What a wonderful surprise. This night just keeps getting better and better."

"C'mon, let's get you and Socks inside." He opened the door for her and led her up the walk.

"This is so beautiful. I can't wait to thank them." She opened the front door and was greeted by the sight of a Christmas tree filled with ornaments and twinkling white lights. "They did the tree too?"

"I would have helped, but as you probably know, men can't decorate."

"This is really special." She placed the pet carrier on the ground and opened the door. Socks stepped out, slowly checking out the surroundings. "You're home, kitty. Don't you recognize the place?"

"She's probably never seen a Christmas tree."

"Luckily it's artificial or she'd try to climb it."

Socks walked over to the tree and swatted at an ornament on a low branch. "Okay, I guess we have to do a little re-decorating."

Tish cracked open one eye and saw Socks in the bedroom window, watching the large snowflakes fall. She leaned up and looked out at the scene which resembled a Currier and Ives Christmas card.

She rolled over and saw the other side of the bed was empty.

Then she heard the coffee machine gurgling.

She got up, decided to put on Spence's oxford shirt and headed to the kitchen.

Spence was already there, setting two cups on the table. "Morning, sunshine. Merry Christmas. And I like the outfit."

She walked over to him, threw her arms around him and gave him a strong hug. "Merry Christmas, fiancé."

"I like the sound of that. Though wife will be even better." The coffee pot beeped, he fixed two cups and handed one to Tish. "C'mon, let's go sit in the living room, enjoy the tree and watch the snow fall. It's beautiful."

"No argument here." She headed into the living room, then

what she saw under the tree stopped her in her tracks. "What the hell? What's all this stuff under the tree?"

"They're called presents."

"Where did they come from?"

"Well, it wasn't Santa. You were way too naughty last night to make his list."

She crouched down next to the tree to take a closer look. "So you did all this?"

"I got A.J. to hide them in your closet. I got up in the middle of the night and put them out."

"All this stuff is for me?"

"Yeah. Well, except for that basket of cat stuff for Socks. I didn't wrap it since I knew she wouldn't care."

"You didn't have to get me all these gifts. My God, the engagement ring was more than enough."

"Well, when we were first dating I figured I needed to get you something for Christmas so I started out with something small and not too forward. Then as our relationship got stronger I kept getting upgrades. So you can follow the progression if you open them left to right."

"You continue to amaze me. All this for me." And then it dawned on her. "Well, I do have one gift for you, but I didn't have the chance to wrap it yet."

"I don't care. Bring it on. But I already got what I wanted for Christmas. You."

"Awww." She grabbed her purse from a chair, reached inside, and pulled out a small square box. "Sure hope you like it because it's all I've got."

He took the box from her, opened it, and his face lit up. "Oh, this is gorgeous." He took the silver antique pocket watch from the box and studied it.

"I know you love old watches but I hadn't seen you with a pocket watch."

"I don't have one. I've been looking but never found one I

liked. This is perfect. Even has a beautiful chain. Where did you find it?"

"Estate sale down the street. The glass was broken and it didn't work. The watchmaker fixed it and said it's probably a hundred and fifty years old."

"Thank you, Tish, it's perfect. I love it."

She pointed at it. "You haven't seen the inscription. I had it engraved."

He looked at it and bit his lower lip as he read it aloud, "*To Spence, for all time. All my love, Tish.*" He looked up at her, his eyes moist. "And now it's the best Christmas present I've ever received."

They lay back, spent, as the flickering fire sent light dancing around the bedroom. "Young lady, you have proved by theory beyond a shadow of a doubt."

"What theory?"

"About women who look and act conservative in public. Once the glasses come off and the hair comes down, she's a hellcat in bed."

"Being on top makes me a hellcat?"

"No, but I never expected you to be so...aggressive. Not that I'm complaining. I like that you take the initiative."

"What can I say, I enjoy making love to you." She took his hand, entwined her fingers with his, then leaned on one elbow to face him. "Speaking of love, I wanted to ask you—"

"Tish, sex with you is incredible but I can't possibly go a fourth time today. My God, you're insatiable."

She laughed a bit. "Not that. And trust me, I am beyond satisfied right now."

"Good. I was worried you'd kill me before the wedding. Though I'd die happy. So what did you want to ask?"

"I was curious...when did you buy the engagement ring for me?"

He scratched his chin. "Uh…let's see…I guess it was the week before the trial."

"Do you remember the exact day?"

"Not really. Why, does it matter?"

"I was wondering when you decided you were in love with me."

He leaned up and turned to face her. "Oh, I see what you're up to. You're not fooling anyone with your little lawyer's trick, young lady."

"What?"

"You're trying to figure out if I fell in love with you before you fell in love with me. Because neither one of us wanted to say it first."

"I'm just curious—"

"Hold it right there. I have a question for *you*. When did you have the pocket watch engraved?"

"About a week before the trial. I don't remember what day."

"Uh-*huh*. So I guess this will forever be unresolved."

"Tell you what, I'll borrow a line from a Tom Cruise movie and say *you had me at whoa.*"

"I'd say that's a very accurate focal point for me as well."

"I have another question."

"What's the deal, does this bed convert into a witness stand?"

"I promise, just one more."

"Fine."

"What is it about my eyes that seems to do things to you?"

He signed and smiled as he locked eyes with her. "Ah, my Kryptonite. You want the secret now that we're going to be married so you can use it against me."

"No, I'm just curious. I mean, I've had people tell me I have really pretty eyes before, but I've never had a reaction quite like yours."

He gently brushed her hair back from her face. "Well, the first time, it was the color. Reminded me of the water in the Caribbean.

But then as I got to know you it was more of that *windows of the soul* thing. And in a way you're like the Caribbean. Deep, peaceful, relaxing, comfortable. I look into your eyes and I see a little bit of paradise that is your soul."

"That's so beautiful, Spence. Thank you."

"Oh my God, she took a compliment."

They both laughed as Socks jumped on the bed. Tish stroked the cat as she lay down between them. "She's sure glad to be home."

"That makes three of us. Of course, we wouldn't be in this position without her."

"What do you mean?"

"She's the reason I knew Brent had paid off the jury."

"Huh?"

"She was in my office, on my desk. I had taken off my watch and she wanted to play with it, so I took it away and told her it was not a toy, that it was expensive. And that's when what I'd seen on the jury hit me. A Rolex watch on a blue collar guy. If Socks hadn't gone after my watch, I probably wouldn't have made the connection. So I called my friend Kayla who's a private investigator I grew up with in my old neighborhood and she got all the evidence. She didn't get it to me until right after the verdict came in. I brought it to the judge and the rest is history."

"So it wasn't some woman you didn't know who gave it to you."

"I wasn't going to tell Judge Winston I was having my own client investigated. Though she probably figured it out. She can look the other way like any other New Yorker to do what's right. Anyway, without Socks, none of that would have happened."

"Maybe not the verdict, but you would have ended up here eventually."

"Oh, really?"

"Hey, what was I going to do with an engraved watch? And what were you going to do with an engagement ring?"

"Very true. Your cat just made things a lot easier."

"She's not my cat, Spence. She's *our* cat. So this is the perfect fairytale ending. We will live happily fur-ever after."

Socks hopped off the bed in the middle of the night and made her way to the kitchen to get a snack. Her person had left out some treats for her. She ate a few, took a drink of water and headed back to the bedroom, stopping for a moment next to the tree she couldn't climb. Socks looked out the window to watch the falling snowflakes against the streetlight. She wondered if it would be fun to catch one of them.

She trotted back to the bedroom and hopped up on the bed, then lay down and went to sleep between her two favorite people, stretching out her front paws over the woman's leg and the back ones over the man's.

So they couldn't get away without her waking up.

Finally, she had reached her goal, getting them in the same place. In her home.

Acknowledgements

Cats have always been a part of my life.

When I was about seven my dad gave me a puppy, his theory being that dogs were for boys and cats were for girls. Well, I wanted a cat. So one day later he found another home for the dog. (Somewhere there's a photo of me holding the puppy on a leash, looking like I'd just been fed a dinner of liver and Brussels sprouts.)

My grandparents lived around the corner, and my grandmother liked to feed to stray cats that lived in the neighborhood. I'd go over after school and she'd let me bring the food out to them. They'd follow me like the pied piper, but of course when I tried to pet them they'd run away.

Except for one. A beautiful, long-haired, black and white kitten. She'd come right up to me and let me play with her.

Mom said I could have a cat if I took care of it. You know, that thing about teaching kids responsibility. So I brought the kitten home. My mother said she was "cute as a button" so we named her Buttons.

Buttons lived eleven years, and that cat had a clock in her head. My mother told me that every day she'd jump in the front window at three o'clock, waiting for me to walk home from school. Cat care came before homework as Buttons loved to be brushed. Allowance money often went for cat toys. And so the obsession with cats began.

Since then I've had many cats, and they all seem to find me. Strays, orphans, special needs kitties. I seem to attract cats that need help, or simply a home. I think cats have a sixth sense which brings them to cat people. And they also know when a family "has an opening" for a cat.

So this book is for Buttons, my first cat, who introduced me to the unique relationship that's possible with an animal. There's nothing quite like the connection you feel when a cat locks eyes with you and looks right into your soul...and lets you feel the unconditional love of a pet.

Bonus Material

PAW PRINTS ON MY HEART
by Nic Tatano

Pandora looked up at the couch and knew she wanted to jump, but for some reason she didn't. Her mind told her back paws to spring, but nothing happened. "What is my problem?" she asked herself.

"Your mind is scrambled," said the voice. "you've had a stroke."

Pandora turned and saw the golden tabby smiling at her. "Who are you? And what are you doing here? This is my house. Get out."

"Don't you remember me?" asked the angel-cat.

"I've been a solitary house cat for seventeen years. How would I remember you?"

"We were friends before you came here. I'm your escort."

"Escort. To where?"

"You're going home."

"I am home," snapped Pandora.

"Don't you remember anything about your mission? Your job as an orphaned kitten?"

Pandora looked up at me and meowed as I lay back on the couch. "She wants to come up," my wife said.

I patted my lap, waiting for her to jump but she didn't. She meowed again. I reached down and picked up the Siamese and lay back with her on my chest. "She's getting too old to jump," I said, as I stroked her soft fur and enjoyed the purr I got in return.

The next morning I walked out of the bedroom and found Pandora sleeping. In the litter box. (Thankfully it was clean.)

"What are you doing in there?" I said, as I scooped her out and brushed her off. I looked into her ice blue eyes and for the first time I didn't get a look of recognition. I put her down and she staggered away, walking like she was drunk, favoring her left side.

My wife scratched Pandora's head and she began to purr, but it was clear our cat had somehow changed.

I cooked a sunny side up egg as always and gave Pandora the yolk, her favorite food. She stared at it but didn't seem to know what to do. I put a little on my finger and wiped it across her mouth, and she licked it off. Then she began to eat.

"I think she's had a stroke," said my wife. "But she's not in pain. She still purrs."

Pandora finished the yolk and just stood there. She tried to wash her face but wasn't doing a very good job of it. Egg yolk coated her long whiskers. I picked her up and looked into her eyes, hoping for that familiar look that always seemed to go right into my soul.

Nobody was home.

But she continued to purr.

She spent the whole day sleeping. I noticed later in the afternoon that the level on her water bowl hadn't changed. It was clear we were going to have to remind our cat to eat and drink. I dipped her chin into the water but she didn't drink. After several failed attempts my wife put water in an eyedropper and squirted it into her mouth.

Something clicked. Pandora drank two bowls of water.

Still, we were faced with the decision I had always dreaded. We kept coming back to two simple facts.

She wasn't in pain.

She still purred.

And the one complicated fact that trumped all.

I simply couldn't do it.

I thought of my late father who had spent the last 59 days of his life in a hospital, hooked up to tubes and machines and not knowing where he was half the time. I know he would have traded those last days for one day at home on the couch watching the Mets.

So we decided to let nature take its course and let her spend her last days at home on the couch, watching the birds.

***

"So let me get this straight," said Pandora. "We're actually angels on some sort of mission?"

"Correct," said the tabby, shaking her body so that her wings appeared.

"You've got wings," said Pandora. "They look ridiculous. Can you fly?"

"They're mostly symbolic," said the angel-cat. "Personally, I find they just get in the way. I generally take them off when I get home."

"So tell me about this mission."

"Well," said the tabby, "we pets are angels who report on the behavior of certain humans. For most people having a pet is normal. But you chose the assignment to be an orphaned pet. You really beat the odds surviving as long as you did. Adopting an orphan takes a special kind of pet owner. What people will do to save a helpless animal is a good indicator of their true being."

Pandora struggled with the concept, her mind still misfiring. "So how they took care of me…shows what kind of people they are?"

"Your mind isn't totally gone."

Pandora looked up at her people. The man and the woman were both

Stroking her head. She struggled to remember her mission, but it was still fuzzy. "So my job is just to report on how I was treated?"

"Yes, along with your normal duties as a cat. You know, unconditional love, keeping them guessing about what kind of food you like, sensing when your master is having a bad day…"

"I can still feel that," interrupted Pandora. "I can't leave just yet."

***

On October 1st, 1988, Myra (my fiancée at the time) heard some noise in her parents' barn. When she investigated she found two white kittens in the bottom of an old fish tank, abandoned by the mother cat. She brought them inside and fed them with an eyedropper. The next morning one had died. The surviving kitten needed constant care. Myra found a tiny baby bottle from a doll house, filled it with cream and egg yolk and honey, microwaved it a few seconds and held it near the kitten's mouth. She grabbed it with both tiny paws and sucked it dry.

But the realities of work presented a problem. Myra was a school teacher, gone all day. There was no way this kitten could go eight hours without food. But as a television feature reporter I had a flexible schedule and my apartment was just a few miles from the station. We decided I would take the kitten since I could scoot home and give her a bottle of our homemade formula.

We made her a bed out of a styrofoam beer cooler. We lined it with a heating pad, added a teddy bear along with a ticking clock and placed the kitten inside. She quickly adapted to her new home, and cuddled with the stuffed animal. She was warm and safe. We quickly found out she was extremely curious, even for a cat, and named her Pandora after the character from Greek mythology known for her curiosity.

Now I've had cats all my life, despite the notion that men should be drawn to dogs while felines belong with women. When I was about seven my father brought me a dog even though I had told him I wanted a cat. Giving a child a dog that had to be walked in the middle of a Connecticut winter was not a wise choice versus a self-cleaning kitty, and dad soon found a new home for the dog while I adopted one of the strays from my grandparents' yard. I named her "Buttons" and she was the best companion an only child could have for eleven years.

Over the years I've had numerous cats, but in this case I learned two things. First, Siamese cats are born white. They get their points (dark mask, socks and tail) as they grow older. They're also a bit neurotic and very vocal, howling for no reason at all. Second, orphaned cats that are bottle fed by humans tend to be a bit on the wild side, never having had a mother cat around to discipline them. In essence, Pandora didn't really know she was a cat, having been basically raised by wolves. Combine the two and you end up with a cat that has more personalities than Sybil. Most people thought Pandora was a bit unusual, and they wouldn't be wrong.

She liked launching sneak attacks at people, including me. She could be a loving, purring kitty one moment and the next go into full blown Tasmanian devil mode, complete with hissing, spitting and biting. Once I got a call from the apartment manager who told me the pest control man was chased out of the room by a "vicious twenty pound cat." I invited her over to meet Pandora. The cat didn't disappoint. She turned into a sweet, seven pound fuzz ball who even gave the manager a lick. "What a sweet cat," she said. I could almost see Pandora smiling when she left.

There was no gray area with Pandora. She either loved you or she didn't. And there was no common denominator. She loved Kathie's husband. Hated my sister-in-law's boyfriend so much she charged him when he entered the house. If you were a single guy she licked your head. If you were under the age of seven, you feared for your life. She refused to leave the house when we went on vacation. She liked her cat-sitters, Chris and John. Curiously, they both owned a Siamese. Pandora must have sensed this.

And for those who maintain cats cannot recognize faces, consider this. My friend Ray would visit and turn his back to Pandora. No reaction. The minute he showed his face she turned into a Halloween cat, complete with arched back and growl.

Veterinarians knew to maintain their distance. One was having a particularly hard time getting the troll out of the pet carrier, so she told her assistant to "get the falcon glove." She then gave Pandora her shots wearing body armor used to handle giant birds of prey.

Pandora was horribly jealous of Myra when we got married. She liked to sneak up on her when she had just stepped out of the shower and was drying her hair. Pandora would jump straight up, snort, and bite my wife in the backside.

She often slept in the guest room, which made things difficult when we had actual guests. Turndown service from Pandora meant a gift on the pillow for these interlopers, and it wasn't a mint.

She had a weird game she liked to play in which she would wait for us to go to bed, then scratch and howl at our bedroom door. When I'd open the door she would run away. It reminded me of that old practical joke in which kids would light bags of manure on fire, throw them on someone's porch, ring the doorbell and take off.

Siamese are one-person cats, and I was her person. Being a

night owl and cats being nocturnal, we bonded during the late hours of the evening. I noted she was particularly loving when I had endured a bad day. It is hard to stay mad when a bundle of fur jumps in your lap and purrs.

I noticed that turning the computer on always brought her out of one of her many hiding places. While working on a novel for long periods of time she would always jump in my lap and go to sleep.

She was the original laptop.

✳ ✳ ✳

After two days of the vacant look from Pandora it was apparent she wasn't getting any better. Still not in pain, still purring, but clearly confused. She would stare at a wall for hours. She couldn't seem to remember to groom her hind quarters, which meant a guy who had never changed a diaper now had to clean the backside of a furry animal equipped with claws.

"I want my cat back," I told my wife.

"Her personality may be gone. All we can do is make her comfortable."

"I want my cat back. If only for a day so I can say goodbye."

***

"It's time to go," said the angel-cat.

"No," said Pandora. "I told you I still sense the bad day. He needs me."

"You Siamese are soooo stubborn. We have a joke that all Siamese should be sent to south Florida instead of heaven."

"Why?"

"Because you're already wearing black socks."

"I don't get it," said Pandora.

"If you were a cat in Miami you would."

"If you're going to tell me jokes then fix me so I can understand. Put me back the way I was."

"I can't fix your body. You're seventeen years old. You can't run around like a kitten anymore."

"Then fix my mind. You heard my person. He wants to say goodbye and so do I. I don't want to see him with water in his eyes anymore. Besides, if you're going to explain this mission I'm on then I'll need a clear head." Pandora sat down and put her nose in the air. "I'm not going anywhere."

The tabby looked up for a moment and then back at Pandora. "Okay. But just for a while. Then you realize you have to go."

"Fine. Only after I deal with his bad day and get to say goodbye."

"Deal."

***

I walked through the house wondering where I'd find Pandora this time. Litter box? Staring at a wall? Instead she was sitting up next to her food dish, and began the loud Siamese chant as soon as she spotted me.

I crouched down next to her and tilted her head up to look in her eyes.

She looked back and licked my nose. Then she nudged her food dish and started yakking again, as if to say "Okay, I'm back, now where's my egg yolk?"

My wife and I were amazed. She ate, she drank, and most important, she recognized us. She was moving slowly and still couldn't jump, but it was definitely Pandora.

She was back.

We'd made the right decision.

For the next three weeks Pandora was her old self, at least mentally. She was smiling again. (Cat owners know what I mean.) She slept next to her favorite toy, a wind-up stuffed cow. She walked very slowly, but wasn't favoring either side. Jumping

272

of any kind was history. And we settled into a routine with her grooming ritual. She couldn't reach around to take care of her backside, so I got a tub of baby wipes and dealt with it. I now have newfound respect for anyone who works in a nursing home.

Watching the little Siamese deal with her limitations was inspiring me. I'd gone though the worst year of my life career-wise, and had been losing the most important thing any creative person can possess.

Hope.

But Pandora wasn't quitting on me or herself. Each day she took forever to get across the room, but she did it.

"She hung in there for you," my wife said.

In Greek mythology, Pandora is the first woman on earth. Her name means "all-gifted." You probably remember the tale in which she is given a box and told not to open it under any circumstances, but her curiosity gets the best of her. Pandora opens the box and lets all the evil out into the world. She tries to close it, but is too late. The only thing left in the box is Hope.

In this case, she gave it to me.

My hope returned. I started making some career calls which panned out.

Things began to turn around.

And just when they did, Pandora turned as well.

***

"You're done here," said the angel-cat. "He's doing better."

"I know," said Pandora.

"We have to go. Today." The light behind the angel-cat was growing brighter. "Just follow me."

"Can I just say goodbye one last time?"

"Okay."

Her final day was a Sunday. That morning I found her laying in a sun square, lethargic and unwilling to eat or drink. Even worse, she wasn't purring.

I stayed with her all day, watching football while stroking her head. When the game ended I went to the kitchen to get something to drink and I heard a loud meow.

It was the first sound she'd made all day. For a Siamese, it meant something.

I ran back to the living room and got down on the floor next to her. She stretched out her two front paws and looked at me. I took her paws in one hand, stroked her head with the other. She took one more breath and was gone.

***

"Are you done yet?" asked the angel-cat.

"Filed my report a little while ago," said Pandora.

"How do you feel?"

"Physically I'm like a kitten again. I can run and jump like I used to. I also like the fact you can eat all you want up here and never have to use the litter box. I sure don't miss hacking up furballs or going to the vet. I hated riding in cars."

"It's not that bad," said the angel-cat.

"All cats hate cars," said Pandora. "Ever see a cat hanging its head out of the car window?"

"I guess you're right," said the tabby. "So…do you miss your people?"

"I miss them a great deal, but I don't feel badly about it. Strange."

"That's normal up here. It's not possible to feel badly about anything. You get to keep all your good feelings, though." The tabby twitched her whiskers. "So, do you want another assignment, or do you want to wait for your people?"

"I'll wait," said Pandora. "And in the meantime, I'll watch over them."

***

It is much too quiet in the house these days. Without a talkative Siamese, the proverbial "peace and quiet" leaves me cold. We've had a magnet on the fridge for years which reads "a home without a cat is just a house." No kidding.

I look at Pandora's pictures quite often, a favorite one now the screen saver on my computer.

I spend a lot of time wondering where cats souls go when they die.

Is there a cat heaven filled with mice and birds and sun squares? Do they share heaven with people? Is her spirit hanging around the house? If they do share
heaven with us, will I be able to talk with her and ask her things I've always wanted to know, like "what was your problem with Ray?" My friend Laurie once told me "if there are no dogs and cats in heaven, I don't want to be there." The mere concept of a perfect afterlife should include your loved ones, human or otherwise.

And I wonder how Pandora came to be in my life, and I in hers.

Friends who stopped by always asked to see her, finding her many mood swings "entertaining." She had an incredible personality for a cat, an incredible devotion to me. I miss her terribly, her crazy little games, her running to greet me at the door.

While she was alive I often told friends how I'd bottle fed her, how I had saved her life.

Funny, it was the other way around all the time.